Elizabeth Ferrars and The Murder Room

》》 This title is part of The Murder Room, our series dedicated to making available out-of-print or hard-to-find titles by classic crime writers.

Crime fiction has always held up a mirror to society. The Victorians were fascinated by sensational murder and the emerging science of detection; now we are obsessed with the forensic detail of violent death. And no other genre has so captivated and enthralled readers.

Vast troves of classic crime writing have for a long time been unavailable to all but the most dedicated frequenters of second-hand bookshops. The advent of digital publishing means that we are now able to bring you the backlists of a huge range of titles by classic and contemporary crime writers, some of which have been out of print for decades.

From the genteel amateur private eyes of the Golden Age and the femmes fatales of pulp fiction, to the morally ambiguous hard-boiled detectives of mid twentieth-century America and their descendants who walk our twenty-first century streets, The Murder Room has it all. **》》**

The Murder Room
Where Criminal Minds Meet

themurderroom.com

Elizabeth Ferrars (1907–1995)

One of the most distinguished crime writers of her generation, Elizabeth Ferrars was born Morna Doris MacTaggart in Rangoon and came to Britain at the age of six. She was a pupil at Bedales school between 1918 and 1924, studied journalism at London University and published her first crime novel, *Give a Corpse a Bad Name*, in 1940, the year that she met her second husband, academic Robert Brown. Highly praised by critics, her brand of intelligent, gripping mysteries was also beloved by readers. She wrote over seventy novels and was also published (as E. X. Ferrars) in the States, where she was equally popular. *Ellery Queen Mystery Magazine* described her as 'the writer who may be the closest of all to Christie in style, plotting and general milieu', and the *Washington Post* called her 'a consummate professional in clever plotting, characterization and atmosphere'. She was a founding member of the Crime Writers Association, who, in the early 1980s, gave her a lifetime achievement award.

By Elizabeth Ferrars
(published in The Murder Room)

Toby Dyke
Murder of a Suicide (1941)
  aka *Death in Botanist's Bay*

Police Chief Raposo
Skeleton Staff (1969)
Witness Before the Fact (1979)

Superintendent Ditteridge
A Stranger and Afraid (1971)
Breath of Suspicion (1972)
Alive and Dead (1974)

Virginia Freer
Last Will and Testament (1978)
Frog in the Throat (1980)
I Met Murder (1985)
Beware of the Dog (1992)

Andrew Basnett
The Crime and the Crystal (1985)
The Other Devil's Name (1986)
A Murder Too Many (1988)
A Hobby of Murder (1994)
A Choice of Evils (1995)

Other novels
The Clock That Wouldn't
  Stop (1952)

Murder in Time (1953)
The Lying Voices (1954)
Enough to Kill a Horse (1955)
Murder Moves In (1956)
  aka *Kill or Cure*
We Haven't Seen Her Lately
  (1956)
  aka *Always Say Die*
Furnished for Murder (1957)
Unreasonable Doubt (1958)
  aka *Count the Cost*
Fear the Light (1960)
The Sleeping Dogs (1960)
The Doubly Dead (1963)
A Legal Fiction (1964)
  aka *The Decayed Gentlewoman*
Ninth Life (1965)
No Peace for the Wicked (1966)
The Swaying Pillars (1968)
Hanged Man's House (1974)
The Cup and the Lip (1975)
Experiment with Death (1981)
Skeleton in Search of a
  Cupboard (1982)
Seeing is Believing (1994)
A Thief in the Night (1995)

The Clock That Wouldn't Stop

Elizabeth Ferrars

An Orion book

Copyright © Peter MacTaggart 1952

The right of Elizabeth Ferrars to be identified as the author of this work has
been asserted in accordance with the Copyright, Designs and Patents Act 1988.

This edition published by
The Orion Publishing Group Ltd
Orion House
5 Upper St Martin's Lane
London WC2H 9EA

An Hachette UK company
A CIP catalogue record for this book is available from the British Library

ISBN 978 1 4719 0694 7

www.orionbooks.co.uk

I

BEFORE STARTING her breakfast, Alex Summerill went to the telephone. When a man's voice answered her, she began rapidly : " Daniel, please will you tell me what I'm to do about this business of having a third eye that doesn't work like my other two ? Here have I been looking at people's faces for the past forty years and thinking that they were pretty or plain and nice or nasty, but not seeing *evil* in them. And I got along all right like that. I don't like seeing evil. It makes me stay awake at night or dream bad dreams. But when that detestable camera you gave me gets people down on paper, that's all it ever seems to show me. Evil. Cruelty. Treachery."

Her own face had flushed excitably while she was speaking and her free hand made passes in the air, as if she felt that these gestures would help the man at the other end of the line to understand what she was talking about.

He appeared to do so with surprisingly little difficulty.

" Who is it this time ? " he asked.

" My assistant, Vivian Dale."

" That nice girl who's getting married ? Oh, nonsense. You've known her for years."

" No, not Henrietta," said Alex. " I told you, she's left me already. Vivian's the new one. She's been working for me for a month now. And I've been thinking how lucky I was to get her. And I took the photographs for fun, chiefly because I thought she was so pretty she'd make a wonderful subject. And I made the prints last night and I've been in a terrible state ever since. Because, don't you see, Daniel, I can't possibly afford to have anyone in that job whom I don't trust absolutely. It'd be a perfect goldmine for anyone with a slight leaning to blackmail or anything like that."

" Now, now, let's keep the melodrama for later," he said. " All that's happened, so far as I can make out, is that you've taken some photographs of your Miss Dale, and they're not very satisfactory. Well, throw them in the waste-paper basket and take some more."

1

"That's precisely what I'm going to do—I'd thought that out all by myself," said Alex. "But if the second lot come out with the same expression as these I shall get rid of her. I must. I can't take any risks with my work."

"Probably the poor girl just isn't photogenic and can't look like her normal self in front of a camera," said the man's voice. "That happens to lots of people."

"But she does look her normal self, that's what's so awful!" said Alex. "If I'd simply found a face that I'd never seen before, I'd know that what you've just said was true and I shouldn't be worrying at all. But now that I've seen this dreadful face on paper, I've *recognised* it, don't you understand? I know that I've seen that same expression on her face again and again and not liked it, and yet just looked away because I didn't want to have to think about what it meant. I think I must be beginning to find out what a fool I've always been about people. I must have been, mustn't I? I can't ever have looked at their faces properly before."

"Very few people do look at faces properly," the man said. "And I should let myself calm down before saying anything about this to anyone else."

"Of course, I shan't say anything to anyone else. I shouldn't dream of telling anyone but you, and I've told you only because it's mostly your fault, getting me to mess around with this photography business. Besides, I want you to look at the photographs and tell me what you think."

"Certainly," he said, "if you think that'll help you."

"When shall I come and see you?"

"Come and have lunch with me to-day."

"Yes, that's a good idea—no, wait a minute, I've an appointment. I'm having lunch with Henrietta. She's coming to London for the day and I believe she's bringing her young man to show him to me. After lunch I'm going to take them shopping to buy them a wedding-present and I don't know how long that'll take. But I should think I could be free by three o'clock. So I'll come along then, shall I?"

"Anything you say."

"Bless you," she said. "It's lucky for me you've retired and are as idle as you are nowadays, because this is urgent—really terribly urgent, and I couldn't bear to wait."

"I'm not idle," he said. "I merely dispose of my time

now according to my own inclinations, and your claims on it have always come high. But don't expect me to take one look at your pictures and say that poor Miss Dale is a murderess, an adultress or anything else undesirable. I've never yet heard of anyone being condemned just for having a certain sort of face."

" I wonder. When you see these pictures, I wonder if you won't say one of those things straight off," said Alex. Putting down the telephone, she went to the table and sat down to breakfast.

When she had finished she did not start immediately for the office. The evening before she had brought some work home with her and now, for half of the morning, she sat at her desk at the window of her sitting-room, busily writing. The window overlooked the narrow strip of her London garden, where from the time when the first crocuses and snowdrops opened in the grass until the fading of the last chrysanthemums, she could always see the gleam of flowers. But just now the earth was bare, the laburnum, stopping across the lawn, was a sooty skeleton of a tree and only the holly bush in the corner had its leaves and a sprinkling of red berries. The January sun, shining through a haze of cloud, spread a pale light over the desk by the window.

Alex's work consisted of writing letters. These letters all began with such words as, " Dear Distracted Wife," or " Dear Depressed," or " Dear Hopeful." They were all signed, " Your friend, Alice Summers." What they contained was the best advice and comfort that Alex was able to give to women with faithless husbands, men with faithless wives, parents with difficult children, children with unaccommodating parents, girls who were afraid they might never get married, young men who wanted to know how to discover a perfect woman. Alex wrote these letters for a column called " Ask Alice Summers," that appeared every Thursday in a daily newspaper.

She always did a great deal of her work at home. She liked the feeling of intimacy with her correspondents that arose from remaining in her own pleasant sitting-room, seated at the old mahogany desk that had come from her grandmother's house in Clifton. For Alex took her work very seriously and in spite of the fact that she was highly paid for giving advice, that which she offered was probably no worse than her correspondents would have received from any other well-meaning, warm-hearted person.

When she left the house later in the morning, the time was nearly twelve o'clock. In her handbag she had the six prints of the photograph that she had taken of her assistant, Vivian Dale. The letters that had just been written were in a leather brief-case. Alex's face showed no signs of the worry in her mind, but, brightly made-up under the veil of her small hat, looked fresh and charming. She was a small woman, naturally blonde, grey-eyed and with a moderate, quite attractive plumpness. Seeing her that morning with the look that she usually had of being on her way to some agreeable appointment, it would have been easy to believe that she was a woman who had never done a hard day's work in her life. In fact, she had supported herself and her son, who was at a public school, since the death of her husband fifteen years before, and the first few years at least had not been easy.

Arriving in Fleet Street, she paid off her taxi, entered the building of the newspaper for which she worked, and took the lift up to her own office on the fourth floor. On the way she exchanged, as usual, a few remarks with George, the liftman, on the subject of pools. George had an idea that she brought him luck and sometimes persuaded her to fill in his coupons for him, which she always did with her eyes shut. To-day he told her that her last attempt had won him eight shillings, but Alex knew that he was generally over-optimistic in his calculations.

Opening the gate for her at the fourth floor, he said : " I took Miss Selby up again a few minutes ago. Is she coming back to work here ? "

" No, this is just a visit," said Alex. " She's getting married a fortnight on Saturday. She'd a young man with her, hadn't she ? Well, that's the one she's marrying."

" She hadn't any young man with her as I noticed," said George.

" She hadn't ? Oh, I do hope he wasn't too shy to come," said Alex. " I've been looking forward to seeing him. I hardly know anything about him yet. I haven't even seen his photograph so far . . ." She stopped herself. She did not want to think about photographs all the time.

4

" She looked kind of different from what she used," said George. " She only said good-morning, she didn't say nothing else. I almost felt she didn't remember me."

" Excitement, probably," said Alex. " After all, one would have a good deal on one's mind if one were getting married a fortnight on Saturday."

" That's right, or maybe she's got a throat like me, and didn't feel much like talking," said George. " Everyone's got a throat this weather. I got a yellow medicine for mine, wot the doctor give me when I was in hospital with my rupture. This morning when I got up I couldn't hardly speak, but the wife give me a spoonful of my yellow medicine and it done wonders. Any time you get any trouble with your throat, Miss Summers, you tell me and I'll bring you some of my yellow medicine along."

Thanking him, Alex left the lift and started down the corridor.

In her office, she found Vivian Dale and Henrietta Selby, sitting facing one another across the desk that was now Vivian's but at which Henrietta had worked for four years. Both girls were smoking cigarettes and both were laughing.

Alex's first thought as she saw them there together was that they were such a nice-looking couple of girls, it must be unspeakably foolish of her to be worrying about the one any more than she had ever worried about the other.

They both said, " Hallo, Alex," at just the same time and Henrietta sprang up and came to meet her, holding out her hands.

" How lovely to see you again," she said. " It feels ages since I saw you last. And it feels ages already since I left here. It doesn't make sense that it's only a month."

" I can't believe it's nearly as long as a month," said Vivian in her softer voice. " I'm still in such a state of confusion."

" That, of course, is nonsense—Vivian is competent to the last degree," said Alex. " Well, Henrietta, my dear, how are you ? You're looking marvellous."

But this was not quite true. As George had just said, Henrietta did in some way look different, as if some nervousness or strain had taken a little of the bloom from her face. It was the other girl, who had remained seated at the desk and

5

who was now reaching out towards a pile of papers, who really looked marvellous, disturbingly marvellous. Henrietta Selby was certainly a pretty young woman, but Vivian Dale, with her composed and delicate and rather emotionless features, had a finished beauty that kept taking Alex by surprise. She could never quite keep its quality in mind and so never got used to it. Even to-day, with the face in the photographs fresh in her mind, Alex felt the usual little shock of pure admiration, tinged with a trace of natural envy.

Vivian was very slender, gracefully and finely made, with a look of fragility about her that was completely contradicted by her energy, except when now and then she had moods of lassitude, when she seemed suddenly to have no life in her at all. She had a pale, clear skin and chestnut hair that grew in short, soft curls. Her eyes were large and dark, with a way of watching steadily the eyes of anyone with whom she was talking, though without showing much of the thoughts that were passing in her own mind. But she had a swift, sweet smile that momentarily took away the impassivity of her face and that seemed to reveal her as a gay and gentle as well as a very intelligent person. She usually dressed in daring colours, bright blues or greens or yellows, with glittering touches of bizarre jewellery.

Henrietta was the shorter of the two girls and only slightly less slender than Vivian, but there always seemed in some way to be more of her, more talk, more laughter, more red in her cheeks. She gave herself away more and showed more interest in other people. She usually dressed in not very expensive suits, seldom wore a hat on her smooth, dark hair and had never quite lost the look of having grown up in the country. She looked younger than her age, which was twenty-five, and probably would always do so, even when she had grown matronly, which was likely to come about in quite a few years' time, at least if she married happily and had children.

" We'll go out and have lunch straight away, shall we ? " said Alex. " As soon as I've unloaded these letters on Vivian. Only where's Conrad? He isn't waiting around downstairs, is he, afraid of coming up ? Or are we going to pick him up some-where ? I was thinking we'd have lunch at Colonna's, but if he's waiting somewhere that isn't convenient for that——"

" No, he isn't waiting," said Henrietta. " Actually he didn't come up to London with me to-day. He's starting a bad cold. He got up this morning with an awful throat."

"Oh, dear, what a pity—I did so want to meet your Conrad. But George just said to me that everyone has colds this weather."

Not believing for a moment in Conrad's sore throat, Alex reflected that she would probably hear the truth about the quarrel that had stopped Conrad Moorhouse coming to London with Henrietta, over the second cocktail at Colonna's.

But here Alex was wrong. In the taxi to Greek Street, Henrietta talked about her aunt, with whom she had gone back to live on giving up her job in London. She talked about her aunt's new house, her aunt's wedding-present, her aunt's boarders, and then, over her martini at Colonna's, became more silent rather than more talkative. Fingering the stem of her glass, she gazed down into it as if the pale liquid had begun to hypnotise her and her face became remote and thoughtful.

Alex started talking about some rugs that she had seen in a shop in Victoria Street. She said that she thought Henrietta and Conrad might like one as a wedding-present and suggested that after lunch she and Henrietta might go and see if Henrietta liked the rugs as much as Alex did herself.

Henrietta raised her eyes briefly, saying : " You're a darling, Alex. But you know that you've got much better taste than I have. I'll like anything that you do."

" Haven't you the time to come with me this afternoon, or don't you like the idea ? " Alex asked. " Would you sooner have something different ? "

" No, I'd love the rug," said Henrietta. " But . . . Well, I'm worried to-day, I know you've noticed it already. I've got something on my mind. It's . . ." She hesitated a long time. " It's Aunt Jay. And—and this wedding and everything. It isn't that I mind having a proper wedding, and Aunt Jay's set her heart on it. But I think it's much too tiring for her and too expensive."

" Is that all that's worrying you ? " asked Alex.

She thought that Henrietta hesitated again before she answered.

" Yes, that's all."

" Well, it doesn't sound much of a worry to me," said Alex.

" Some things are worth while even if they do cost a bit more and wear one out. One can always rest and economise afterwards."

" Yes, I suppose so. But you see . . ." Henrietta had started drawing patterns on the tablecloth with the prong of a fork. " Ever since the fire in the old house, Aunt Jay's been different. She doesn't seem to have the same energy any more. I know her heart's troubling her and she says and—and she does very queer things. You'll see what I mean when you come down. You are coming, aren't you ? " There was a trace of anxiety in the question.

" Of course," said Alex. " I wouldn't stay away for anything. Vivian's going to drive me down on Friday afternoon."

" It'll soon be over, anyway," said Henrietta. " Then, as you say, she can rest. Perhaps that's all she needs, really. She's got too excited over the whole affair and it's come too soon after the shock of the fire and that poor old man getting killed, and then the move to the new house and so on . . . Aunt Jay always used to want this new house, yet she doesn't seem happy in it. I believe she'd sooner be back in the old ramshackle dump on the other side of the cove. By the way, talking of houses, Conrad and I think we've found a cottage that we're going to buy."

" Good," said Alex. " Have another martini. And don't worry about the wedding. As I remember Miss Clyde, she was a rather formidable old rake who was obviously pining for more excitement, not less of it. Whereabouts is this cottage ? "

" It's about half-way between Aunt Jay's and Sharnmouth," said Henrietta. " It's a glorious little place, at least it will be when we've done a good many things to it. Conrad isn't particularly handy, but I think we'll be able to do most of them ourselves. Only I wish you would come and take a look at it and advise us about it . . . Oh, I say, isn't that a good idea ? " A new note came into her voice. " Do come, please come. You could, couldn't you ? Come a couple of days early and advise us about the cottage. If Vivian's with you, you can deal with your mail down there."

Even less able than most people to resist an invitation to give advice, Alex smiled, hesitated and said that she must think about it.

But if there was anything on which she enjoyed advising even more than on affairs of the heart, it was on old buildings, gardens, furniture and decorations. In her spare time she sometimes wrote articles about these things for the women's magazines, under the name of Alexandra Soames. So Henrietta had only to repeat her invitation, with an appearance of growing excitement over her own suggestion, for Alex to admit that she would be delighted to go down to Sharnmouth two days earlier than she had intended and give her opinion on the cottage.

" And you will bring Vivian, too, won't you ? She looks as if she could do with a few extra days of country air," said Henrietta with what struck Alex as a slightly curious insistence. She had not realised that the two girls, who, so far as she knew, had met only about six weeks before, when Henrietta was helping to instruct Vivian in the taking over of her job, had become so friendly.

" Talking of Vivian . . ." said Alex.

" Yes ? " said Henrietta.

" Oh, nothing," said Alex, her own more cheerful spirits suddenly evaporating. " Except that I've an important appointment at three o'clock, so we mustn't be too long over lunch, if we're going to Victoria Street to look at those rugs."

II

AT THREE O'CLOCK that afternoon, Alex Summerill climbed the stairs to the photographic studio of her old friend, Daniel Whybrow, which was in a flat on the top floor of a tall house in a square near Victoria. Reaching the flat, Alex found the door ajar and, pushing her way in, walked familiarly along a short passage and entered the big, bright room at the end of it.

The room was not unduly full of photographic apparatus, although a camera, some lamps and reflectors were grouped in a corner. One wall of the room was covered with photographs, a few of which were framed, but most of which were fixed to the walls with drawing-pins and frequently changed.

Nearly all of them were portraits. The wall opposite was covered with books, many of which were fine editions, but in other parts of the room, on tables, chairs and carpet, there was a far-flung spray of paper-covered detective stories.

Daniel himself was not in the room, nor, apparently, in the flat. Alex was not unduly surprised or put out by this. Taking one of his cigarettes from a half-empty packet on the mantelpiece, she picked up one of the detective stories and sat down in a deep chair in front of the blazing fire.

About a quarter of an hour later, she heard Daniel come into the flat. Hurrying and panting slightly, he came into the studio, his arms full of paper bags.

" I'm so sorry, I hoped I'd be back before you got here," he said, " though I left the door open, in case. It occurred to me that you'd probably want some tea and that I hadn't any milk in the place, or any cakes, and that the cigarette supply was dangerously low."

She smiled up at him. " D'you know, you're nearly always out when I get here ? I'm always having to let myself in. I think you must half-want to avoid me."

" No," he said, " certainly not that. But perhaps I do enjoy the thought of your coming in here as if the place belonged to you, and of my finding you here when I get back. A kind of trick on myself, I suppose."

Cautiously he slid the paper bags out of his arms on to a table.

He was a tall man, gaunt and slightly stooping and about fifty years old. He had fine, bony features, bushy, dark eyebrows, dark eyes and a dark skin that had wrinkled rather deeply for his age. The wrinkles were those that come early in any thin and mobile face and did not really make him look any older than he was, though, combined with his hair, which Alex had never known anything but the grey that it was now, they helped to give her a confused feeling concerning his age. She had always felt that he was immeasurably older than she was herself.

" I've barely finished a large lunch so we needn't think of tea yet," she said. " But come and look at these photographs, Daniel. I haven't looked at them since the morning and now I'm almost afraid to look, in case they turn out to be even more horrible than I think."

" Or in case they turn out to have nothing whatever the matter with them ? "

" Meaning that then there would be something the matter with me ? " Opening her bag, Alex took out the envelope containing the prints. " Well, take them—take them over there and look at them by yourself and then tell me what you think."

Daniel took the envelope and carried it over to the window. Alex did not watch him, but her gaze on the fire grew more intent as she sat waiting for him to speak.

It was some time before he said anything. It was longer than she had expected. Then he said softly, " A beauty. Oh, a real beauty."

" Is that all ? " she asked.

" Except that she has the evil eye and is probably a witch," said Daniel.

" No," said Alex, " please be serious."

" I am serious," he replied. " Three centuries ago she would certainly have been burnt at the stake. And I should have gone to see it. It would have been wonderful."

" No," said Alex. " I want your serious opinion, Daniel. I really want to know what you think."

" I've just told you."

" You haven't."

" What makes you think not ? "

She considered. " Well, for one thing, you'd never have gone near a witch-burning."

" Are you so sure ? "

" Of course. You're far too civilised."

" Three hundred years ago I could have allowed myself, in some respects, to be less civilised. And you asked for my serious opinion. Well, I've given it. Your Miss Dale is a witch and I advise you either to burn her or to become her intimate friend. No other course of action will be safe."

Alex frowned. " I almost believe you mean what you're saying and you do think there's something wrong with her ? "

" Oh, I do. I certainly do. No young woman of thirty should have quite so much knowledge and power in her face."

" Thirty ? " said Alex sharply. " Twenty-three."

" Thirty," said Daniel. " At least thirty."

" But she told me she was twenty-three," said Alex, " and I'm sure she doesn't look any more. That's to say . . ." All at once she began to feel unsure. Frowning more deeply, she started trying to recall exactly the face of her assistant, as she had seen it that morning in her office. But as usnal, Alex found that she could hardly remember at all what Vivian Dale looked like.

" Then, that's one lie she's told you," said Daniel, picking up the photographs and bringing them across the room to her. " Look, there are lines here which would be quite impossible to find in the face of a girl of twenty-three. If you like, I'll enlarge these prints for you, so that you'll see what I mean. I'll enlarge them to well over life-size, so that you can study the texture of the skin."

Alex took the prints from him and looked at each in turn.

" Of course, that isn't a very terrible sort of lie, is it ? " she said.

" Probably not," he agreed.

" Only she seems rather. too intelligent for that sort of thing," said Alex. " And at only thirty. That's still quite young, after all."

" Some people can feel very old at thirty," said Daniel and unconsciously he ran a hand over the hair that had turned grey so young. " If they're lucky, they sometimes discover some extra youth later on. But an important question here, so it seems to me, is what she was doing during those seven years that she didn't mention. A young woman with that face will almost certainly have done a good deal. What did she tell you she'd been doing before she came to you ? "

" She said she'd just come from a secretarial college," said Alex, " and so she had. She had their diploma and a particularly good recommendation. And before that she'd been at Oxford."

" Did you check on that ? "

" No. She was obviously so much better educated than me that it never occurred to me even to wonder about it."

" How did she come to you ? "

Alex hesitated, then she said, " Daniel, I believe these pictures really have you worried for some reason. They aren't just pictures of a nice girl, are they ? You do think there's something I ought to look into ? "

Daniel shrugged his shoulders. " Remember Duncan," he said. " ' There's no art to find the mind's construction in the face.' "

" Duncan was a silly old fool," said Alex. " That's why he got murdered."

" Not necessarily," said Daniel.

" But I've simply *got* to make up my mind about the girl ! " Alex exclaimed. " You understand why, don't you ? She handles all the mail I get as Alice Summers and types out the answers, most of which, let me remind you, don't get published in my column and in fact could never get published anywhere without starting up all sorts of trouble. If you saw the things that people write to me ! People write to me about the most fantastic things, Daniel. The most intimate things and sometimes the most terrible things. I never can understand why they should, except that most of them, poor souls, haven't got anyone on this earth to whom they dare talk honestly. But if a bad sort of person had access to their letters, the blackmail she could start demanding ! The secret love affairs she'd know about, the swindles people have worked on their best friends, and the crimes—yes, actually the crimes ! I simply daren't think of what the consequences could be."

" Where d'you keep all these letters ? " Daniel asked.

" Oh, I destroy them as soon as I've dealt with them," said Alex, " unless I feel I must keep them to cover myself in some way. But the point is, my assistant reads my post before I do. She sorts letters out and chucks away the merely crackpot things, the silly, anonymous, insulting things that always turn up, and the proposals of marriage and so on. Then some of the regular queries she types answers to straight away, merely giving them to me to sign. So you see, if some really important letters went missing, I'd never know about it. She could have hidden them before I'd even arrived at the office and there'd be no possible way of my finding out."

" What's puzzling me at the moment," said Daniel, " is why you never worried about these risks before."

" That's because I had Henrietta working for me for four years," said Alex. " No one on earth could ever have suspected her of anything dishonest. And before her I had dear old Miss White, who'd worked in the place for thirty years."

"Did you ever take Henrietta's photograph?" Daniel asked.

"No, I . . ." Then she saw the point of his question and with some indignation added: "No, I'm not quite such a fool as you think. I know Henrietta really well and I'm very fond of her. She's a good, sweet person."

"But you've never taken her photograph?"

"No, but I will, if you like."

"It isn't what I like that matters at the moment," he said. "But this same kind of thing has happened once or twice already. You've taken a photograph of someone you thought you liked and immediately you've started to see all kinds of things in their faces that you'd never noticed before. With the other cases, as I remember them, there couldn't have been any serious consequences, but it's clear that they've helped to undermine your trust in your own judgment of people, and that isn't very nice for you, particularly now that something's turned up where I agree the consequences certainly could be very serious. So I thought perhaps we ought to try and find out what's happening to you and that we might begin by getting you to experiment on some other people you know. Me, for instance. Or yourself. Or Henrietta."

"I always hate all photographs of myself," said Alex, "and you would only look a little ghoulishly handsome. I trust Henrietta absolutely."

"Well, then," he said, dismissing it, "suppose we return to that other question I asked you. How did Vivian Dale come to you?"

"As a matter of fact," said Alex, "she came in a rather odd way. She simply wrote to me out of the blue, saying that she would like to work for me. It was a very nice letter. I liked it. So I wrote back and said I was sorry I had an assistant who was a perfect treasure, but that if by any chance she should leave me, I would bear Vivian's name in mind. I'm not sure why I bothered to do it, except that there really was something unusually attractive about the way she wrote. And then only a few days later, Henrietta told me about her engagement and said she would like to leave in about a month's time. So then I wrote to Vivian and asked her if she would like to come and see me. She came, and I was so impressed by her that I took her on at once. The only worry I had was that she seemed to me rather too good for the job. Of course, I realised that she'd thought of it as a way of getting started in journalism, and that she was really very ambitious, whereas Henrietta never wanted to do anything but go on being my assistant until some sufficiently nice young man had the sense to marry her. But I don't mind a bit of ?mbition in Vivian. At least, I don't think I do. I don't think I've been storing up secret suspicions of her simply because the poor girl happens to have beauty and brains. Though I believe you're wondering if that isn't the trouble, aren't you, Daniel? I believe you're wondering if these photographs have simply brought to the surface some sort of jealousy or envy or something."

" Well, I dare say they have," he said, " but still the fact is, it *is* a strange face . . . I wish I could have her for a model. Would she consider it, do you think? "

Alex laughed. " I could ask her—if you think you'd be safe with her. But I dare say she'd be no worse than some of your other lady friends."

" Meanwhile," he went on, " I've just had a constructive idea. I'm going to write you a letter, Alex, confessing all the sins of my private life."

" Don't I know most of them already? "

" Not these, you don't—not these horrible crimes. I don't know them myself yet. But when I've thought out something really juicy, I'll write to Alice Summers and tell her all about it. Then I'll let you know that the letter's been posted and you can wait to see if it ever turns up."

" But that's a brilliant idea! " said Alex, enthusiastically.

" As a test," he said, " it's scarcely infallible, unless the girl does pocket the letter. Still, if it reaches you safely, you'll feel at least a little more confidence in her, won't you?

" Of course, I shall. It's a wonderful idea. When will you do it? "

" This evening. Then all being well, the letter will reach you to-morrow, or at latest the day after."

" You mustn't use your own name," said Alex.

" No, I'll call myself—I'll call myself Paul Brown."

" And use a typewriter. She may have seen your handwriting."

" Oh, I'll take every precaution."

" While I'll be concentrating on those seven years. Oh, Daniel . . ." She smiled at him. " I feel so relieved. What on earth should I do without you ? "

" Some day we might make an experiment to find out," he said. He added thoughtfully, " It might be good for both of us."

Alex had looked back into the fire. After a little while she said, " Actually it's most unlikely that there's anything really wrong, isn't it ? "

" Who can tell ? " said Daniel. " Evil does exist."

" Yes, but——"

At that, however, for the time being, she left it.

III

IT WAS the next day.

Looking up from her desk to smile at Alex, Vivian Dale said, " Good-morning."

She was wearing one of her brightly-coloured dresses, of a green that was almost emerald and that contrasted vividly with her curling, coppery hair. The dress had a tight bodice and a full, swinging skirt. She had a heavy jet bracelet on one wrist. On the desk before her was a pile of letters, several of which had not yet been opened.

Trying to look as if she had no wish to observe her, Alex crossed to her own desk. It did not escape her that Vivian gave her a keen look, which suggested that the girl had immediately noticed that Alex had something unusual on her mind. As she dropped into her chair and turned to face Vivian again, Alex thought, " The girl's too damn clever. I'm sure that that's all that's the matter with her. But what on earth did she want to come here for, upsetting simple souls like me ? "

Aloud Alex asked unconcernedly, " Anything interesting this morning ? "

" Not so far," said Vivian.

She seemed to have nothing more to say, but went on

slitting envelopes and glancing quickly over the letters that came out of them.

"By the way," Alex went on, unable to endure a silence just then, "Henrietta wants me to go down to Sharnmouth a couple of days before the wedding, so that I can look over a cottage she and Conrad have found. She wants you to come, too. You can manage that, I suppose?"

"Of course," said Vivian.

"I don't know Sharnmouth," said Alex, still talking for talking's sake, while she watched Vivian pick up the next letter. "In summer it's rather resortish, I think, but in winter it's probably nice and quiet."

"Inhabited solely by the dodderingly aged, the hopelessly infirm and the mildly lunatic," said Vivian. "Those little seaside towns always seem to have a basic population of the dead and the half-dead who come out to sun themselves on the promenade when the summer visitors go."

"Well, we'll all be old some day," said Alex.

"I wonder . . ." But Vivian said this staring at the letter that she had just opened, so that Alex could not be sure whether the words were a comment on her own or on the letter.

"What do you wonder?" she asked quietly after a pause.

"I meant, I wonder how many of us will ever get old," said Vivian, her eyes still on the letter. "For some reason I can never imagine it of myself. But if I do . . ."

"Yes," said Alex.

"I certainly shan't settle at a place like Sharnmouth. I shall always stay where there's plenty of life, even when all I can do is watch it—life and people!" It was said with an intensity which seemed to take Vivian herself by surprise, for her cheeks reddened noticeably.

Alex heard herself making the rather fatuous remark, "Well, that may happen sooner than you think."

Vivian seemed to make an effort to concentrate her attention on Alex, but her eyes were abstracted.

Alex went on, "Getting old, you know, sooner than you think I think." She hesitated, then said decisively, "Just tell me something honestly, will you, Vivian? You're quite a bit more than twenty-three, aren't you?"

Slowly, Vivian lowered the letter to the top of the pile before her. Across the room, Alex could see that it was a typewritten letter of some length. Furious with herself for having brought out that question at just that moment, and with so little thought as to how to handle the matter, Alex noticed that the flush on Vivian's cheeks had grown even brighter and that there was an unusual glint in her eyes.

" What makes you think that ? " she asked.

" Well, it's true, isn't it ? " said Alex.

" Yes, it's true," said Vivian. " I suppose I was stupid to think I could get away with it."

" It's one of the things that nearly always gets found out sooner or later," said Alex.

" I'm thirty—nearly thirty-one," said Vivian.

" That's what Daniel—that's what I thought," said Alex.

" But is it important ? " Vivian asked. " Are you going to be very angry about it ? "

" That'll depend on why you did it."

" Just feminine weakness, I suppose."

" No—it's that that's worrying me—that wouldn't be in character," said Alex.

" Isn't character a rather complicated thing to lay down rules about ? "

" Well, in this case it's just that you're very intelligent and you're very well educated and you're very good looking, so that you've no possible need to pretend that you're younger than you are," said Alex. " I mean from vanity, or anxiety about getting married or getting jobs or anything of that sort. I can't help feeling——"

" You can't help feeling," said Vivian, thoughtfully smoothing the letter on the pile before her, " that I'm really concealing something else besides my age."

More than a little annoyed with her for having grasped the point so quickly, Alex nodded.

Vivian gave a sigh. " Well, I'm very sorry about it. I suppose I shouldn't have done it. I was concealing, you see, where I'd spent about six years of my life. The first few jobs I tried to get after coming out, I didn't conceal it and to my great surprise, I didn't get the jobs. Everyone was very nice about it, of course. Everyone would have liked to help me if they could, but they just didn't think that the jobs they had to give me would be suitable work for me. So eventually I had the bright idea of dropping those six years out of my life and joining my three months at the secretarial college on to my time at Oxford. And it worked. I got the job." She smiled. " Perhaps if I'd known you better, I'd have trusted you. Naturally, I wish now that I had. Yet, I'm not sure . . . It was always the kind-hearted people who turned me down."

Quickly, Alex said, " You spoke of coming out, but you didn't say what you came out of. It wasn't . . ." She stopped, her thoughts hovering in acute agitation between visions of prisons and lunatic asylums.

" It was a T.B. Sanatorium," said Vivian.

Alex relaxed in her chair. She instantly felt intensely ashamed of her suspicions, yet the sense of shame was so pleasant and reassuring after the horrid sensation of doubt of the integrity of another human being, that she almost enjoyed it.

" But good heavens, my dear, why ever should you have thought that you had to conceal that from me ? " she asked warmly. " I only wish I'd known before. I'd have made sure that you were taking proper care of yourself and not doing too much and——"

" That's just it ! " said Vivian. " I told you it was the kind-hearted people who were worst. Would you have given me the job if you'd been afraid that I couldn't do as much hard work as other people ? "

" But are you quite well now ? " Alex asked. " Are you quite sure you're quite well ? "

" Quite well—quite sure," said Vivian.

Alex, in her new mood of relief and apology, found that she was looking at the girl with new eyes. She realised that six years of illness could explain a great deal of what had seemed strange about Vivian. They had been six years spent out of contact with the ordinary world, with suffering and fear always in the air. Vivian's changing moods of energy and lassitude, her look of knowing more than was good for her and yet at the same time of a certain childishness, which had made it possible for her to convince Alex that she was only twenty-three, were now all easy to understand.

" I was never a bad case anyway," said Vivian. " A bit obstinate, but not serious. Now look, there's a letter here . . ." She stopped, picked up the typewritten letter on the top of the heap before her, and standing up, brought it across the room to Alex. " Would you mind looking at it now and telling me what to do with things like that—because the fact is that my first impulse on reading it was to put it very quickly in the fire."

Alex lifted her eyebrows. " So dirty ? "

" So dangerous," said Vivian.

Alex took the letter and dropping her eyes for a moment, saw the signature, " Paul Brown " at the bottom.

Casually she asked, " Why dangerous ? "

" Because if certain people knew that that man had written that letter and that you'd read it, it might seem to them a good idea, I'd think, to have you put out of the way. Me, too." Vivian went back to her desk. " Not to mention Mr. Paul Brown himself."

Alex read the letter.

It ran : " Dear Alice Summers. Will you please tell me what a man is to do who saw a murder committed five years ago and who kept his mouth shut about it because he didn't want his family to suffer. I have always felt pretty bad about it and now my family is grown up and can take care of itself I would like to put things right if I can. But I do not want to go to prison. After all, I only saw the man push the old fellow into the road and bash his head in and run his car over him, so when I said in court I saw the accident and that the old fellow ran right out in front of the other one's car, I was only concealing part of the facts. But was this perjury all the same and would it mean prison ? My conscience feels awful but I do not want to go to prison. It wouldn't be fair on my children who are doing very well now. I should say that the man in the car is someone whose name you know as well as I do and whom no doubt you think is a respectable and honourable man, like I used to do before I got to know better. I should say, too, that as a result of what I said I saw, I have been able to give my children very good educations and they are both doing fine now, whereas if I had spoken the truth I was given reason to believe that I should not see either of them again. So you see how good comes out of evil, but still I feel very bad about it and should like to get even with the old bastard, as well as putting things right for the old chap's daughter, who is a fine girl and would get all the money if her brother got what was coming to him. But I do not want to get into any more

trouble than I can help. What do you advise me to do ?
I think you are a sensible woman who will understand my
problem and not be too hard on me, because I always read your
column and notice you are never hard on anyone, even the
ones I would like to kick up the backsides. Thanking you in
anticipation, please advise yours truly, Paul Brown."

As she finished, Alex, to her dismay, found that she could
not check her laughter, though she knew that Vivian was
watching her keenly and with some surprise.

" Murder, intimidation, blackmail, perjury ! " Alex said
happily. " What a lovely letter ! I don't wonder that you
were a little startled."

" D'you often get things like that ? " Vivian asked.

" No, just occasionally," said Alex.

" What will you write back ? "

" Oh, I shan't answer it."

" Why not ? "

Alex considered. " Well, I can't really believe that Mr.
Brown is suffering very acutely from his disturbed conscience
and is in desperate need of help and comfort from me."

" What will you do with the letter ? "

" I think burn it, as you suggested."

" But oughtn't you really to hand a thing like that over to
the police ? "

" Perhaps, and in the past I have handed them letters once
or twice," said Alex. " But generally, if I think it would
be foolish on my part to enter into the matter, I destroy them.
I won't swear that it's the right thing to do, but I do feel that
I have to justify the confidence people have in my secrecy.
It's only when I've thought that dangerous consequences
might follow my saying nothing that I've gone to the police.
And on one of those occasions the whole thing turned out to
be a hoax. People do think it's fun to hoax me quite a bit,
you know."

" Then d'you think this letter's a hoax ? "

" What do you think yourself ? " Alex asked interestedly.

Vivian gave a laugh. She seemed to like the question, but
she did not answer it at once. When she did, there was still
amusement in her voice. " If you like, I'll tell you what I was
really thinking. I was thinking how very easy it would be to
find out who the people are who are mentioned in this letter.

Mr. Brown seems to think he's concealed their identities by not mentioning their names, but in fact there can't have been so very many cases of some fairly prominent person being involved in a motor accident in which his own father was killed by him—and where a Mr. Paul Brown gave evidence at the inquest that it was an accident. Though, of course, his real name won't be Paul Brown. But allowing for that, you or I could easily find out who this murderer was and cash in on our knowledge, couldn't we . . . ? Tell me, d'you never think of things like that yourself ? I'm always thinking up that kind of idea. It must mean that there's a real streak of criminality in me."

Something prickled up Alex's spine. She did not know whether she wanted to laugh or to get angry at having her mind so easily read, but for a moment she felt almost afraid, as she might have felt at the sudden unreasonable suspicion that there was a third person hiding in the room.

Then she laughed and said, " Well, let's get on with the job."

Later that day, talking to Daniel Whybrow on the telephone in her home, she tried to describe that moment of superstitious dread.

He said lightly, " It's as I said then, she's a witch. How do you feel about the photographs now ? "

" I haven't looked at them again," said Alex, " and I'm going to put them into the fire without looking at them."

" So you're still nervous ? "

" No, I feel a fool. Vivian answered all my suspicions in the most innocent way possible. And the more carefully I look at her now, the more I think that those pictures aren't like her in the least. I must have done something wrong with the lighting. I'll take some more of her another day. Oh, by the way, that letter from Paul Brown . . ."

Daniel gave a chuckle.

" I told her I was going to burn it, but in fact I shall keep it always. Thank you so much, my dear Daniel. Reading it was a wonderful experience."

She rang off. Then she took the photographs of Vivian out of her handbag and dropped them into her sitting-room fire.

IV

AT THE TIME it looked as if that was to be the end of Alex's suspicions of Vivian Dale. But a fortnight later, something happened which brought them back, terribly intensified. On the morning of the Wednesday on which Alex and Vivian were to leave for Sharnmouth, a letter which gave Alec one of the worst shocks that she had ever had in her life came to her house. The post was delivered just after Vivian had arrived there, so Alex thrust into her handbag the three or four letters that the postman had pushed into her letter-box and then did not trouble to open any of them until she and Vivian were already some distance from London. If Alex had read the letter sooner, neither she nor Vivian would ever have gone to Sharnmouth.

The letter, written inexpertly on a typewriter and with no address at the top or signature at the end, read :

" So that's what you are, Alex Summerill, a snake in the grass, a low crook, imposing on unsuspecting people. I wrote to you in the simple faith that you would at least respect my confidence, even if you could say nothing to help me, and you write back to me making threats and demands. But let me tell you that the name for that is blackmail and you can be made to pay for it as heavily as I for my crime. So do not imagine that in me you have found a helpless victim. Desperate people can discover desperate courage. We shall meet this week-end. Take care of yourself then, Alex Summerill."

Alex read the letter twice. Then she went on staring at it, her mind gone rigid with disbelief while a sense of cold had spread through her body. At her side, Vivian was giving all her attention to her driving. Her face was as composed as usual. Her calm gaze was steadily on the road ahead.

For a moment Alex tried saying to herself, " Mr. Paul Brown's overdoing things." But she knew that this letter had not come from Paul Brown.

Yet it had come from someone who knew the real name of Alice Summers, as well as her home address.

Folding the letter carefully at last, Alex put it back into its envelope, and after a thoughtful look at the envelope, put it into her handbag. Taking out her cigarette-case, she held it out to Vivian.

" Cigarette ? "

" Thanks." Without looking round, Vivian groped for a cigarette.

Alex struck a match.

" Really, you ought not to smoke," she said as she lit a cigarette for herself.

" I suppose not," said Vivian.

" But you smoke a good deal, don't you ? "

" It depends on what I'm doing."

" Didn't the doctors tell you not to ? "

" They may have. But at a certain point I stopped bothering about what they said."

" Rather reckless, wasn't it ? "

" Probably I am a bit reckless. It's easier to live that way."

" Yes—you are a bit reckless." Settling back in her seat, Alex took quick nervous puffs at her cigarette, turning her head to stare through the window beside her at the wintry fields. They were silvered with frost and quiet and empty.

" You don't mean I'm driving recklessly, do you ? " said Vivian. " I'll go slower if you prefer."

" You drive beautifully," said Alex. " You do everything beautifully. You're a very accomplished person. If I were half as talented as you are, I'd be quite satisfied with life."

Vivian glanced at her questioningly, but Alex was still gazing blankly at the bare hedges.

She was thinking, " The postmark is Sharnmouth. That letter came from somebody who knows Henrietta. That's how the person knew my name and address. When I saw her, Henrietta was worried about her aunt. She'd been saying and doing queer things. Perhaps the letter came from her aunt. Or from someone else at the guest house . . ."

For the moment, that was as far as she could get. She was still clinging to the feeling that this could not really have happened to her. She had done nothing to bring such a catastrophe on herself. She had only allowed herself to be duped, and was that so wrong of her ? Should one's mind always be full of suspicion ? In fact, for the last fortnight, she had been feeling deeply ashamed of her suspicions of Vivian and had been only too glad to be free of them.

Too glad. That was the trouble.

A feeling of physical distaste for the nearness of the girl beside her had filled her, but it did not occur to her to tell Vivian to turn the car back to London. Rather, Alex wanted to reach Sharnmouth as quickly as possible. She wanted to talk to Miss Clyde and convince her that she, Alex Summerill, would be utterly incapable of doing what the letter now in her handbag had suggested. And surely that would be easy. Surely no one who had met her and spoken to her could possibly believe such things of her. It would all be perfectly simple to straighten out. Of course it would be.

As the dreadfully slow hours of the drive passed by, however, a number of doubts accumulated in Alex's mind. For one thing, it was possible that the letter had not been written by Henrietta's aunt. But whether it had or not, the truth about who had written it might not be easy to prove. For to walk up to a woman one scarcely knew and ask her if it was she who had received a blackmailing letter in response to one she had written, confessing to some crime, would be a very awkward thing to have to do. Then there was the threat in the letter. At first Alex had given it hardly any consideration, but as time went on, she began to feel more and more that it was not pleasant to be threatened. Then there was the question of whether or not she ought to go to the police.

From that thought she recoiled blindly. But it remained with her, nagging at her with the persistent suggestion that it was the only sensible thing to do. Besides, it was almost certainly her duty. If Vivian Dale were a blackmailer, then merely to sack her and leave her to continue her activities elsewhere could scarcely be called a responsible way to act.

If Vivian were a blackmailer. . . .

But suppose she was not?

Suppose it had not been Vivian who had intercepted the first letter from Sharnmouth, but someone else? Hundreds of people worked in that Fleet Street building. Someone whom Alex had never even met might have a key to her office and have been in the habit of interfering with her post for years. It was possible, too, that the letter from Sharnmouth had never even been posted. It might have been in Sharn-mouth itself that the theft had taken place.

Presently Vivian commented on Alex's silence. " Something wrong ? "

Alex said that she had a headache, adding untruthfully, " I always get a headache when I travel."

" How horrid. Don't you take anything for it ? " asked Vivian sympathetically.

" Oh, aspirins and so on sometimes, but I forgot to bring any," said Alex.

A few minutes later, passing through a village, Vivian stopped the car outside a chemist's shop.

" I'll get you some Veganin," she said.

" Don't bother," said Alex. " Please don't. Just drive on and don't bother."

But Vivian jumped out of the car, ran into the shop and came out with a tube of Veganin and a glass of water. Alex had to take the pills. But at least from that time on, Vivian did not bother her with conversation.

They had lunch in Wincanton, coming out after it into a chilling and thinly-falling drizzle of rain. The rain continued as they drove westwards, making the dusk come earlier than it would have on a clear day. There was very little traffic on the road and the world seemed to Alex a desolate place. Later, a grey glimpse of the sea was bleak and forbidding.

She had thought of these few days in Devonshire as bound to be sunny, filled with a soft western warmth. Yet the day seemed only to grow colder and colder the farther they travelled.

Sharnmouth lay in a hollow, with wooded hills behind it and steep bare cliffs rising on either side of it. The small town, with its Regency crescents and squares, its prim little esplanade, its old-fashioned hotels, its neat civic gardens, its rigorous exclusion of the vulgar and its curiously luxurious shops, had a charm that at any other time would have appealed to Alex. She would probably have wanted to stop and have tea where she could sit and look at the sea. But to-day she had only a furious impatience to reach her destination.

Henrietta had sent her a map, drawn by herself in pencil, of the last few miles of the drive. It was not easy to follow, for Henrietta had forgotten to mark a number of the turnings.

But at last, after the road had taken a wide curve behind the cliffs and then had risen steeply through the woods, to emerge into the open about a quarter of a mile from the edge of the cliffs, they saw the lights of a house some distance ahead across the shadowy landscape.

" That must be it," said Alex. " There should be a lane off to the right here—yes, there it is—and then some white gates."

" How's the headache now ? " Vivian asked, as she slowed the car to turn into the lane. It was very bumpy and she had to proceed with care.

Alex did not answer. It cost her a physical effort to exchange a word with the girl beside her.

The white gates, described by Henrietta, appeared after a few minutes. As Vivian swung the car in at the gates and brought it to a standstill in front of a stone porch, she sat back, pushed one hand through her curls and gave a long, rather shuddering sigh. The sigh might have meant mere weariness or it might have been the expression of some other and greater strain. Turning in her seat, she looked deliberately into Alex's face.

Her steady, probing, unrevealing gaze made Alex move hurriedly. Getting out of the car, she went quickly up the steps to the green door of the house and grasped the brass bell-pull hanging beside it.

It was Henrietta who came to the door. In the light of the hallway her cheeks were warm and red, her dark hair gleamed and her eyes were bright with welcome. She greeted Alex and Vivian with a laughing embrace for each, then said, " And this is Conrad."

Across Henrietta, Conrad Moorhouse smiled at Alex.

His appearance took her by surprise. He had been described to her by Henrietta in an enthusiasm, slightly blurred by confusion, in such a way as to make Alex expect a big, beaming, blundering, simple-hearted young man with freckles, yellow curls and his thoughts deep in agriculture. The only actual facts that she had known about him were that he was thirty-two, six feet tall and a member of the agricultural advisory service in the district. She now found that the freckles and the yellow curls were entirely absent. Though his hair was fair, it had only a slight wave in it, while his skin had a deep, even tan. If his heart should turn out to be simple, his thoughts at least would certainly be those of a complex, rather highly-strung person, while the beaming smile that Alex had envisaged was in reality only a slight and charming curve of the lips and a friendly lightening of the very blue eyes.

When he had shaken hands with Alex, he turned to Vivian. She had been in the doorway, looking back at the car and asking Henrietta whether or not she should leave it in the drive. Turning now towards Conrad, she met his eyes and immediately a hot flush travelled over her neck and cheeks. Conrad, on the other hand, turned quite pale, while every trace of expression was wiped from his face. They shook hands stiffly, staring at one another with blank eyes.

Henrietta said cheerfully, " Now come and get warm. You poor things must be frozen."

Apparently she had noticed no strangeness about the meeting between Conrad and Vivian.

Opening a door, Henrietta led them into a big room, full of easy-chairs, with a fire blazing in a wide, brick fireplace and bright curtains drawn over the windows. It was a comfortable room with impressionist prints on the walls, bookcases full of books, a radio and plenty of ash-trays. Yet there was something about it that was not quite homely. Its comforts had been conscientiously supplied for the paying guests who used the room, but it was easy to tell that it had never been allowed to become the true background to the life of any particular person.

Two elderly women were sitting in chairs on either side of the fireplace. Though Alex had met Henrietta's aunt only once, she knew at a glance that neither of these was Miss Clyde. One, in fact, could scarcely have been any relation of Henrietta's, for she was Japanese. She was short and stout, dressed in a shabby blue woollen dress and a grey, knitted cardigan. Her black hair was streaked with grey, taken straight back off her high forehead and twisted in a thick plait at the back of her head. She was holding a book of verse in her hand. When Henrietta introduced her as Miss Takahashi, she made a bobbing movement with her head and gave a sudden hoarse laugh which faded away into a quiet little giggle.

The other woman was a gaunt, grey person with wild, wispy, grey hair and a deeply-wrinkled skin. She was dressed in a shapeless grey tweed suit with a very short skirt and thick, greenish, hand-knitted stockings. Henrietta introduced her as Mrs. Wakely. The name stirred some memory in Alex, though at first she could not recall what it was. Mrs. Wakely's only greeting was to raise her bushy, grey eyebrows and give Alex and Vivian a penetrating stare.

" Aunt Jay's lying down," said Henrietta, " but I'll go and tell her you're here. Then I'll show you your rooms. I'm afraid I've had to put Vivian right up on the top floor——"

She was interrupted by Miss Takahashi suddenly getting up, slipping behind her chair and then, keeping close to the wall, running out of the room.

" She's awfully shy," Henrietta explained, " but she's a dear when you get to know her."

In a surprisingly thin, high voice, Mrs. Wakely said, " A very intellectual woman. Cultured. Truly cultured."

" That's quite true," said Henrietta. " She's making a translation of some Japanese poems for some special edition. But you'll never manage to get her to tell you about it. She's far too modest."

" Unlike some," said Mrs. Wakely into the air before her.

Alex heard a quiet laugh from Conrad. " That's me Mrs. Wakely's getting at. You'll find it her dominant pre-occupation just now. Still, we're really very good friends, aren't we, Mrs. Wakely ? "

" WE," said Mrs. Wakely, plainly not referring to herself and Conrad but to some other, more imposing conglomeration of persons, " do not believe in chemical fertilisers. The govern-ment does. The government is systematically poisoning the people. Mr. Moorhouse is a servant of the government."

" There you have it in a nutshell," said Conrad with a sigh. " Couldn't have been better put. You've such powers of expression, Mrs. Wakely, you're always bound to win in an argument."

" Don't tease her," said Henrietta in a whisper.

" She loves it," he whispered back.

Mrs. Wakely suddenly fixed her bleak grey eyes on Alex. " WE believe in natural manures," she said. " Don't you ? "

" Oh, yes," said Alex.

Henrietta slipped her arm through Alex's. " Let's go upstairs, shall we ? " she said. " Conrad can be getting some drinks out while we're gone. And then I'll call Aunt Jay."

" Don't disturb her if she's resting," said Alex.

She thought a shadow passed over Henrietta's face, but the girl said nothing. She took them out and led them up the stairs. On the way, with an apparent return of cheerfulness, she went on : " Mrs. Wakely doesn't hold with drinks, except mead, which we haven't got, so with any luck she'll clear out to her room when she sees Conrad doing things with bottles and glasses. Then you won't have to sit and listen to the glories of compost, or even to the sad confession of Mrs. Wakely's crime."

" A crime ? " said Alex quickly.

" Well, once in her life she fell from grace and used some chemical fertiliser on a crop of tomatoes," said Henrietta. " Her husband ate some of the tomatoes and immediately developed symptons of food-poisoning."

Alex felt disappointed. She had not traced the writer of the letter, for one could worry seriously over being blackmailed for a crime of that order.

" Does her husband live here too ? " she asked.

" No," said Henrietta. " It was he who was killed in the fire in the old house last year. I told you about it."

" Ah, yes, then that's why I thought I'd heard the name," said Alex.

" You'd think she wouldn't want to stay here, so close to a place with such frightful memories, wouldn't you ? " said Henrietta. " But she won't leave. She goes out hunting for herbs and things on the cliffs and keeps pottering all round the ruins. Here you are," she went on, opening a door on the first landing. " This is for you, Alex. I'll take Vivian up to her room and come back in a minute to see if you've got everything you want."

The room was a large, rather sparsely furnished bedroom, a pleasanter room for a summer visit than for a winter one, though a radiator kept it reasonably warm. The room was at a corner of the house and had windows facing two ways, one of them a french window with long curtains drawn across it. As soon as she was left alone in the room, Alex went to this window, opened it and stepped out on to a small balcony.

The evening was bitterly cold. Drawing the door shut behind her so that the bedroom should keep its heat, Alex clutched her fur coat about her and peered out through the dusk at the sea. She could see its glimmer in the cove below her and hear the surf grinding softly on the shingle. A dark mass of cliffs rose facing her on the far side of the cove. Against the skyline a shape that looked like a house jutted up between two groups of trees. The smell of the sea was sharp and fresh in the cold air.

After a minute or two the door behind her opened and Henrietta joined her on the balcony.

" I thought I'd find you here," she said. " One always has to take a look at the sea when one first gets down to it. It's a kind of ritual, isn't it ? "

" I didn't realise you were quite so close to it," said Alex.

" You can go straight down from the garden to the beach, if you don't mind scrambling a bit," said Henrietta. " So you could from the old house, too. The trouble there was to reach it any other way. The so-called road to it was rather a myth. It was practically impossible for cars, which meant that Aunt Jay got only the hardiest sort of summer visitors. From that point of view this place is far better. It's paying her far better already than the old house ever did."

" Is that the old house over there ? " Alex pointed at the shadowy form on the top of the cliffs.

" Yes," said Henrietta. " In the dark like this it looks fairly solid, but it's really only a skeleton, all charred and horrible. I hate seeing it there."

Alex suddenly realised that Henrietta had come out on to the balcony without her coat. " You'll freeze to death ! " she exclaimed and hustled her inside.

" I've told Aunt Jay you're here," said Henrietta. " She's getting up. She'll come to the sitting-room." She started towards the door.

" Henrietta——" Alex began.

The girl stopped.

" Henrietta, about that fire and the old man who died in it . . ."

" Yes ? "

" Did no one you know of ever drop hints that there was anything wrong about it ? I mean, could your aunt have been worrying about stories of that sort ? I'm asking because of a very strange letter I had to-day."

" To-day ? " said Henrietta in a startled voice.

" Yes, this morning."

" No—I don't know—I don't think . . ." Henrietta's eyes, usually so candid, seemed suddenly to have lost all expression. They did not avoid Alex's, but met them with a steady, unrevealing stare. All at once it made Alex think of Vivian's way of looking at her.

After a moment Henrietta went on, " At the inquest it was decided that the whole thing was just a ghastly accident. It was something to do with the electric wiring. It was all terribly old and apparently it had been put in at all sorts of different times without any regard for regulations. As long as I can remember, it was always going wrong. So Aunt Jay was criticised a bit, though not very harshly, for not having taken more thorough precautions. All the same, I do think it upset her and that she'll never forgive herself for what happened to that poor old man. It was all rather strange, because he was supposed to be going to the cinema with them that evening."

" Was everyone else at the cinema then ? " asked Alex.

" Yes, but Mr. Wakely never turned up. The others had gone into Sharnmouth earlier to do some shopping and have tea, and he was to have met them at the Rialto. But he never came. They never found out why. The fire didn't start till much later in the evening and the body was in the bedroom." She had become very pale while she was talking. " About that letter——"

" I'll show it you, if you like," said Alex.

She took it from her bag and handed it to Henrietta.

The letter was so short that it could have been read in a moment and handed back to her. But Henrietta went on looking at it as if it had far more to tell her than had been set down there in words.

At last Alex asked her, " Can you make any guess who sent it ? "

" It's just some lunacy," Henrietta muttered. " I shouldn't take any notice of it."

" I don't think I can quite do that," said Alex.

"But that's how you always did treat the crazy letters you got."

" Are you sure this one is just crazy ? "

" Yes." Henrietta gave her back the letter. Without saying anything more, she went out of the room.

With a sigh, Alex put the letter back into her bag. All at once she found that she was deadly tired. Tired and wretched. Scared, too. She had a quick wash, changed her dress, gave herself a fresh make-up and went to the door. As she opened it, she had the second bad shock of the day. She was so startled that she took a quick step backwards. For standing there motionless, only just outside the door and looking as if she might have been waiting like that in ambush for half an hour, was a huge, red-haired, red-eyed old woman.

V

HER HAIR was so red that it looked ready to burst into flame. Her face was a dull white mask. She was at least six feet tall with wide, sagging shoulders and a flabbily fat body. She was dressed in a black dress, long and shapeless, with a black shawl over her shoulders. The ends of the shawl were held together by one enormous hand pressed against her bosom. An extraordinary collection of rings of all descriptions glittered on the fingers of the hand. Its nails were painted bright red. Her eyes were greenish, red veined and red lidded, and were fastened on Alex's face in steady, bitter concentration.

After her first revulsion, Alex managed to say, " Oh, Miss Clyde—good-evening."

" Good-evening," said Henrietta's aunt. " I'm very glad to see you, Mrs. Summerill."

The tone was one of deep irony. In fact, it seemed to Alex that she had never in her life had to stand up to such a blast of hatred. It left her speechless. She had no idea how to approach this ogrish old woman.

Alex was also horrified by the change in Miss Clyde. It was about two years since Henrietta had brought her aunt to the office to meet Alex and Alex had taken the two of them out to lunch. Miss Clyde had then been a jolly, swaggering old creature, almost smart in a raffish fashion, and though perhaps she had been rather formidable, she had had the attractiveness of anyone over seventy who could still vigorously enjoy life. There had been no suggestion then in her personality that in another two years she would have turned into this toppling wreck of a human being.

" I'm very, very glad to see you," Miss Clyde repeated menacingly. " You cannot imagine how afraid I was that something might occur to prevent your coming."

Alex felt that she had never before been so directly threatened.

" What could have prevented it ? " she asked mildly.

" An accident of some sort," said Miss Clyde. " Accidents happen."

" I suppose they do," said Alex.

" One never can tell when one's going to meet with an accident," said Miss Clyde. " A bursting tyre, a slip on a staircase, a gas-tap left on by mistake, a short circuit in the night when everyone's asleep, starting a fire that burns one to a cinder."

Alex thought she understood. That accident in the other house had turned the poor old thing's brain. She hadn't been able to bear the death of Mr. Wakely. It had preyed on her mind till she had gone stark, staring mad.

Coming out of her room, Alex said, " In general, I'm a very lucky person. I've been in very few accidents."

" There's a first time for everything," said Miss Clyde. " And insurance will only help other people, not you."

" That's if I'm actually killed."

" That's what I was thinking of."

At that point Alex could not help laughing. But she was annoyed with herself to hear that the laugh came out of her sounding like a nervous giggle.

Under her arm Alex had the bag with the unsigned letter in it. She now felt no doubt whatever that the letter had come from Miss Clyde. But Alex could not bring herself to refer to it. She thought that first she would feel her way and try to arrive at a clearer understanding than she had at present of Miss Clyde's state of mind. In fact, if Miss Clyde was not quite sane, it might be best not to refer to the letter at all.

Miss Clyde led her down to the sitting-room. There was now no one in the room, or so Alex thought at first. Miss Clyde advanced to a table on which stood a decanter and some glasses. She looked at them and in a tone of deep disgust said, " Sherry ! " Then she turned and went out of the room without another word.

Alex went towards the fire and sat down in one of the deep chairs near it. It was as she did so that she discovered her mistake in thinking that the room was empty, for a voice from a corner of it remarked, " Hallo there."

Alex looked round, replying, " Hallo."

A man who had been sitting cross-legged on the floor, twiddling the knobs of a radio, got up and came across the room towards her.

" Don't think the old lady despises liquor in general," he said. " It's just that she considers sherry a soft drink. She'll probably be back in a moment with the gin, bless her. You're Mrs. Summerill, I take it ? "

" Yes," said Alex.

" Glad to know you, Mrs. Summerill. I'm Tally," he said.

" How do you do, Mr. Tally ? " said Alex.

" No, just Tally." He sat down facing her. " In full, Thomas Theodore Tally, but folks just call me Tally."

He had a queer way of speaking. It was as if a dozen different accents had been melted down together in his voice. He was a shortish man and very thick-set, though he was not particularly fat. His face was the fattest thing about him. His cheeks, his jaw, his thick lips, his short shapeless nose, all looked heavy and fleshy and almost as if there might be no bone behind them. His skin was coarse and florid. His eyes were large and round and staring. Alex thought his age must be in the later thirties, but his dark hair had already receded a long way from his forehead. He was dressed in a loose-fitting, light-coloured suit and the pattern of his tie was so enterprising that if she had not heard him speak, she might have presumed that he was an American. He had big hands with coarse dark hairs on them, and on one finger he wore a large ring with a cat's-eye set in it. Altogether he was an unlikely kind of man to find staying in mid-winter in a Sharnmouth guest house.

" Staying long ? " he asked her.

" Only till after the wedding," she replied.

" Busy woman, eh ? Off back to London. Ah, London . . ." He leant back, crossing one short, thick thigh over the other.

" What wouldn't I give to be going back to London ? "

" Then are you staying here long ? " asked Alex.

" Who can tell ? I've got to stay here till the bosses say I can leave. A dog's life. What wouldn't I give for a nice little business of my own ? "

" In London ? "

" Maybe. Maybe not. Maybe not in this blasted country at all. After all, why stay here ? Why stay here if you've got the chance of going somewhere else, eh ? Would you ? "

" I just might," said Alex.

" What for ? Meat on the ration, one egg a week, no fuel, no cars, trains late and falling to bits and the government saying don't-do-this, don't-do-that."

" Where would you go then if you had a free choice ? " she asked.

" I'd not go anywhere in particular. Keep moving, that's the best thing. Every place you think of has disadvantages. One place it's the food, another place it's the mosquitoes, another it's the women, another it's fever. Some places you can't find anyone to talk to and some places you can't get a quiet hour to yourself. Some places you never see the sun and some places you get to hate the sight of a blue sky. So keep moving and then you get a bit of everything. What's more, you can call your soul your own."

" It sounds to me as if you're in the habit of doing that," said Alex.

" That's right. Citizen of the world. Graduate of the University of Hard Knocks."

" And now you're stuck in Sharnmouth."

" That's right. Sharnmouth. God Almighty ! "

" Have you been here long ? "

" Here in this house ? About three months. Can you imagine that ? But maybe you haven't seen the other inmates yet."

Alex did not reply to this immediately and after a pause he went on, " I get it—sorry. Shouldn't have said that, with you a friend of the girl's and asked down for the wedding and all. Bad form and all that. Sorry, sorry ! But mind you, I like the old lady. Tough old girl, lots of spirit. And Henrietta now, I could go for her. But I haven't a chance. I'm not her type. Shouldn't be even if that young chap wasn't around.

36

She's the romantic type, likes them tall and handsome. Still got lots to learn." He chuckled.

Alex still could not diagnose his accent. There was some undercurrent in his voice that seemed familiar and an occasional echo that she was almost able to recognise, but these were lost under layers of imitation American and occasional experiments with the pronunciation of a B.B.C. announcer.

He went on, " I expect you wonder what I do in Sharnmouth."

" Yes, I do," she said.

" But you're a lady, eh ? You wouldn't ask a personal question. But why don't you if you want to ? People like you to ask questions. Shows that you take an interest in them."

She smiled. " What do you do then, Mr. Tally ? "

" Just Tally, please. I'm in insurance. Not very interesting, eh ? Touting insurance round these damned Devonshire backwoods. God Almighty ! "

" You've a car I suppose ? "

" You bet I've a car."

" Then why live in Sharnmouth at all ? Particularly in a remote spot like this. Wouldn't Plymouth, say, suit you better ? "

He gave a bark of laughter. " There—caught me out right away, that's what you've done. I might have known you would. Put your finger right on my soft spot. The fact is, my dear, I like it here. Would you believe it ? Me, T. T. Tally, citizen of the world, graduate of the University of Hard Knocks. I like the country. I like the sea. I like to walk out on the cliffs at night and see the stars in the sky. But don't tell anyone."

Henrietta and Conrad came in then. Muttering something about having gone to help the two Barton sisters who worked as cook and housemaid, in the kitchen, Henrietta poured out sherry and handed it round. A few minutes later Vivian came down. As she came into the room Alex saw Tally's dark, pug-dog eyes almost fall out of his head with excitement.

" No one," he declared loudly, " told me about this."

Leaving his chair, he started fussing about the room until he had succeeded in placing himself in a chair next to Vivian.

Vivian and Conrad did not look at one another.

Miss Clyde did not reappear as Tally had foretold, but after a short while the group in the sitting-room was joined by two more guests, who were introduced by Henrietta as Monsieur and Madame Perrier.

" But don't you go getting the idea from her madam-ing me like that, that I'm French," said the woman to Alex. She was a plump, very brassy blonde of about forty-five in a tight black suit and a frothy lace blouse. " I'm as English as you are, dear. No, it's my husband who's French, as you'll realise the moment he opens his mouth. He can't get hold of proper English any more than I can get hold of the lingo over there. Still, we manage to find plenty to say to each other, don't we, Pierre ? " She nudged her husband with an elbow and gave a little squeal of laughter.

He nodded solemnly and said, " Yes—yes, naturally."

He was a big man, almost as tall, thought Alex, as Daniel Whybrow, but there was a look of lean, muscular strength about him that Daniel did not possess. His skin was deeply tanned, his eyes and his hair were dark, his features were sharp and handsome. When he smiled, a gold tooth flashed in his mouth. He would have looked well wearing ear-rings and a piratical scarf around his head.

" So you've come to the wedding, have you, dear ? " Madame Perrier went on as she sat down near to Alex. " My, what a thrill it's been for us in our quiet lives here. When first Mr. Moorhouse came to stay here, I said to Pierre, I said, ' Next time our little Henrietta comes down here to visit auntie, you'll see what you'll see,' I said."

" My wife," said Monsieur Perrier in his slow, careful English, which gave a seriousness and caution to his speech which did not match very well with the rest of his personality, " is very romantic."

" Well, wasn't I right ? " cried Madame Perrier. " Wasn't it a dead cert from the start ? If you could have seen them together that first week-end—oh, my ! "

Alex, remembering Henrietta's face when she had come back to the office from that first week-end and had made casual mention of having met a man called Moorhouse, thought that Madame Perrier had been quite right in calling it a dead cert. But seeing the discomfort that appeared now in Henrietta's

face at this jocularity about her deepest feelings, Alex came
to her help.

" So you've been staying here for quite a while, Madame
Perrier ? " she said. She found this, if anything, even odder
than that T. T. Tally should have chosen Miss Clyde's guest
house as his residence.

" That's right, dear," said Madame Perrier. " Dead and
alive too, but that's what we need. Pierre had a bit of trouble
with his health. An old wound, you know. He was in the Free
French Marine and got torpedoed a couple of times. So he
had to give up his job and take a long rest and it happened
that I had a bit of money saved up in England that I couldn't
get out of the country. So here we are, and dear Miss Clyde's
been an angel to us, a real angel."

Her husband nodded his confirmation. " It is very nice
here," he said. " I fish. I like to fish. It is more nice here
than at the old house. In the old house was all draughts.
Here one has the central heating. Very nice."

His wife beamed at him. " His English really is getting on,
isn't it ? "

" Splendidly," said Alex, trying not to puzzle over the
question of how Monsieur and Madame Perrier had managed
to keep themselves entertained in Sharnmouth for even longer
than she had at first realised, for if they had stayed in the old
house they must have been in Sharnmouth for more than a year.
But after all it was not difficult to shift her thoughts from that
problem, for there were others weighing on her mind that were
far more worrying.

At dinner Conrad sat next to Alex. Miss Clyde came in
only after everyone had sat down at the table and took her
place at the head. No one seemed disturbed by the fact that
she sat there without speaking and only pecking at the food
on her plate. Only Henrietta seemed to mind this. By the time
the meal was half-done, she was looking as if she might burst
into tears at any moment. Yet, although she kept on looking
anxiously at her aunt, it seemed to Alex that the real cause
of Henrietta's distress was something quite different. Alex
realised that Henrietta had not recovered her cheerfulness
since reading the letter that Alex had in her handbag. She
kept thinking about Henrietta's behaviour on reading the
letter. She had said something that had struck Alex as odd.

But Alex could not remember what it was. Her thoughts kept exploring this small gap in her memory like a tongue exploring a hole in a bad tooth. She could not keep away from it and when Conrad spoke to her, she only half took in what he said, finding herself at one point replying quite stupidly to a question of his with the bewildered query, " My cold ? Is my cold better ? But I haven't had a cold, have I ? "

" Oh ? " he said, looking puzzled. " Wasn't it because of a cold, or flu or something, that you couldn't have lunch with us ? "

" Lunch ? . . . But it was you who had a cold, wasn't it ? " she said.

" No," said Conrad.

They looked at one another.

Then Conrad said softly, as if he wanted no one else at the table to hear : " Didn't you have a cold ? "

Alex shook her head.

" Didn't Henrietta go to your house and see you in bed ? " he asked.

" No, we had lunch together at Colonna's."

The blue of his eyes seemed to brighten with a flash of anger.

" No—listen," said Alex, as if she were replying to something he had said, " Henrietta seems to have played a little trick on us both. She must have felt for some reason that she wanted to see me alone. You mustn't be worried by a thing like that."

" Mustn't I ? " he asked ironically. " What sort of reason was it ? "

" I'm not sure," said Alex. " Something to do with her aunt, I think. She was worried about her and about all the fuss of the wedding. Nothing serious, I assure you."

" Did she spend the whole morning with you ? "

" No, we just had lunch."

" She told me she wanted to go up to London the night before because she wanted to go out to your house fairly early in the morning."

" Possibly she wanted to do some private shopping—a surprise for you, perhaps."

" Do you really think so ? "

" Certainly."

Conrad looked at her dubiously, then he smiled. "I'm sure you're right. Jealousy is just about the most ridiculous of the human emotions, isn't it? I've never really known before what all the talk about it meant, but now I get crazily jealous whenever Henrietta's out of my sight. But don't mention it to her. It's my private problem. Promise?"

With a laugh, Alex promised. "But she's probably just as jealous of you as you are of her," she said.

She thought that his eyes moved uneasily, almost as if they were about to snatch a swift look at Vivian, seated beside Tally. But they returned to meet Alex's steadily.

"She has no cause," he said.

Then he took a long look at Henrietta.

Alex felt a stab at her heart. It was years since anyone had looked at her like that. Fifteen long years. She started aimlessly crumbling the bread on the table beside her and trying to listen to what Monsieur Perrier, on the other side of her, was trying to tell her of the joys of fishing for mackerel in the cove.

After dinner Miss Clyde disappeared. So did Miss Takahashi. The others gathered for coffee in the sitting-room. As soon as she was able, Alex excused herself and went up to her room. The headache, which in the afternoon had been a fiction, was now a reality. Henrietta accompanied her to her door and looked as if she were intending to suggest coming into the room for a talk, but with an abrupt change of mind, she said good-night and went downstairs again. Alex went in alone.

Every drawer and cupboard in the room was open. Her suitcase had been turned upside down. Her belongings had been tossed all over the bed and floor.

Closing the door sharply behind her, she stood staring incredulously at the mess.

It was plain that the room had been thoroughly searched.

VI

ALEX DID NOT often lose her temper. She seldom felt the inclination to shout, stamp and start throwing things. However, if Miss Clyde had happened to walk into the room at that moment, she would have been told a number of unpleasant things about herself.

As Alex imagined the huge, grotesque old woman with her dyed hair and great, clumsy, beringed hands pawing over Alex's intimate belongings, carelessly tossing her most treasured nylon and silk on the floor in a search, presumably for some letter that Alex had never even seen, her anger made her face burn and her body tremble. Her first impulse was to find Miss Clyde and furiously demand an apology.

Second thoughts stopped her.

It was important to consider carefully what steps would actually be the best in handling the horrible situation, finding out the truth about the letter that had disappeared and somehow approaching Miss Clyde with it and reassuring her.

It was also necessary to bear in mind that just possibly the letter in Alex's handbag had not come from Miss Clyde, but from someone else in this curious household and that it had not been Miss Clyde who had searched her room.

Slightly calmed down, though still muttering angry words to herself, Alex set about collecting her scattered belongings.

She had only just begun this when there was a tap on the door. When she answered it, Vivian came in.

One glance at Vivian's face told Alex that she was in the grip of a temper which, unlike Alex, she had not attempted to control. Seeing the angry brilliance of Vivian's eyes and her tight-drawn mouth, Alex was reminded for the first time for days of the face that she had last seen disappearing into ashes in the heart of her sitting-room fire.

" So they've done it to you, too ! " cried Vivian, looking round. " Can you tell me, please, what sort of house this is we've come to ? "

" Come in and shut the door," said Alex.

Vivian came in. As she closed the door behind her, some of the tension of her anger relaxed.

" I'm sorry if I sound unreasonably rattled," she said, " but it feels rather queer, when one's on a visit, to find that one's room has been searched."

" But did they find anything ? " Alex asked.

Vivian looked at her in astonishment.

" What d'you mean ? " she asked.

" I was thinking of a letter," said Alex. " A letter of some importance appears to have gone missing."

" But why on earth search through my stockings for it ? Oh ! " The idea seemed suddenly to reach Vivian. " Not something to do with your mail ? "

" Apparently," said Alex.

" Well, luckily they didn't have a chance at that. I had it with me in my handbag."

" Did you have some premonition that someone might come looking for it ? " asked Alex, her tone flat and cold.

" No, but I always feel that those letters are rather a responsibility," said Vivian. " And from now on, I'll feel rather inclined not to move a step in this house without taking all my luggage along with me."

" Yes," said Alex with a sigh. " I'm sorry about it, Vivian— if you really don't know what I'm talking about."

The girl gave her a sombre look.

" Just what have we got into here ? " she asked quietly.

" I don't know yet," said Alex. For the life of her, she could not decide whether Vivian's behaviour implied innocence or merely excellent acting.

" The people here—the guests, I mean—aren't quite what I was expecting. That spiv from Marseilles and that awful little man, Tally . . ."

" How d'you know Monsieur Perrier comes from Marseilles? " asked Alex.

" I heard him talking French to his wife. One couldn't mistake the accent."

" So you're a linguist, too, Vivian, among all your other accomplishments ? "

" Only French and German," said Vivian.

" Well, there's nothing we can do about this to-night," said Alex, " so let's go to bed."

Vivian nodded and said good-night, but after that she still lingered. " I know you're worried about something," she said. " Can't I nelp with it in any way ? "

Her face had the gentle and appealing smile that came to it only rarely.

" Not now," said Alex. " Thank you. Good-night."

As soon as Vivian had gone, Alex started muttering again in an angry undertone, furious with herself for being unable to make up her mind how seriously she suspected Vivian of being a barefaced liar, a thief and a blackmailer.

In bed, after about an hour of attempting to sleep, but finding her mind still remorselessly active, Alex started composing a letter to herself. It ran :

" Dear Alice Summers, I wish you could advise me. I think I am more worried than I have ever been in my life. I have been accused of an extraordinarily horrible action and I cannot decide what I ought to do about it. I suspect a certain other person of being guilty of this action, but I have no proof of it, and since the person whom I suspect of suspecting me I also suspect of being mad, I do not want to start badly by making a lot of false accusations. It is all an awful mess, because of course the old lady may not be mad at all, but only upset in her conscience. Yet I really had a horrible feeling for a few minutes this evening that she was dangerous and that I ought to look out for my safety, at least until I can persuade her that I didn't try to blackmail her about something she confessed to me. Which is absurd, when you think that she's Henrietta's aunt. Henrietta's such a dear. I do hope she's going to be happy with Conrad. He's got a great deal of charm, but he isn't at all what I expected. Still, Henrietta's behaved pretty oddly herself to-night. There was something she said this afternoon when I showed her that letter that somehow didn't fit in—only I can't remember what it was—and then there was that story about Conrad and his cold. Conrad never had a cold, and I never had a cold. It was George at the office who had a cold and George told me . . . What did he tell me ? Something I want to remember but can't . . . He told me about his yellow medicine, but there was something else . . ."

Her thoughts were growing drowsier, flowing into each other in a confused and darkening stream and somehow they were no longer in the form of a letter to herself but had become a part of a telephone conversation with Daniel Whybrow.

" . . . And Vivian was quite right," she felt herself to be saying. " Those Perriers and the little man Tally don't look the right sort to be staying here. And I can't help feeling that Conrad ought to have been something a bit more—well, bucolic. But perhaps that just means that I've never understood Henrietta. Perhaps, in fact, I've never understood anyone. How does one start understanding people ? One reads their letters and one does one's best to answer them helpfully and perhaps all the time one doesn't understand what they're all really about, so that one oughtn't to rush in with advice of any sort. I can't see how to go about things here at all, except that of course I see it would help if I could find that letter that's gone missing. But if Vivian's got it, she won't have it with her here. Or will she ? Will she, won't she ? . . . Please advise me, Daniel . . . It's such a long time since I've had anyone to advise me . . ."

The muddled murmur of her thoughts gradually whispered their way into a series of restless and disturbing dreams.

She woke before it was light and switching on the lamp beside her bed, she looked at her watch and saw that it was seven o'clock. She could hear no noise of movement in the house, but a soft, surging sound from outside reminded her of the presence of the sea. As soon as the beginnings of day-light appeared, she got up, dressed, put on her fur coat, went downstairs and let herself out of the house into the twilit garden.

It was a small garden, formed into two or three terraces because of the slope of the cliffs. Some steps led downwards at the side of it and descending them, Alex found herself on a path that circled the small cove about twenty feet above the beach.

For the first time she saw the cove properly.

The steely grey sea was dotted with seagulls, riding quietly on the swell. Rocks were piled on each other at each end of a short, curved strip of clean, grey shingle. Some way out to sea a small boat with two men in it was being rowed by one of them towards the shore. They had a dog in the boat with them, and though it was too far off for the sound to reach her, the way that the dog was lifting up its head suggested that it was barking excitedly. She stood still for a minute or two, watching the boat, thinking that it must be a very cold morning for fishing and that a barking dog could hardly be any help.

On the skyline on the far side of the cove she could now see clearly the shape of the house that had been burnt down. It was an ugly and desolate thing to see. The sky was cloudless, turning a clean, pallid blue as the sunshine began to sparkle in it.

Alex walked briskly along the cliff path, feeling a delightful sense of relief at being out of the house behind her. But she had not gone far when she heard someone whistling behind her and glancing back, she saw a man in a camel hair overcoat following her. The face was almost hidden in the turned-up collar of the coat, but she recognised the nearly bald head and the stocky figure of T. T. Tally.

Reluctantly she waited and let him catch up with her.

Shuddering yet deeper into his splendid overcoat, he asked her, grinning, " Do you always come out as early as this on a January morning, Mrs. Summerill ? "

" Do you ? " she asked.

" Not likely," he said. " But I had an idea when I heard you going out that you might be aiming to take a look at that old place over there. It's always got an uncanny fascination for visitors. But it isn't safe. Beams and bricks fall on your head, if you aren't careful. There are plenty of notices up, saying it isn't safe, but I know from experience you can't trust women to bother about notices. Anything that says, ' Keep Out,' they generally take as a particularly pressing invitation to come in. So I reckoned I'd better come after you and stop you."

" That was very kind of you," said Alex, " but I hadn't intended to go so far."

" If you want to see it, I'll show it you," said Tally. " I know which bits are safe and which aren't. But there's nothing to see, really. It wasn't an old house or anything like that. If you've seen blitzed buildings, that's all it's like."

" Really, I just came out to take a look at the sea," said Alex.

" Ah, there's nothing like it, is there ? 'Specially in winter. Queer thing, I'm never really happy away from the sea. Doesn't seem natural in someone like me, does it ? To look at me, you wouldn't think I'd care what went on outside a pub or off a racecourse, eh?—I can tell that's what you've been thinking from the way you've looked at me. ' A tout, that's all he is,' you've been thinking. Quite right, too, in general. Only, I like the sea. It's quiet and empty. It doesn't talk at you all the time. It gives you a chance to think. Funny thing, my kid's just like me in that. She was always on at me till I sent her to a school by the sea. That's where she is, in a swank place at Bournemouth, the best I could do for her. I always do the best I can for that kid. She's worth it, she's a wonder. I'd never have thought I could produce a kid like that. You got any kids, Mrs. Summerill? "

" A boy," said Alex. " But he's nearly seventeen already."

" Mine's eight," said Tally. " Lovely kid, golden hair, blue eyes—just like her mother. Met her mother in the U.S. Couldn't believe my luck when she seemed to want me. Got married and thought I was all comfortably settled for life with a nice cosy cutie. But one day I came back home and she wasn't there any more. Don't blame her. I'm not much good and never have been. And anyway, she left me the kid and the kid's wonderful. Always taking me by surprise being such a looker and saying and doing the things she does. I've got some photographs of her back at the house that I'd like to show you if you're interested."

He paused hopefully and Alex said that she would be very interested indeed to see the photographs. Then she suggested that they should turn back to the house.

As they reached it, they met Madame Perrier, wrapped in a shabby coat of dyed squirrel, walking down the drive towards the house. It looked as if she had been out for an early morning walk in the direction of Sharnmouth, except that the very high-heeled shoes with amazing platform soles that she wore, were not at all suitable for walking along a country lane.

Greeting them cheerfully, she explained : " I've just been seeing my husband off on the bus. He's going up to London for the day. Poor old Pierre, I do hope to goodness he doesn't get lost. I told him not to bother with the tubes and buses but just to take taxis and blow the expense. But you know what men are, they will get independent and try to do things their own way. And then he's always likely to go and buy me some terribly expensive present that I could do quite well without." She simpered girlishly.

" What's he gone up for ? " Tally asked.

Rather coldly, Madame Perrier replied, " On business, Mr. Tally."

" Didn't know he had any business," said Tally.

She did not reply to this but her stare grew haughtier.

" All right, all right," said Tally with his impudent grin. " A gentleman doesn't keep asking questions. Think I don't know that ? My dear old girl, people have been trying to hammer that into my head since I could talk. I can still remember my poor dear ma saying to me, ' The next time yon say wot or why, young Tom, I'll tell you wot and why with this flat-iron.' " He went into the house.

Madame Perrier spoke confidingly to Alex. " You'll find Tally does need putting in his place sometimes, dear. He can be very crude in his manners. But his heart's all right. He's very obliging and he'll do any little thing for you any time. He's been a great help to Miss Clyde in the house. He'll always fix anything that gets broken and so on. But he's inquisitive and he presumes. You just have to keep him in his place."

She followed Tally indoors.

Thinking that a strong, cheap perfume is singularly unpleasant out of doors on a fresh, bright, winter's morning, Alex lingered a moment in the garden, then went in too in search of breakfast.

She found that the table in the dining-room had been laid, but that the breakfast itself had not yet appeared. Going upstairs to her room to leave her coat there, she saw Miss Takahashi on the staircase that led up from the first to the top floor of the house. On catching sight of Alex, the little Japanese ran down a few steps towards her, laid her finger on her lips, looked round mysteriously, then started excitedly beckoning Alex towards her.

Alex went to the foot of the staircase.

From a couple of steps above her, Miss Takahashi bent down and whispered in her ear : " I want to tell you about this house. Very funny house. I want to tell you about it. Very funny here. Very funny people. I want to tell you what happens here. Very, very funny."

" I'd be only too glad if you would tell me about it," said Alex. " It's time somebody did."

Again Miss Takahashi laid her finger on her lips and darted a wary look all round her.

" I tell you about the bathroom," she whispered. " Very funny bathroom. You turn on the tap, you wait, nothing happens, you wait, you wait. Be careful. Water comes suddenly. Comes very, very hot. Be careful. Very funny bathroom. You turn on tap, nothing happens. You wait, the water comes hot, terribly hot. Be careful."

" I see," said Alex.

" I tell you about Mrs. Wakely," Miss Takahashi went on rapidly. " Very funny woman. She leaves all her things in the bathroom. Not nice. Bathroom is for everybody. I never leave anything in the bathroom. But Mrs. Wakely very funny woman. She leaves towels, sponges, soap in the bathroom. She hangs up her clothes to dry in the bathroom. Bathroom is used by gentlemen but Mrs. Wakely is very funny woman, she hangs up her clothes to dry over the bath in the bathroom. No one can take bath till they move Mrs. Wakely's clothes. I never leave my clothes there. Nobody leaves their clothes there. Bathroom is for everybody. But Mrs. Wakely leaves all her things in the bathroom. She leaves her towels and her sponges and her soap and her toothbrush. Not nice to leave all your private things in the bathroom. Bathroom is for everybody. Mrs. Wakely is very, very funny woman."

The thought of Mrs. Wakely's funniness seemed suddenly to become too much for Miss Takahashi, for clapping a hand over her mouth she erupted behind it into a wild explosion of silent giggles.

Alex took the opportunity this gave her to thank Miss Takahashi for her useful information and disappear into her room.

Downstairs in the dining-room a few minutes later, Alex found Henrietta and Conrad.

" Tell me," said Alex, " does Miss Takahashi always say everything three times ? "

" Always," said Henrietta. " She's an odd little soul. So far as we've been able to find out, she's got hardly a friend in the world and hardly any money, and she spends her time in her room working on those poems she's translating. When she first came, she took down all the pictures in her room and the only things she has on the wall now are a Japanese scroll of some sort and a picture of Shelley. Nobbling you on the staircase to tell you things seems to be her only form of social relaxation."

" I don't think she misses much of what goes on in the house," said Conrad. " Now when shall we go and take a look at this cottage that Henrietta's lost her heart to ? Straight after breakfast ? "

" That'll suit me," said Alex.

" Since he hasn't mentioned the fact," said Henrietta, " I may say that Conrad's heart is also pretty well lost to the place. All right, we'll go after breakfast. But what about Vivian ? Would she care to come too or would it bore her terribly ? "

" Bore her terribly," said Conrad a little too quickly.

From the doorway, Vivian's voice contradicted him, " Oh, no, I'd love to see the cottage—that is, if I shan't be in the way."

" Good," said Henrietta, smiling at her cheerfully as she came in.

But Conrad turned away with a curious twisting of his mouth that had no resemblance to a smile.

When they set off after breakfast, Henrietta drove the car and insisted on Alex sitting beside her. Conrad and Vivian got into the back seat together. Throughout the drive they were both quite silent. Yet when the car stopped at a small stone cottage and Henrietta, producing a key, led Alex up the path to the low, moss-grown porch and into a dim empty room with paper hanging in strips from the walls and cobwebs clouding the air, Alex saw over her shoulder that Conrad made a quick gesture towards Vivian, catching her by the elbow and muttering something in her ear. Then the two of them wandered away into the cottage garden.

" Oh," said Henrietta, seeing it too, " he's showing her the outside first. Perhaps you'd have preferred that too, but I wanted to show you this room. I know it's in a terrible state, but I thought one could make it so lovely if one set about it the right way."

Looking round her, Alex tried to set her professional mind working on the subject. She knew that Henrietta was watching her with a look of anxiety on her face, an anxiety perhaps a little too acute to be caused only by Alex's slowness in giving a verdict on the room. Once Henrietta glanced uneasily at the door, but immediately afterwards she turned her back on it, as if to check any impulse to repeat the glance.

Alex managed to say one or two things about the room and about the little, stone-floored kitchen that opened out of it. She knew that Henrietta was right about their possibilities and that with a little money and a good deal of effort, they could be made very attractive, but other questions crowded Alex's mind so that she could not keep it on matters of paper and paint.

Intending to say something about the condition of the floorboards, she found herself saying instead, " Henrietta, I know something's awfully wrong down here. I can see that you're terribly worried by something. I know that you came to London on purpose to talk to me about it and then for some reason or other lost your nerve. Well, why don't you talk ? Aren't we old friends ? Can't you take me into your confidence ? "

Henrietta responded with a quick, wide-eyed glance, then looked down at the ground, scraping the toe of her shoe along a dust-filled crack in the floor.

" Yes," she said in a hurry, " I knew you'd see it if you came. That's why I really wanted you to come down early, much more than because of this cottage. Things are all wrong at the house, aren't they ? You can see that ? "

" I can see that your aunt's changed completely since I saw her last," said Alex.

" Yes, and the people in the house," said Henrietta. " Those Perriers and Tally. There is something wrong about them, isn't there ? I'm not just imagining it ? Conrad says I am, but he hasn't been here long enough to have known what it used to be like before they came. Why on earth should people like that want to stay at Aunt Jay's ? "

" Henrietta, you know that letter I showed you yester-day——"

" Yes." But Henrietta's face immediately became blank.

" Did your aunt write that ? "

" Perhaps."

" Have you any idea why ? I mean, have you any idea

51

about the crime that she says she confessed in the letter that I never got ? "

" That you never got ? "

" The one that's apparently been used to blackmail her with."

" Who do you think did get it ? " asked Henrietta.

" Naturally that's what I've been wondering myself. And since I've seen Tally and the Perriers, I've been wondering if it isn't just possible that that letter went missing down here before it was ever posted."

Henrietta nodded slowly. " That might be it . . . Anyway, I believe Aunt Jay's afraid of them, or anyway of Tally. I believe that's what's the matter with her. It's since Tally came here in the autumn that she really changed. Though that could be coincidence, couldn't it ? After all, Conrad came here about the same time as Tally, and of course she isn't afraid of him."

It seemed to Alex as if there was something challenging in those last few words, almost as if Henrietta expected Alex to contradict her.

" I should have thought Pierre Perrier was a much more frightening sort of person than little Tally," said Alex. " And the Perriers stayed in the old house, didn't they, before the fire ? About that fire, Henrietta—I know this sounds a wild question, but is there any possibility that there could have been some serious trouble between the Perriers and Mr. Wakely ? "

" Oh, no ! " said Henrietta. " No, Mr. Wakely was the most completely harmless old thing——"

She stopped because just then Vivian and Conrad came into the cottage.

The inspection of the cottage went on.

It was upstairs, in one of the low-ceilinged bedrooms, that Alex felt a grip on her elbow and found that it was now she who was being prevented by Conrad from following Henrietta round the cottage.

Bending his head close to her ear, he said to her in a fierce whisper, " You've got to get rid of that girl, somehow, Mrs. Summerill. She's got to be got away from here immediately."

VII

ALEX DREW away from him. Some violent feeling had made the lines in his face deepen so that it looked years older. There was something intimidating about that sudden look of age.

" You mean Vivian ? " she said.

" We can't talk here," he replied.

" Perhaps you'd prefer a cosy chat in the garden," Alex suggested rather acidly.

" I don't want a cosy chat anywhere," he said. " I'm just telling you, get rid of her. She'll make Henrietta unhappy."

" You've met Vivian before, then ? "

" Of course I've met her before. You saw that yesterday, didn't you, when we met ? I saw you notice what happened then. It was quite a shock I had, seeing her like that."

" But you must have been expecting her. You knew she was coming."

" I knew that a Vivian Dale was coming. I'd known her by a different name."

" When was this ? "

" Soon after the war. In Paris." " But I said we can't talk here," Conrad said again. " And if she's in a decent job and you like her, I don't want to upset things for her. I just want to get her away from here."

" In that case, why don't you discuss it with Henrietta instead of with me ? " said Alex. " Mightn't that really be the wiser thing to do ? "

He gave her a look as if he thought her the stupidest woman on earth. But Henrietta called them just then from the other room, and they had to drop the discussion.

Following the two girls into the second bedroom, Alex took an interest in cupboards and shelves and talked about the modernising of the bathroom. Then she was taken downstairs again and shown the garden. Then they drove back to the guest house. Again Alex sat beside Henrietta in the car, while Vivian and Conrad sat in silence in the seat behind them.

As if she had been waiting for the sound of the car to announce their return, Miss Clyde came to the door to greet them. Standing in the doorway, leaning against a doorpost, she waited while they got out of the car, making little bowing movements of her head, fixing her eyes dully on each face in turn. Her flame-red hair hung in wisps down each side of her face, looking as if it had not been combed that morning. Her eyes seemed even more bloodshot than they had the evening before, while the yellowish-grey pallor of her cheeks made her look desperately ill. It was only on coming near to her that Alex realised that at least a part of Miss Clyde's trouble was that she was drunk.

As Alex approached her, Miss Clyde spoke abruptly. " My friend," she said hoarsely. " My old friend. You are my friend, aren't you, my dear ? All my worst enemies are my best friends. Ha, Ha ! You can't think how I laugh over that sometimes. They think I think they're my friends. But I know what they're like. Oh, yes, I know all about them."

Her bleary glance slid round to Vivian. For a moment Miss Clyde seemed puzzled by her presence, then she pointed a long finger at her, making it look rather as if it were the barrel of a revolver. She barked at her, " Friend or enemy ? "

Vivian answered lightly, " Enemy, of course."

Miss Clyde gave a cackle of pleased laughter. " That's right, my dear, I like that. Enemy, she says. That's more than anyone else says. They all say they're my friends. They'll do this for me and that for me. Everyone wants to help poor old Aunt Jay. What I say is, give me a few enemies. I'd sleep better at night in a houseful of enemies." She gave Vivian a beaming, loose-lipped smile. " I like you, dear. I can't quite remember who you are, but you must stay here. You must stay as long as you like. But Alice Summers is my best friend. And everybody's friend. ' Your friend, Alice Summers.' That's how she signs all her letters, doesn't she ? And she makes a lot of money out of being everybody's friend. Much more than I've ever made, honestly letting rooms to honest people, ha, ha ! She writes lots of letters and she gets paid for it. Oh, yes, you'd never dream how much she gets paid. But one day she might get *paid out* instead, mightn't she ? I wonder if she's ever thought of that. She might get paid out by one of her own dear friends. Take care of your friends, Alice Summers. It's much better to have enemies."

Her voice had risen on the last words almost to a screech. Then she turned and strode unsteadily towards a room at the far end of the hall.

Alex knew that this room was Miss Clyde's bedroom and office, the only room in the house that was solely for herself. Henrietta immediately hurried after her aunt. Conrad hesitated, but finding that Vivian was looking at him, he turned and strode off through the garden. For an instant Alex saw on Vivian's face a look of intense pain and anger, then she went quickly into the house and upstairs.

At Alex's side a voice spoke. " What did I tell you ? Gin. Poor old girl. It's been the ruin of many a good woman. Which doesn't mean that a drop wouldn't do you a lot of good at the moment from the look of you. How about it ? "

It was T. T. Tally. Dressed in corduroy trousers and a high-necked, emerald-green sweater with the initials, T. T. T., knitted into it in white across his chest, he was standing in the doorway of the sitting-room.

" I fix good drinks. Come along and try," he said.

" So you aren't working to-day," said Alex, following him into the sitting-room and dropping despondently into a chair. " Oughtn't you to be scouring the countryside, trying to sell insurance ? "

" What, when there are lovely women around ? "

Mrs. Wakely, who was in a chair by the fire, said frigidly, " He never does any work. He just sits around talking and drinking."

" And what is there better to do in the world ? " he asked, pouring out a glass for Alex and another for himself. " Particularly when one's got a lovely woman to drink with." He lifted his glass to Mrs. Wakely.

She gave him a glare and went on speaking to Alex. " Mind you, I will say this for him, he takes quite an intelligent interest in the question of the fertilisation of the soil. Much more so than that young man of Henrietta's, who's merely a mass of conventional prejudices and believes anything he's told in a government pamphlet. That's how they grow up these days. All spoon-fed, no independence of judgment. We were different. We thought for ourselves. When my husband and I first became aware of the extreme danger to our society of the systematic destruction of the productivity of the soil——"

Tally interrupted by murmuring : " Excuse me," and with a wink at Alex which suggested that it was her own fault if she chose to sit and suffer while Mrs. Wakely rode her hobbyhorse, he gulped his drink and trotted out of the room.

This had made Mrs. Wakely lose the thread of her thoughts. " What was I saying ? " she asked.

" You were talking about your husband," said Alex discreetly.

" Oh, yes . . . My poor husband. You'll have heard all about his death, of course. Such a wonderful man, such a deep thinker, so sincere. People wonder at my staying on here, I believe, but the truth is, I feel closer to him here than I should anywhere else. Besides . . ." Her bleak grey eyes had softened for one tragic, self-revealing moment, then they grew colder than before. " Sometimes," she said, " I wonder."

Alex stirred uncomfortably. She felt just then that she could endure Mrs. Wakely's hobbyhorse far more easily than Mrs. Wakely's wondering. But still an intense curiosity kept Alex seated.

" I wonder," said Mrs. Wakely, " about that barking dog."

" *What* dog ? " asked Alex, startled.

" No doubt you'll laugh at me," said Mrs. Wakely. " A great many people laugh at me for my opinions. I've been laughed at for this. But still I keep thinking about it so much that now I can hardly bear to hear a dog barking . . . Rather inconvenient in the country," she added with an uneasy little smile.

Alex had noticed that Mrs. Wakely's manner was growing more excited. At the same time Alex found herself trying to remember some thought of her own about a dog that had barked. But for the moment she could not think what it was.

" You see, only the day he died," said Mrs. Wakely, " my husband said something to me about a barking dog. He said, ' I'm going to the police about a barking dog.' At least . . ." Her gaze grew confused. " I think that's what he said. ' I'm going to the police about a barking dog, Addie.' That's my name, you know—Adelaide. I think he said it, but sometimes I start distrusting myself when I think about him. I think about him so much, you see, that sometimes I think I must be making up some of the things that I remember about him."

" But that doesn't sound like the kind of thing you'd trouble to make up," said Alex.

" No, that's what I think. But Miss Clyde said I must have made it up or got muddled about it somehow. I was very ill for some weeks after Roland's death and what I remember so clearly might possibly have been some silly sort of dream."

" He said this to you on the day he died, the day of the fire ? " asked Alex.

" Yes, in the morning. We were all going to the cinema in Sharnmouth, Miss Clyde, Miss Takahashi, the Perriers and Roland and me. It was a French film with that wonderful actor, Raimu, in it, and Miss Clyde thought it would be nice for Monsieur Perrier to see it. He hadn't been long in England then and could speak even less English than he can now. We decided to go to the five-thirty performance, because that meant we could do some shopping in Sharnmouth first, have tea at the Holly Bush Tea Rooms, go to the cinema and get home in time for a late supper. We'd all agreed on it about a week before when Miss Clyde first saw the notices of the film and at that time Roland had said he'd come in with the rest of us in the early afternoon. But then on the morning of the day he said to me that I must tell the others that he wanted to go on looking for some herb on the cliffs and that he would meet us at the cinema. I reminded him that it was quite the wrong time of the year for the herb he mentioned, and he said, ' None of them will know that.' So I asked him what he really wanted to do during the afternoon. And he said, ' I'm going to the police about a barking dog.' "

It was then that Alex remembered the dog she had seen in the boat in the cove in the early morning.

Speaking very fast in her agitation, Mrs. Wakely went on, " At the time I thought it was just a joke of Roland's. He was never a very sociable man and I thought he was looking for a way of avoiding the shopping and the tea party. And when he didn't come to the cinema, I felt sure that that was all it was. And when I heard that his body had been found in bed, I thought he'd spent the afternoon having a nice quiet read and had dropped off to sleep and overslept himself. That all sounds probable, doesn't it ? Much more probable than that he'd been meaning to go to the police about a barking dog and that somebody stopped him——" She checked herself abruptly, staring at Alex with a look of terror in her eyes.

Alex thought that this must be the first time that Mrs. Wakely had ever put the half-formulated, terrible thought into words and that the sound of them, making a bald statement of murder, had turned out to be more than she could bear.

" Much more probable," Alex agreed, perhaps too hurriedly, feeling herself infected by Mrs. Wakely's fear. " After all, there wasn't any barking dog, was there ? "

" Not that I know of," said Mrs. Wakely.

" And he hadn't mentioned one at any other time ? "

" No, I don't think so. Though now that I think of it . . ."

She paused and Alex was aware of a great desire to prevent her going on. She did not want to have to think about fire and death and barking dogs and murder. She wanted to be able to say soothingly to Mrs. Wakely that she was letting her imagination torture her unnecessarily. But Alex said nothing.

" I remember his saying something about a dog being able to see much farther than you'd think," said Mrs. Wakely, " because a dog had apparently seen him standing on the cliffs and had started to bark when the boat was quite a long way out to sea."

" The *boat* ? " said Alex.

" Yes, the dog was in a boat," said Mrs. Wakely. " But that couldn't have had anything to do with it, could it ? "

" No," said Alex. " No, of course not."

Mrs. Wakely got up then and went out of the room.

Alex felt the same sensation of sudden cold in her body as she had felt the day before in the car after reading the anonymous letter.

At lunch Miss Clyde did not appear. Since Monsieur Perrier was in London and Conrad had gone on an advisory visit to a farmer in the neighbourhood, the big table in the dining-room seemed empty. Only Tally talked. He talked about life in a prison camp in Germany, which Alex thought he did in an attempt to impress Vivian, who smiled at him absently but was clearly not listening.

When lunch was over, having told Henrietta that there was some work she must do and Vivian that she wanted her mail, Alex went to her room. After a few minutes, Vivian appeared with the letters and once more upset Alex's plans by seeming to be able to read her thoughts.

" Well," said Vivian, laying the bundle of letters on a table, " go on and say it. Say I ought never to have come when I knew Conrad was here. Of course, I know that I ought not to have come. And now I wish that I hadn't. But I suppose most people do fairly stupid things at some time in their lives, even when they know beforehand that they're going to regret it ever afterwards. I happen to have done quite a number of things like that."

" So you did know him before you met him here ? " said Alex.

" Of course I did—didn't you notice it when we met ? " said Vivian. " Neither of us disguised our feelings very well, though poor, dear Henrietta seemed to notice nothing."

" I shouldn't be so sure of that, if I were you," said Alex. " But why did you come ? "

" Why d'you think ? " Vivian looked almost contemptuous at the question. " I wanted to see him again. I thought—no, I didn't think. I didn't think anything. I just wanted it. There's nothing else to say about it."

" When did you meet him first ? " Alex asked.

" Soon after the war, in Paris."

" I thought you were in a sanatorium then."

" I was, but a sanatorium isn't a prison, you know. One's permitted to take holidays. There are times when being an invalid and being among invalids, who talk nothing but their illness all day long, becomes something that one simply can't bear any longer. One feels it'd be better to go out into the normal world and do a little living and get worse and die, than go on living by the grace of doctors and nurses, with thermometers in and out of one's mouth all day and rest periods and everything one does being watched, while the occasional coffin gets slipped out quietly at night. So I went to Paris."

" And you didn't call yourself Vivian Dale."

" No, I called myself Mary Carter."

" Which is your real name ? "

" Vivian Dale."

" Why did you use a false name when you went to Paris ? "

" D'you mean you don't understand ? It was to leave my illness behind, of course. For a short time I wanted to wipe out everything that reminded me of the sanatorium and of being ill. It was to be only Vivian Dale who was ill, not Mary Carter."

" And then you met Conrad ? "

" Yes, he was in the army. I met him on my first day in Paris. If you want details, I picked him up in a café. He was the first healthy man, not a doctor, whom I'd had a chance to talk to for what felt like a lifetime. And then I fell hopelessly in love with him. And he fell in love with me. He wanted us to get married as soon as he could get back to England. And I agreed. I agreed without stopping to think. I'd have agreed to anything just then. It was so wonderful that I can't bear to think about it now. When I do, by mistake, I feel as if it were cracking me in two."

" But you didn't get married ? "

" Oh, no," said Vivian with a bitter laugh, " our dear Conrad isn't a bigamist. I ran out on him, you see. I deserted him. Poor, poor Conrad."

Her tone annoyed Alex and checked the sympathy she had been starting to feel. It seemed to her that Vivian's manner had become too dramatic and somehow rather false.

" Why did you do that ? "

" Why ? " cried Vivian. " *Why?* " She stared at Alex in a kind of shocked astonishment. " Because I wasn't Mary Carter, I was Vivian Dale. I wasn't a healthy woman, fit for marriage, I was a tubercular invalid with no right to burden anyone with my useless existence."

" Didn't you tell him ? "

" Of course not. He'd have felt he had to go on and marry me, or wait for me, or do some stupid, noble thing about it all. So I just walked out one night and went back to the sanatorium. I didn't write to him. I was very ill for a time after I got back. I thought I was going to die. But then I began to get well surprisingly fast, because—I'm sure that was the reason—I'd somehow got myself to believe that I'd something to live for. You see, I knew where Conrad's home was and I thought that if I could get really and truly cured, I might——" She stopped. Her lips closed, trembling.

Alex was silent, too, fighting a confused battle with her sense of pity on the one hand and her suspicions on the other.

Presently she said, " Well, you shouldn't have come here.

60

In a way, I can't help sympathising with you, but still you shouldn't have come. You took your decision in Paris and when you discovered that Conrad was engaged to be married, you should have stuck to it."

" It must be awfully easy to say that to somebody else," said Vivian.

" It isn't," said Alex, " even if it's rather easy to see that it's the truth." What she really felt just then was that it would have been much easier if only Alice Summers could have put it into a letter to Vivian. Alice Summers dealt with problems like that every day. " But how d'you feel now that you've met Conrad again ? Are you still as much in love with him ? "

Vivian crossed the room to the window and stood looking out at the grey, calm sea.

" D'you know, I'm not at all sure," she said. " I'm upset, because seeing him again has made me live through a lot of what I went through in Paris and afterwards. But I'm not sure I feel that Conrad's actually the person who made me feel all those things. In any case, you needn't worry about me —or about your darling Henrietta. I'll behave very properly and not speak to him any more than I can help. I had to have one talk with him to put one or two things straight, but from now on I'll do my best to avoid him. If you like, I'll go back to London to-morrow."

" That might be best," said Alex.

" It would certainly be pleasantest for me," said Vivian with a little snap of venom in her voice. " You needn't worry though about Conrad and your Henrietta. She'd be able to hold him even if I did try to get him away from her. Conrad's —well, he's rather a fool in some ways. That may be why I'm not sure any longer about being in love with him any more, because I'm five years older than I was in Paris and I've got to like different qualities in people. But Henrietta's clever. I believe she's ever so much cleverer than you've ever realised, perhaps than most people have ever realised. That's partly where the cleverness comes in. So you'll find she can look after herself very nicely. I shouldn't worry about her at all, even when there's a dreadful and desperate person like me around." She laughed again, this time softly, as if she had some private joke to enjoy, and went out of the room.

VIII

FOR THE next two hours, Alex tried to work. But the letters she wrote seemed to lack all her customary warmth of tone and confidence in dealing with other people's problems.

In each letter she felt inclined to write : " My dear X, I'm in a mess myself and haven't the faintest idea what I ought to do about it. So couldn't you please advise me ? "

Fortunately the letters were all of types that she had received a thousand times, so she was able to write her answers more or less from memory.

While her pen ran on, her thoughts became more and more entangled in visions of Miss Clyde. The old woman seemed to have taken up her quarters in Alex's brain and to be lurking about in all the spare corners of it. Alex kept trying to trap these visions into conversation, but they all appeared to be deaf.

The room grew dusk. At first Alex took no notice of it, going on with her work until she could hardly see the words she was setting down on the paper. But at last she had to get up and turn on the light. The yellow brightness in the room, after the shadows, had the effect of making her come abruptly to a decision. She would go to Miss Clyde now. The old woman had had several hours in which to sober up and should be in a condition to be made to understand the preposterousness of her accusations.

Alex went downstairs. As she went along the passage to Miss Clyde's room, she saw no chinks of light showing round the door, which made her half-expect to find the room empty. But when she tapped on the door, Miss Clyde's voice answered immediately : " Come in, come in ! " From the impatience in her tone, it sounded as if she were expecting somebody.

Entering, Alex said, " It's I, Miss Clyde. May I talk to you ? "

" Yes, yes, come in," said Miss Clyde, as if it were Alex whom she had been expecting.

The room was almost in darkness, for the curtains had been drawn half-way across the windows, excluding most of the little remaining light of the early evening. Though there was no fire in the grate, the room, warmed by a big radiator, was stiflingly hot. It was a small room, crowded with all the hoarded litter of a lifetime, as unlike as possible the well-arranged comfort of the rest of the house. Photographs in silver or velvet frames, furniture decorated with tassels and fringes, large pots filled with drooping green plants, pale prints of young ladies and gentlemen in romantic costumes, little carved Indian tables and bookcases full of unfriendly-looking, unread Victorian classics, crowded all the corners, ledges and bare spaces of wall in the room. The only touch of modernity was a small electric clock standing on the corner of a writing-table.

Miss Clyde lay on a divan against the wall, under a crimson satin eiderdown. Her feet, still in their slippers, stuck out from under the end of the quilt. Her head was propped up by a great pile of pillows, with her flaming, tousled hair tumbled across their whiteness. Alex could scarcely see her eyes in the shadows, but they seemed to be staring up at her intently.

" Why didn't you come sooner ? " Miss Clyde asked as Alex crossed the room towards her. " Nobody comes to see me. They leave me to lie here alone, to sleep or to die, for all they know or care. Nobody cares about me any more. I've been lying here counting. I've been saying to myself, ' I'll count up to five hundred and if no one's come to see me by that time, I'll show them. I'll show them what it means to be neglected when you're old and ill. Yes, I'll count up to five hundred and then I'll show them.' But it's difficult counting up to five hundred, d'you know that ? Two hundred or three hundred's easy, but somewhere after that I always lose count. I've tried keeping a check on the hundreds on my fingers, but then I always forget whether I've counted my thumb or not. All the same, I'll show them. Why didn't you come sooner ? "

It seemed to Alex that Miss Clyde had not really taken in who she was.

" I thought you'd like a good rest," she said. " You must be very tired, with all the excitement of the wedding on Saturday."

" It's not the excitement," said Miss Clyde. " It's the fear." Pointing imperiously to a small, beaded, fringed and tasselled chair, she went on : " Come and sit down. Come and talk to me. I'd got to four hundred and twenty-nine when you came in. I hadn't lost count yet. I'm all right when I make a real effort. My head's as clear as anybody's. But the fear preys on my mind. Have you ever been afraid ? "

" Very often," said Alex.

" But so afraid that your blood doesn't move round in your body. Afraid for your life and afraid of what will happen when you die."

" Yes—once in a car accident," said Alex.

" Ah. Was anyone killed ? Whose fault was it ? "

" I'm not sure that it was anyone's fault."

" You mean it was your fault, don't you ? "

" No, I wasn't driving."

" It must have been your fault. That's why you were so afraid. You're afraid like me, but pretending not to be. I'm glad of that. It amuses me. You look so innocent, but you're as bad as I am."

" Perhaps we're none of us too good," said Alex.

The old woman giggled. " You look good, you sound good, but there's no telling, is there ? I shouldn't wonder if you've got all the crimes of the world on your conscience. That's what I have, you know. All the crimes of the world. And that's a terrible state to be in at my age, my dear, with so little time left. Death so near, you know. Terrible, isn't it ? I'm just a poor old woman who never meant to do anyone any harm. You do believe me, don't you ? It was an accident. You must believe it ! "

" Of course," said Alex, giving up all thought of the mission that had brought her to the room and wondering if she could possibly bring any comfort into the clouded mind of the poor, crazed old creature. " I'm sure you never harmed anyone in your life. Everyone knows that it was an accident."

Another giggle came shockingly from under the crimson eiderdown.

" That's right, that what they think, the fools. But I'll show them. D'you know what I'm going to do ? I'm going to count up to five hundred and then I'm going to write to the police. Nobody ever thought I'd do that. Henrietta told me to write to that Miss Summers of hers, but she's a blackmailing bitch, my dear, always talking to me about a barking dog.

Don't listen to her. It was nothing to do with a barking dog. The poor old man, the poor old man. Oh, God, be merciful to me . . . I'm going to write to the police about a blackmailing bitch, not a barking dog. When I've counted up to five hundred. That'll show them."

" Miss Clyde, did you say *Henrietta* told you to write to me ? " asked Alex, leaning closer to the bed.

But she could see at once that the question made no impact on Miss Clyde's consciousness. After her last words, her eyes had closed. In the deepening darkness it had become almost impossible to see her features or the bright colour of her hair. Her face was only a blur, framed by a darker blur, looking like a battered paper mask tossed down on the pillow.

Alex waited for a few minutes until deeper breathing suggested that Miss Clyde had actually fallen asleep. Then Alex got up and walked softly to the door. In a way, her heart was lighter than when she had come in. The babblings of poor old Miss Clyde had no need to be taken seriously. But Alex blamed Henrietta for not having told her more explicitly of her aunt's condition, or got Miss Clyde weeks ago into the hands of a good doctor.

Alex opened the door. As she did so, footsteps retreated rapidly down the unlit passage.

She groped for a light switch. But before she had found it, whoever had been listening at the door had gone. Turning on the light, Alex thought for a moment that there was no one about, then she saw Miss Takahashi standing half-way down the stairs. She had one finger on her lips, while with her other hand she was eagerly beckoning Alex towards her. Since the footsteps had gone in the direction away from the staircase, Alex knew that it could not have been Miss Takahashi who had been the eavesdropper.

Walking to the foot of the stairs, Alex asked her, " Did you hear someone run down that passage just now ? "

Miss Takahashi made motions of pressing her fingers still more secretly against her lips. Then she pointed at Miss Clyde's door and whispered : " Poor woman. Very sick. Very funny woman, always worrying, got very sick now. Very funny woman to worry about what can't be helped. Got very sick from worrying, poor woman. But very good to me when I am sick. I am very glad to help her if I can, but very hard to cure sickness from worry. Very funny to get sick from worry. Very funny woman."

" Yes," said Alex, feeling that that was really all there was to say about it.

Miss Takahashi darted down a couple of steps, and leaning closer to Alex, she whispered even more inaudibly, " Mustn't keep you talking when you're busy. But I watch, you watch, perhaps if we watch we help her. I always watch. No one knows, but I watch all the time."

Then she clasped her hand over her mouth and had one of her fits of silent, explosive mirth, in the midst of which she turned and ran off upstairs.

Alex stood looking after her. Then she looked again along the passage, realising that if Miss Takahashi wanted Alex to share in her watching, she seemed to have no intention of sharing with Alex any information about what she had almost certainly seen. With a shrug of her shoulders, Alex went to the sitting-room.

She found Conrad there alone, twiddling the knobs of the radio. He had just succeeded in tuning in to some Chopin, but after only a few bars of this he went looking for other sources of distraction.

Alex went to the fire and sat down beside it.

After a minute or two Conrad left the radio and came to the fireside. He did not look at Alex, but resting both hands on the mantelpiece, stood staring moodily at the flames.

" Well, I've been having a talk with Vivian Dale, alias Mary Carter," said Alex.

" Oh, yes ? " It sounded as if he were trying to suggest that the subject had no interest for him.

" She told me an intriguing story," said Alex.

" She was always good at that," he said.

" You don't want to hear it ? "

With the toe of his shoe, he kicked at a smouldering lump of coal. " Not very much."

" Of course, if it's true, I ought not to tell it you," Alex went on.

" It probably isn't true."

" What makes you say that ? "

" Because Mary's imagination was always singularly vivid."

" I'm not going to pry," said Alex, " but there's one thing

I do insist on asking you and that is, how much does Henrietta know about it now ? "

" Nothing," he said.

" Then go and tell her," said Alex. " Go and tell her quick."

He gave a laugh and flung himself into a chair. His blue eyes shone angrily with reflections from the fire.

" And I didn't even enclose a stamped, addressed envelope for the advice, Miss Summers," he said.

She flushed. " No," she said, after a moment, " you didn't. I'm sorry."

He hesitated, flushing also, then said, " No, *I'm* sorry. That was a rotten thing to say."

" It's a rotten habit, giving advice," said Alex. " Sometimes I can't seem to stop myself. But you see, I'm very fond of Henrietta."

" Strange as it may seem, so am I," he said. " But this situation with Mary—Vivian—has taken me by surprise and I want to think it out. I've a certain responsibility . . . ." He stopped and got restlessly to his feet again.

" Towards Vivian ? " Alex asked apprehensively, thinking of what such a responsibility usually implied.

" No," said Conrad, with an odd glance at her that Alex could not interpret. " Towards someone else. Which makes me anxious to know what Vivian's really after. Because that isn't me, whatever you may think. She never had much use for me, except when I looked at someone else. Then it amused her to lay traps for the other person to get entangled in and hurt. That's partly why I want to be very careful what I do about Henrietta. Because "—his voice dropped—" I never imagined that anyone could be quite so precious to me as she is."

" I should think you could tell her absolutely anything you wanted to," said Alex, " if you used the tone in which you said that."

" Except, you know, that there are a good many things she doesn't tell me," he said " And that complicates things, because it means she distrusts me quite a lot."

" You mean because of those colds that you and I didn't have ? "

" And some other things since then."

" Well, Vivian's said that she'll leave to-morrow and I'll

see that she does," said Alex. " That at least should make the situation easier for the moment."

Conrad stabbed again with his shoe at the lump of coal so that it collapsed in flaming fragments. Watching these, he muttered, " I'll deal with her, anyway. Don't be afraid. With her and the old woman. It's my responsibility."

He left her then abruptly.

The flames from the piece of coal that had just been broken made a gay crackle in the fireplace and sparkled brilliantly against the blackness of the chimney. The surge of heat made Alex move her chair back from the fire. The room seemed to her to have become very warm, which was a strange feeling on such a cold winter's evening. She thought that the cause of it was probably her nerves and that perhaps she had a temperature. Sometimes when she had become over-excited, or worried, she did develop a slight temperature, enough to make her feel uneasy and depressed, though not to make her think of herself as ill. It would be just like her to have this happen now, with Henrietta's wedding the day after to-morrow.

The wedding. She had almost forgotten about it. No one else seemed to be talking about it or treating it as an event of much importance. Presumably this was because of Miss Clyde's condition, for it must have become quite clear to anyone who had been living in the house during the past fortnight that there was little chance of Miss Clyde playing her part normally at any wedding.

If only Henrietta had brought herself to speak more clearly about her aunt during that lunch at Colonna's, thought Alex, the advice that she would have given her then would certainly have been quite different.

" If I'd had any sense," Alex's reflections continued, " I'd have seen she was really seriously worried about something and could probably have got her to talk about what was on her mind. But my own silly mind was too damn full of a lovely white wedding to sentimentalise over and all that nonsense. If only I'd understood the situation, I'd have told her to get a special licence and go off to the nearest registry office, in a tweed suit, a raincoat, or anything that came to hand, and then come home and deal with her aunt. But I couldn't stop thinking about those horrible photographs of Vivian and so I never really bothered to make her talk . . ."

From the doorway, a voice said, " So the lady is all alone."

It was Tally. He walked across the room to her, smiling cheerfully.

" All alone and thinking," he said. " And they looked pretty sad thoughts, which is a pity. Nothing's worth getting all that depressed about, anyway when you're our kind of age. After all, one can always have a drink. What about it ? "

" Presently," said Alex, smiling back at him and thinking that in this house of worries, there was something rather comfortable about him.

" Perhaps you want to go on being alone," he suggested. " Just say the word if you do. I get that way myself sometimes, though generally when the fit comes on, I like a bottle of gin at my elbow. A room, a bath, and a bottle of gin, that's civilisation." He sat down facing her. " Nice and quiet here, isn't it ? I like the way it gets quiet here in the evening. No cars, no trains, no people in the streets under your window. Just listen a moment how quiet it is."

Alex listened, then said, " Yes, not even a dog barking."

Afterwards she was never able to make up her mind what had made her say that. Had she said it innocently, using the image that most easily expressed for her the silence that surrounded the house on the cliffs ? Or had the dog that had barked its way into the conversation of one person after another with whom she had talked that day got its fangs into her thoughts already, so that she could not get free of him ?

The effect on Tally was extraordinary.

All the good humour vanished from his face. Springing from his chair, he crossed to where she sat and bending over her, his face close to hers, taut with a look of anger and violence, he demanded : " What do you know about a barking dog ? "

IX

ALEX DREW away from him sharply.

"What," she said, "are you talking about?"

He went on staring into her face. Then his expression changed. He straightened and turned away.

"Sorry," he said. "Sorry, sorry, my mistake."

"You don't make sense," said Alex. "What do you want to know about a barking dog?"

"It's just something I've got on my mind," he said. "Something important to me."

"Then I'm sorry I can't help you," she said. "I might just as easily have said just now that I couldn't even hear an owl hooting."

"Yes, I know," he said. "I know, forget it. But if ever anyone talks to you about a dog barking . . ."

"Well?"

"Maybe you might just mention the fact to me."

"I might," she said thoughtfully, "if I knew why you were so interested."

He looked at her again with his round, pug-dog eyes sardonic. "So someone has been talking to you about it, eh?"

"About what?"

"That damned dog. You're interested in it yourself. You'd like me to tell you something about it."

"I'd certainly like you to explain a little more than you have your own curious behaviour just now when I used a very ordinary phrase," she said.

"I said I was sorry, didn't I?"

"Which was certainly proper in the circumstances, but not enlightening."

He gave a laugh. "My dear, it seems to me I've been sizing you up all wrong. I thought from the look of you, with that nice fair hair of yours, and your smile and your pretty clothes and that stuff you write, that you were one of the fluffy ones. Fluffy and gentle and easy to get along with."

" Not quite a cosy cutie, but say half-way along the road to it ? " Alex suggested.

" That's it, that's it exactly. Whereas you're really a pretty cool customer. Well, I dare say I should have guessed it. Being successful at anything takes toughness. I dare say you've had to be pretty tough to hold on to that column of yours. And pretty shrewd, eh ? I dare say you know a lot more about people than anyone would think from reading that blah blah stuff you turn out each week. D'you know, I envy you a gift like that, I really do. Wonderful just to be able to sit down and write that sort of thing and have the cash come rolling in. If only I could do something like that."

" At any rate," said Alex, who had flushed with annoyance at his description of her work, but who was determined not to argue with him on a matter so personal, " you have a gift for evasion. It was a barking dog we were talking about, weren't we, not my journalistic successes ? "

" A barking dog, that's right." Instead of going on, he started to hum a little tune. He stared at her while he did so. He looked as if he were trying to make up his mind about something, but at the same time not to let her guess what he was thinking about. At last he shrugged his shoulders. " I'll tell you one thing," he said, " but the trouble is you won't take me seriously. That dog's not a good thing to talk about round here."

" Why not ? "

" I wish I knew."

" Then Mrs. Wakely's right——"

He interrupted sharply : " I said, don't talk about it."

" You might explain a little more," said Alex.

" I can't," he said. " I don't know much more. I only know it's not a good thing to seem to know more about it. That old man who went up in smoke, he'd started talking about a barking dog. Poor old geezer . . . Well, we don't want any more fires, do we ? "

" You're making a very horrible suggestion," said Alex. A certain new idea about T.T. Tally had just entered her mind.

" I'm not the first to make it to you though, am I ? " he asked shrewdly. " Now you take my advice, my dear, and even if you hear dogs howling all round the house, don't go

71

remarking on it. Just stick to it that this is a nice, quiet place. Only if you hear someone else talking about a barking dog—not Mrs. Wakely, she's bats, she doesn't count—just mention it to me, will you? I could use the information."

Reaching out a stubby-fingered hand, he stroked it lightly over Alex's fair curls, and adding softly, "Blah, blah," he left the room.

Ruffled, puzzled and at the same time more scared than she had realised until that moment by the implications of the conversation, Alex opened her bag to look for her pocket mirror, to make sure that her hair had not been disarranged. She wished that she had asked Tally one more question before he went out. But no doubt the opportunity to do so would arise presently.

It did not arise before dinner. He came in a minute or two after everyone else and taking his place beside Vivian, started again on his prison-camp anecdotes. Vivian, Alex thought, had undergone a change since the morning. She had a pallor that made her look ill and an absent look as if she were deeply engrossed in an absorbing problem. Conrad and Henrietta kept up a strained silence so that Mrs. Wakely had no real competition in delivering a lecture on the evils of sulphate of ammonia.

Miss Clyde did not appear. Henrietta had put a little supper on a tray and taken it to her aunt's room, but on returning to the dining-room had said, " She says she doesn't want anything. I tried arguing, but she wouldn't listen. So I've just left the tray by the bed."

Returning to the sitting-room after dinner, Alex found no one else there but Madame Perrier, who was sitting by the fire with an armful of lacy, pale pink knitting in her lap. When Alex appeared Madame Perrier suggested that it would be nice to have the radio on if there was any nice light music on the programme. Going to the radio, Alex switched it on. For some reason it did not work. After fiddling with the knobs for a minute or two, she gave it up and returned to the fire.

" Well, never mind," said Madame Perrier. " Tally will fix it. He's as clever as can be at things like that. He'll be in presently to listen to the news, then we'll get him to see to it. Whatever he's doing, he never misses the nine o'clock news. He's one of those people who always think a war may just have broken out and that it'd be fatal if he wasn't the first one to know of it. Myself, I don't like listening to the news, I generally go out when he turns it on. It's always so awful, it upsets me. I prefer to think of nice things, like the wedding, for instance. You've no idea how I've been looking forward to the wedding, my dear. Henrietta's such a sweet girl. I'm sure she deserves all the happiness in the world, and Mr. Moorhouse is such a handsome, gentlemanly young man, isn't he? I'm sure it's a perfect match. Only they don't seem very cheerful at the minute, do they? At dinner, I mean, they hardly said a word. A lover's quarrel, I suppose." She looked up from her knitting and cocked a knowing eyebrow at Alex.

"I hadn't noticed," said Alex. She had taken up a book and hoped that Madame Perrier would notice the fact. But Madame Perrier chatted on. She talked about the wedding-dress and about what she herself was going to wear for the occasion, about what Alex would wear, about what Alex was wearing just then and about Vivian's way of dressing.

"A kind of a queer-looking girl, if you don't mind my saying so, dear," said Madame Perrier. "I suppose some people would call her quite good looking, but she doesn't know how to make the most of herself. She's too pale to go about with so little make-up and her dresses aren't what you could call smart, are they? In fact, I should say they were just a bit on the eccentric side, as if she was trying to call attention to herself. And I don't believe she'd mind attracting the attention of Mr. Moorhouse, would she now?" She gave an arch little giggle to show that her remark had of course been meant only as a joke. But while her plump fingers flickered amidst the pink wool, she kept a shrewd eye on Alex.

Having given up trying to read because of Madame Perrier's flow of talk, Alex contributed an occasional yes, or no, or is that so, but she was thinking that in another few minutes, if Henrietta did not appear, she would go looking for her.

Alex had just laid her book down and was about to get up, when Tally came in.

"Mind my turning on the news?" he asked.

"There now, didn't I tell you he'd be in to hear who's declared war on who?" said Madame Perrier. "But you're going to be disappointed to-night, Tally."

" What, no war. Impossible," said Tally, grinning.

" No wireless," said Madame Perrier. " Unless you can put it right."

" Hell," he said, " what's wrong ? "

" Nothing happens when you switch it on," said Madame Perrier, " that's all I can tell you. You're the clever one who can tell us why."

Frowning, as if the thought of missing the news put him out quite seriously, Tally went to the radio.

He appeared to be one of those men who become extremely profane the moment they start handling an even mildly refractory piece of mechanism. As soon as he had made sure that the set was correctly plugged in and would not respond to the switch, he started quietly and steadily swearing while he twiddled knobs and tried hitting the radio in a number of places, in case a little primitive action might do it some good. Nothing resulted except that Madame Perrier made a pained face, and saying " Anyway, I never care to listen to the news," went out of the room.

A minute or two later Tally exclaimed, " God darn it, I'm a fool ! "

" Found the trouble ? " said Alex.

" I ought to have seen it at once," he replied. " One of the leads is broken. Soon put that right, anyway. All I need is a pair of pliers." He hurried out of the room, leaving the door wide open.

It was just then that the lights went out. Both in the sitting-room and in the passage, there was suddenly complete darkness. Alex started to get up but changed her mind and remained where she was. After a winter of power-cuts, it did not occur to her that there was anything remarkable about the failure of the lights. She sat still.

Almost immediately someone shuffled cautiously into the room. It was Madame Perrier's voice that exclaimed, " There—another cut ! We've been having them about twice a week since the beginning of December. Oh, dear, I can't see a thing till my eyes get used to the dark." Her shadowy figure came towards the chair that she had left a few minutes before. " We've let the fire get too low. Isn't that silly of us ? Mrs. Summerill, dear, the coal-box is your side. Suppose we make the fire up a little."

As Alex stooped to find the tongs for the coal, Tally's voice at the other end of the room, said, " Oh, to be in England now that austerity's here ! I ask you, who'd stick it if they could get out ? Who wouldn't sooner be in France or Italy ? Or just think of California now. Blue skies and a blue sea and the mimosa in blossom and all the damned electricity you can use." He came towards the fire. " What's the trouble now ? No coal, I'll bet."

" There certainly doesn't seem to be any," said Alex, who had been feeling around inside the coal scuttle with the tongs.

Tally laughed sourly and sat down. The fire, which had sunk to some glowing cinders, lit up his heavy features with a dull red light.

" If it weren't for my kid," he said, " I wouldn't stay two weeks in the lousy hole. But the trouble is, she's had too much pushing around already. For the first three or four years of her life she was shoved here and left there till the poor kid didn't know if she was going or coming, and now she's got something she likes at last, I haven't the heart to take it away from her. She's happy as can be in that posh school at Bournemouth. So here I am stuck for the next few years, forced to take all the miseries our government can think up for us and not complain."

" You never do anything else but complain," said Madame Perrier.

" Not half as much as I'd like to, all the same," he said.

" I suppose it *is* a power-cut," said Alex, " not a fuse or something."

" Well, it's the whole house," said Tally, "which doesn't look like a fuse. If you don't mind sitting in the dark for a little, I'll look for some candles. There are usually some on the mantelpiece, but they seem to have been used up. These cuts don't usually last long, though."

As he spoke, the door opened again and two figures advanced towards the faint light of the fire. They were Conrad and Henrietta.

" What's wrong with the fire ? " asked Conrad. " If we made it up a bit this could be rather nice. We could have drinks all round and tell ghost stories."

" No coal," said Tally.

From the doorway, Mrs. Wakely's voice remarked, " Then

someone must have been burning it most uneconomically, because the scuttle was full not long before dinner."

" If anyone's got a torch to lend me," said Conrad, " I'll go out and get some more."

" Wait till the light comes on," said Henrietta. " It won't be long, and it'll be easier. That coal shed's such an awkward place if it's dark. But why haven't you lit the candles ? "

" No candles," said Tally. " And no wireless either. The lead's broken."

" Looks like a complete breakdown of all civilised amenities," said Conrad. He laughed. " Hasn't anything else gone wrong ? "

" D'you know," said Alex uncertainly, " I'm almost sure there were candles on the mantelpiece before dinner—tall, tapering, red ones. Or was it last night I noticed them ? " She frowned, visualising the candles quite clearly in their branching brass candlesticks, but not absolutely certain when she had last seen them.

" If so, they've probably been pinched by Miss Takahashi," said Conrad. " She's the kind of person who likes to be provided against all emergencies. She'd hardly go for a half-hour's walk without carrying iron rations with her. I expect she's upstairs scribbling away as usual while Rome doesn't burn."

" I wish you wouldn't refer to things burning," said Mrs. Wakely.

This naturally produced a very uncomfortable silence.

To end it, Conrad returned to his suggestion that drinks all round would help, and with Henrietta striking matches to help him, he found glasses and filled them and handed them round. He had just accomplished this when a man's voice from the hall called out, " Hallo, hallo, why are we all in darkness ? "

" That's Pierre," cried Madame Perrier, starting up. " I've been expecting him by the nine-fifteen bus, but I hadn't realised it was so late already." She tripped over to the door and opened it. " In here, Pierre, we're all in here. It's just another of those wretched power-cuts. How are you, dear ? I've been so afraid you'd lose yourself in London and miss your train and find some frightful foreign brunette to pass the time with. But you came safe home to your old Florrie ! "

She giggled and in the darkness she and her husband were heard to exchange a smacking kiss.

" A power-cut ? " said Monsieur Perrier, coming into the sitting-room. " That is strange. That is very strange."

" Myself, I'd call it one of the commonest events of our daily lives," said Tally bitterly.

" But nowhere else are the lights out," said Monsieur Perrier.

" What—not in Sharnmouth ? " said Tally.

" No, not in Sharnmouth. Not in the cottages by the road. All is in order."

Disgustedly, Tally said, " Then it's something gone wrong in the house. I'd better see if I can find out what it is."

" Perhaps when the wireless went wrong, it fused all the lights," suggested Madame Perrier helpfully.

" Not probable, I'm afraid," said Tally. He turned to Alex and reaching out, took hold of her hand. " You come and hold matches for me, my dear, like Henrietta did for Conrad, then we'll soon see what's the matter. Only finish your drink first."

Since he seemed disposed to keep hold of her hand while she did so, Alex finished her drink rather quickly. " All right," she said, " let's go and see what's wrong."

As she followed Tally across the room, she heard Madame Perrier give a suggestive titter. Alex did not mind this, for she wanted to speak to Tally alone. Ever since she had had that odd thought about him a little while ago, she had been turning it over in her mind, and now she would have a chance to ask him about it. She followed him along the dark hall. Afterwards she remembered that as she passed through the door, her foot struck against some small object on the floor that tinkled as she kicked it.

They went past Miss Clyde's door towards the kitchen. " The fuse-boxes are along here," he said.

" Mr. Tally," said Alex behind him, " there's something I want to ask you."

" Just a minute," he said. " Hold this, will you ? "

The small flame of a cigarette-lighter spurted in the darkness. He handed the lighter to her and turned to open a cupboard just outside the kitchen door. The little flickering light, which Alex guarded from the draught by curving her hand round it, showed the cupboard to be full of fuse-boxes, meters and switches, as well as brooms, mops, dusters and a vacuum-cleaner.

"Mr. Tally," said Alex with determination, "are you a detective?"

He had just been about to step inside the cupboard. But stopping now in its opening, he looked round at Alex.

"Well, well, you do get ideas, don't you?" he said softly.

"It's only an idea," she said.

"That's right," he agreed, "only an idea."

"Then you *are* . . . ?"

"I haven't said so, and you won't either, if you're as smart as I think."

"You see, I've been thinking about your working for an insurance company," she said, "and living out here, and apparently not doing any work to speak of, and the mystery of that house getting burnt down, which an insurance company might be interested in even after it had paid the claim on it, particularly if people started dropping hints and suggesting there was something peculiar about a barking dog——" She stopped because just then Tally bent towards her and kissed her on the lips.

Her hand jerked and the lighter went out. In the way of lighters at critical moments, it refused to light again.

Tally took it from her and, obedient to him, it immediately produced a flame. He held it out to her.

"You shouldn't have done that," she said stiffly as she took the lighter and held it so that it lit up the inside of the cupboard.

"Well, it was a way of stopping you talking a lot of nonsense," he said, "for which you ought to be grateful." He was looking very pleased with himself. "Hold it just a bit higher, will you? . . . There, that's fine."

"Mr. Tally, I'm assuming that you've answered my question in the affirmative," said Alex sharply.

"Hark to her," he said. "Now how does one get to learn to talk like that. Me, I was educated in the University of Hard Knocks and they never taught me much about fine ways to talk—only about how not to talk and when not to talk. My speech is pretty terrible, I know that, but my silence is golden."

"I won't say anything about it to anyone else if you'd rather I didn't," said Alex.

"Fine, fine," he said. "A smart girl, after all. Because you see, my dear, if by any chance any of the things you were suggesting just now should turn out to be true, then it could be that there's somebody around here who isn't a very nice person, if you see what I mean. Who mightn't be very nice to you or to me . . . *God damn some bloody, blundering fool !*" The last words were shouted furiously. The next instant all the lights in the house came on. "Did you ever see anything like that ?" Tally demanded, standing staring at something in the cupboard which Alex, whose ignorance of electricity was not far from complete, supposed, though she could not be sure of it, was probably the main switch.

"Very funny," Tally went on grimly. "Very, very funny." Popping out of the cupboard, he strode straight back to the sitting-room and flung open the door. "Who's the joker in the house ?" he said, glaring round at the company grouped about the dying fire. "Who thought it was funny as hell to turn off the main switch and let us all sit in the dark, thinking there was a power-cut ?"

No one replied. They looked at one another and shook their heads.

"Is that really all it was ?" asked Conrad.

"That was all," said Tally, his face even redder than usual in his anger. "Someone was having their little joke and if you want my opinion of that lousy sort of humour——"

"Sssh !" Madame Perrier broke in imperiously. "We all know what your opinions are like, Tally, when you start shouting like that."

Conrad got up. "I'll go and get some coal now," he said, and picking up the scuttle, went out.

Monsieur Perrier seemed to think that an appearance of being politely amused at the episode might help to ease the feeling of strain in the room.

"A joke," he said. "A funny joke." His gold tooth flashed in his brown, handsome face as he smiled. "We do not mind a joke. Now if you will excuse me, I go and wash."

He also went out.

"I missed the news," grumbled Tally. "If someone hadn't done that, I could have mended the lead in a moment and anyway heard the end of the news."

"Well, get on and mend it now," said Madame Perrier,

" then you can hear the next lot—though why anyone should want to sit and listen to all that stuff about wars and strikes and conferences that don't do anything, and how there's going to be less to eat next month——"

" I wanted to hear about the Test Match," said Tally sulkily, and turning his back on everybody, went over to the radio.

Alex had remained standing near the door. The incident had disturbed her deeply. She could not believe that the lights had been switched off simply as a joke. The atmosphere in the house was not the atmosphere for a joke. But if, after all, humour had been intended, then the humour was of a twisted kind and far from mirth-provoking. She found herself thinking of tall red candles which she was sure had been in the brass candlesticks on the mantelpiece before dinner. Tally was quite right, there was nothing funny about it.

She saw that he was holding what she took to be the two ends of the lead that had been broken and was staring at them with a look of intense concentration in his bulging eyes. Then he quietly dropped them behind the radio, put his hands in his pockets, and strode back to the fire.

" Well, can't you do it ? " asked Madame Perrier.

" I'll do it later," he muttered and flung himself into a chair.

Alex returned to the fire, doing her best not to look in his direction. She did not know if he had realised that she had seen his surreptitious concealment of the two ends of the wire, but if he had he would not welcome any exchange of knowing glances, which might suggest to someone else that he and she shared some item of dangerous knowledge. Alex had taken in the meaning of the warning he had given her in the passage. Yet who was there in the room just then for him to worry about ? Only Madame Perrier and Henrietta.

But a moment later Monsieur Perrier and Conrad were also in the room. They came in together, in haste, but stood still just inside the doorway. Both had shocked faces and Conrad's was noticeably pale. He had not brought the coal-scuttle back with him.

Monsieur Perrier was slightly in front of Conrad.

" Something is wrong," said Monsieur Perrier. " I regret extremely. Just now I go to Miss Clyde's room to announce

80

my return. I see the light on in her room. I knock. She does not answer. I knock again. Again she does not answer. So I try the handle but the door it is locked. So I think, perhaps is something wrong here, so I will go outside to see if I can see inside Miss Clyde's apartment from the garden. On the way I pass Mr. Moorhouse and I explain. He comes with me. We go to the window and the curtains they are not closed. We can see perfectly into the room, and I regret extremely to announce . . ."

He paused, and suddenly looked helpless, as if his English had just failed him completely.

Conrad took over. Coming forward, he put his arms round Henrietta.

"It looks pretty bad, darling," he said. "She's lying on the floor in a very queer position, and we think she's dead."

X

HENRIETTA had stiffened in Conrad's arms and drawn away from him. The look of horror that appeared on her face as she took in the meaning of Monsieur Perrier's words suggested the stupor that might have come as the result of a physical blow. Alex started to go to her, then changed the direction of her steps and walked out quickly into the hall.

From what she had understood of Monsieur Perrier's statement, the door of Miss Clyde's room should have been shut. It was open. Alex ran along the passage.

Just inside the room, looking down at the great sprawled figure on the floor, was Miss Takahashi.

Several people had followed Alex from the sitting-room. Conrad now thrust past her. He caught Miss Takahashi by the shoulder and jerked her round to look at him.

"How did you get in ?" he demanded.

Miss Takahashi looked as if she were much more startled at having a young man lay hands on her than at finding her landlady lying dead on the floor.

"I saw a key on the floor, I picked it up, I knew it was Miss Clyde's key," she said. "I thought it is very funny to find key on the floor. I brought it here, I knocked, no answer, very funny, so I tried door and found it locked. Very funny indeed to be locked on outside, so I unlocked it and came in and saw that there had been some very funny business which must explain how key came to be on the floor, where I found it and picked it up, knowing it to be Miss Clyde's key——''

For once no one waited for Miss Takahashi's information to be given in triplicate.

" How did you know it was Miss Clyde's key ? " asked Conrad.

" There is paint on it in a peculiar pattern that I recognise,'' said Miss Takahashi. "When the house is painted for Miss Clyde some paint drops on the key. I see the key on the floor, I know it is Miss Clyde's key, I think it is very funny to find key on the floor, I bring it here——''

" Just exactly where did you find the key ? " Conrad asked.

" Outside sitting-room door,'' said Miss Takahashi.

Alex remembered then the small object that had tinkled as her foot struck against it, when she had followed Tally out of the sitting-room towards the cupboard containing the fuse-boxes and main switches. That object must have been the key to Miss Clyde's room.

The thought made Alex's head swim so that she almost fainted. Someone who was a murderer had come out of Miss Clyde's room, had locked the door, had come to the sitting-room, dropping the key in the doorway and staying there, talking to the other people in the room, as if he were no different from the rest of them.

" Here, hold up,'' whispered a voice in Alex's ear, and an arm slid inside hers, supporting her. " Come along out if you don't like it.''

It was Tally. Like Alex, he had stood still only just inside the door while the others had crowded past to stand in a hushed group in the middle of the room. But whereas Alex, after one sickening glimpse of the dead woman, had turned away, Tally was even more pop-eyed than usual with fascinated interest.

Alex had seen all and more than she wanted in that one glance at Miss Clyde. She was lying on the floor near the writing-table. She was lying on her side, but with one long arm stretched out across the carpet, the fingers with their crimson nails curling as if she had tried to grasp something as she fell. Her face was terribly distorted and discoloured. There was no blood, but there was a line round her fleshy neck, where something had been drawn tight round it. A chair, which Alex remembered as having stood by the writing-table, was overturned near the body. It looked as if Miss Clyde must have been sitting at the writing-table when she was attacked, had tried to rise, upsetting the chair as she did so, and then herself had fallen, dead or dying.

Conrad, who had been the first to come into the room after Alex, was the first to move out of the petrified group. He crossed to the writing-table and was about to pick up something that he saw there when Monsieur Perrier shouted at him harshly, " Do not touch ! Do not touch anything ! It is for the police to find it as it is."

Conrad drew his hand back. " Yes, sorry," he muttered. But he went on looking at what was on the desk. " She was writing to the police," he said.

Madame Perrier tripped over to his side and looked at the sheet of paper on the writing-table. Though her face was pale, her eyes were brilliant with excitement.

" She didn't get very far with it, poor dear, did she ? " she said. " 'Dear Sir, I wish to inform you . . .' That's when it happened, I suppose. Funny, that ! Whatever d'you think she was writing to the police about ? "

" Someone should telephone the police immediately," said Monsieur Perrier. " I would do it myself, only I am not able to understand well on the telephone."

Henrietta came to life. There was a wild, lost look about her, like that of a child who has strayed out into the midst of the terrifying traffic of the highway and now sees no escape from it, no way back to safety.

" I'll do it," she said and ran out of the room, going to the telephone that stood on a table in the hall.

" We'd all better clear out of here," said Conrad.

" If anyone will listen to my opinion," said Mrs. Wakely, " which I have long since ceased to expect, I think we should all return to the sitting-room and remain there together, because it is essential that no one of us should be able to return to this room alone. There is, of course, no doubt that one of us here is a murderer."

Madame Perrier gave a little scream. " Pierre ! " she cried. " Pierre, that isn't true, is it ? "

" But certainly it is true," her husband replied gravely.

" But who ? When ? Ooooo . . . ! " Her voice soared up again in another louder shriek. " The lights ! It wasn't a joke, turning off the lights ! It was then he did it ! "

Alex heard Tally draw in his breath between closed teeth.

" And there's something else the others don't know yet," he whispered to her, " only I can't see yet how it fits in."

" The wireless ? " she asked.

" Oh, you saw that, did you ? You don't miss much, my girl. Yes, that lead had been cut. But I'll save that for the police, I think."

" And the candles had been taken away," said Alex. " But what on earth could the candles in the sitting-room have had to do with—with this ? "

He did not answer. Though he had gone no farther into the room, he had not moved his eyes for a moment from the body on the floor.

Madame Perrier had gone on shrilly, " Well, it couldn't have been me, anyway, and it couldn't have been Pierre, because all the time the lights were out, I was in the sitting-room, which Mrs. Summerill can vouch for, and Pierre didn't get home until long after the lights went out. And it couldn't have been Mrs. Summerill, and it couldn't have been Tally, because they were in the sitting-room too——"

" But who says it happened when the lights were out ? " asked Tally.

The question brought a sudden silence in the room, during which the voice of Henrietta in the hall could be heard speaking in an unnatural monotone, held steady by a desperate effort, to someone at the police station.

Then Mrs. Wakely asked querulously, " But didn't it ? "

" Maybe it did," said Tally. " Maybe it didn't."

" Why else turn the lights out ? " Conrad asked.

" Why, indeed ? " said Tally. " Only you don't want to jump to conclusions, not when you're dealing with murder. We don't even know how long she's been dead, do we ? "

" Well, if it happened before the lights went out," said Madame Perrier with a note of cheerfulness in her voice, " it certainly couldn't have been me or Pierre who did it, because

I was sitting knitting in the sitting-room and Pierre must have been in the bus coming out from Sharnmouth, or even in the train. And it couldn't have been Mrs. Summerill. And if Mr. Moorhouse and Henrietta were together, I suppose they can give each other an alibi——"

"Only we weren't," said Conrad. "Now let's do as Mrs. Wakely advised and go to the sitting-room."

Miss Takahashi was the first to make up her mind to carry out this suggestion. With her head bent and her hands folded before her, she turned and sped noiselessly out of the room and into the sitting-room, as if it were a burrow in which she hoped to disappear. When Alex followed her a moment afterwards, Miss Takahashi was sitting on a hard chair in a corner of the room, her stumpy feet, in a pair of felt slippers, resting on a bar of the chair, her hands still folded and her face turned away from the people who began to collect in the room. She looked as if she were hoping, by a sheer effort of will, to become invisible.

The result was that Madame Perrier's attention was immediately drawn to her.

"And where were you, dear," she asked in a voice that sounded more cheerful with every moment, "when the lights went out ?"

Miss Takahashi did not answer. But her broad brow creased into a scowl at the blank wall at which she had chosen to stare.

Madame Perrier's eyes grew harder as she looked at her.

"Yes, just where were you, dear ?" she asked again.

Addressing the wall, Miss Takahashi replied, "I talk to the police when they get here. I talk only to the police. I talk to the police and tell them everything I know."

"Good girl," said Tally. "That's the line. No amateur tec stuff for us, eh ?"

Looking offended, Madame Perrier turned to Mrs. Wakely and confided to her in an audible whisper, "Well, I just thought suddenly that strangling was the sort of thing a Japanese might know about. Ju-jutsu and all that, you know."

The words scandalised Mrs. Wakely. "Prejudice !" she exclaimed in an equally audible whisper. "A preposterous prejudice ! Ju-jutsu ! Miss Takahashi is a most cultured woman."

Clearing his throat to make one of his careful speeches, Monsieur Perrier said slowly, " Mrs. Summerill, I beg your pardon for asking the question, but since I am of the opinion that Mrs. Wakely is very wise in asking us to assemble here, may I inquire, where is your secretary ? "

Alex herself had just been thinking about Vivian. She had been the one person besides Miss Takahashi who had not come to the sitting-room after the lights had gone out. Whatever she had been doing in her room, the lack of light had not disturbed her.

" I think she's upstairs in her room," said Alex. " I'll go and get her."

Henrietta, who had just finished her telephoning, said, " I'll come with you."

She said it decidedly, as if she had her own object in coming. Alex did not protest. They went up the stairs together, Alex leading.

As soon as they were out of earshot of those below, Henrietta began to speak. Alex stood still a couple of steps above her to listen to the quick, breathless sentences.

" Alex, what am I to do when the police come ? What am I to tell them ? I mean about Aunt Jay and that letter she was writing. They're sure to ask me if I knew what it was about, aren't they ? But how can I tell them ? "

" Do you know what it was about ? " Alex asked.

" I think so. I think I can guess," said Henrietta. " It's what she wrote to you about. The burning down of the old house. But how can I tell the police about that ? She brought me here to live with her, Alex, when my parents died. She looked after me for years. She was wonderful to me and I loved her. How can I tell the police that I think she . . ." She could not go any further.

Alex finished it for her, " Committed arson and in doing so killed an old man ? "

Henrietta gave a sob and the tears began pouring down her cheeks.

Alex went on, " She was going to tell the police about it herself, wasn't she ? She'd made up her mind to confess to them and try to get some peace of mind. Mr. Wakely's death seems to have been more than she could bear. The thought of it was driving her mad. I think probably she'd want you to tell them all you know. But how d'you know she wrote to me about it ? "

" Because I advised her to," said Henrietta. " I don't mean I knew then what she had to write about. But she'd started getting into a dreadful state and kept talking about a terrible crime on her conscience. I thought—I thought you might be able to help her."

" I never got the letter," said Alex. " Somebody took it and then tried to blackmail her. So then it seems she plucked up her courage to write to the police. But someone prevented it. I can think of two people who might have thought that worth while."

" Two ? " said Henrietta. " I think the only person who would want to murder Aunt Jay, if she knew the truth, would be Mrs. Wakely."

" If you count her, that makes it three," said Alex. " Because if your aunt did burn down the old house to collect the insurance, I should think she probably had some help from somebody, so that person, for one, would have been desperate to stop her confessing to the police."

" And the third ? "

" Well, blackmail's a dangerous weapon, isn't it ? If the victim doesn't give in but turns to the police instead, the blackmailer can suddenly find she's in a worse position than the victim, can't she ? "

" She ? " said Henrietta.

" Well, in this case . . ."

" You mean Vivian ? " Henrietta looked much more startled than Alex thought she should. She had never thought of Henrietta as particularly quick, but felt that her suspicions should at least have got as far as that.

" Oh, but that's impossible," said Henrietta.

" I wish it were," said Alex. " Come along, let's go and find her." She went on up the stairs.

" But you aren't going to accuse her ? " said Henrietta, following her. " You don't actually think she stole that letter and then murdered Aunt Jay ? "

" That's going rather far, I admit," said Alex. " But I'm sure she stole the letter."

" No, no, you're wrong," said Henrietta. " I know—I'm sure you're wrong."

Alex reached the top landing and looked round, not knowing which was the door of Vivian's room. Henrietta passed her and knocked on one of the doors. There was no answer. She knocked again and called to Vivian. When there was still no answer, she looked questioningly at Alex, who nodded. Henrietta opened the door.

The room was still in darkness. Perhaps, thought Alex, if Vivian had gone to bed early, turning out her lights, that explained why she had not come down with the others when the rest of the lights had failed. Perhaps she was asleep now and that was why the commotion downstairs had not disturbed her. Henrietta turned on the light. But she did not go into the room. She remained in the doorway, holding tightly to the door, making a little moaning sound of which she seemed not to be conscious.

On the bed lay Vivian. She was staring towards them with eyes starting out of a hideously discoloured face. She was wearing a pale yellow housecoat that gaped in front, showing a lacey yellow nightdress. She had a bright green slipper on one foot. The other slipper lay in the middle of the room. Seeing her even from the doorway, there was no possible doubt that she was dead.

Alex felt her self-control dissolving. In another moment, if she had gone on looking into the room, she would probably have started screaming. She saved herself by taking hold of Henrietta and jerking her roughly back on to the landing, making her shut the door. A dark wave seemed to be trying to engulf Alex's mind, leaving only a little of it clear and lucid. Fighting against this plunging tide of horror to keep that remnant of sanity, she said in a high, shrill voice, quite unlike her own, " Both of them ! Both of them ! That's why he had to turn off the lights. He had to get up here, and from here back to Miss Clyde's room, or the other way around, without being seen."

" He ! " cried Henrietta. She was shaking. " Why d'you say he ? You don't know anything about it."

" No, I don't know," said Alex. " I didn't think. I just thought of someone on the stairs in the darkness, not being seen by anyone, going from one room to the other. Only I wonder if there was time. I wonder how long the lights were out. How long was it, Henrietta ? "

" I don't know," said Henrietta. " I don't know anything. Anything at all."

" Was it twenty minutes, or half an hour ? They must have gone out just after nine o'clock, because Tally'd just been trying to get the news . . . But I don't know when they came on again . . . Wait ! I know how we can find out."

She plunged down the stairs.

Henrietta behind her, said in an odd, querulous tone, " I don't see why it matters ? It's too late now. It doesn't matter."

But Alex hurried on downstairs. For the moment it seemed to her that nothing did matter but to discover how long the lights had been out. By holding on to this thought she kept herself from slipping under that dark, towering wave. She had remembered that there was a clock in Miss Clyde's room. That afternoon Alex had noticed it as the one touch of modernity in the crowded, overheated room, for it was an electric clock. Therefore, when the lights went out, the clock would have stopped, and when the lights were turned on once more, it would have started again. The amount by which it was now slow would be the length of time that the lights had been out.

She reached the bottom of the stairs and still followed by Henrietta, went to Miss Clyde's room. The clock, as she remembered it, was on the writing-table. She looked at the time on the clock. It was seven minutes to ten.

She looked at the time on her wrist-watch. It was seven minutes to ten.

So in spite of the electric current having been turned off for some period, perhaps as long as half an hour, the clock was right.

The people in the sitting-room had heard her running down the stairs and down the passage to Miss Clyde's room. Monsieur Perrier and Tally came hurrying after her, Monsieur Perrier protesting that it had been agreed that no one was to enter this room again before the arrival of the police.

Henrietta started to speak, but Alex silenced her by gripping her arm. Alex went to the sitting-room. She looked round at everyone seated there.

" May I ask who put the clock right in Miss Clyde's room after we went in and discovered the body ? " she said.

No one answered.

She tried again. " Perhaps whoever did it noticed the time

before putting the clock right. If so, we can calculate just how long the lights were out. This may be an important thing to know, because during the period of darkness two murders were committed. My secretary is also dead. She seems to have been killed in the same way as Miss Clyde. The murderer needed darkness to go from one room to another."

There was a silence. There were no exclamations of horror, of disbelief, of surprise. For an appalling moment Alex felt that they had all been sitting there expecting to hear the news.

Once more she asked, " Who put the clock right ? "

No one answered.

XI

DETECTIVE-INSPECTOR GAFFRON was a big man with enormous shoulders and a paunch. He moved heavily and deliberately, he spoke heavily and as little as possible. During long, frowning silences his own thoughts seemed all-sufficient to him. Whether or not he listened at those times if other people chose to speak to him, was difficult to know. He generally turned away from the speaker, giving him an occasional sideways glance, after which he would cock an eyebrow as if to register slight surprise at the speaker's existence. If he wanted a person to speak, he pointed a pencil at him. But even then he might slowly and silently walk away in the midst of what was being said to him.

Alex observed these characteristics during the earlier part of that first evening after the murder. She noticed too that Gaffron could stare steadily and unblinkingly at a face without showing any reaction whatever to anger, charm, pleading, or obvious lying. Yet there appeared to be nothing intentional in this, no cultivated assumption of a poker-face. So far as there was any expression in his eyes, it was a kind of innocence. As Alex watched him speaking to Henrietta, it occurred to her that if this man should have much cruelty concealed under the quiet surface, he would be terrible.

While other detectives and policemen tramped about the house, and the doctor came and went, while lights flared for photographs and powder was dusted over the furniture in the two rooms where murder had been done, the members of the household stayed in the sitting-room, as quiet as if the taciturn Inspector had infected them with his own habit of silence.

By then the facts known to them all were that Miss Clyde and Vivian had both died of strangulation, a piece of electric flex having been used in each case and left behind by the murderer, embedded in the flesh of the neck. Miss Clyde had apparently been attacked as she sat at her desk, Vivian in the middle of her room, her body then being deposited on the bed by the murderer. On the supposition that the murder had occurred during the period of darkness in the house, it seemed probable that Miss Clyde had been the first to be killed, for it was unlikely that she would have remained seated at her desk for many minutes after the lights had failed. The flex matched a coil of flex on a shelf in the cupboard that contained the main switch.

One by one, each person was questioned by Gaffron, who had settled himself for the purpose in the dining-room. Alex's turn to be questioned came late. By the time it came, she was so tired that she seemed to have no feelings left but of weariness. The slightly feverish sensation that she had had earlier had come back, there was a drumming in her ears and her head ached. She looked at Gaffron as if from a great distance, hardly able any longer to take in anything about him but his bulk and a pink blur where his face was.

But she spoke clearly, though sometimes with long pauses between the words, temporarily losing the thread of her thoughts. Gaffron appeared quite satisfied with this method of answering his few questions and neither hurried nor prompted her. Because he spoke so little himself and showed so little interest, belief or disbelief, in what she had to tell him, Alex began to feel a great urge to make sure that she had convinced him of the truth of what she was saying. Adding more and more details, she ranged wider and wider in what she thought worth telling.

She told him all that she knew about Vivian. This, she realised, was really very little and consisted mostly of what Vivian had told her about herself. Alex spoke of her suspicions of Vivian, admitting that she had had no real reason for them, and told him of the trap that she had set with the help of Daniel Whybrow. She told him how Vivian's behaviour, when the trap had been sprung, had lulled her suspicions, then of the shock that she had had on reading the anonymous letter that had been delivered at her house. Taking the letter out of her bag, she handed it to Gaffron.

He looked at it for a long time, nodded and then pointed his pencil at her, indicating that she was to continue talking.

Alex told him of her belief that the letter had been written by Miss Clyde, in response to a blackmailing letter that had probably been written by Vivian, who must have intercepted the earlier letter written to Alex by Miss Clyde. Alex said that she had been more or less certain of all this after her talk that afternoon with Miss Clyde. It had been plain then that Miss Clyde had considered herself guilty of the death of Mr. Wakely and that she had resolved to confess this to the police.

" She was rambling terribly, not at all in her right mind," said Alex, " and I couldn't possibly know if the guilt was real or something she'd built up in her own imagination. That's what I was rather inclined to believe then. But as I was leaving the room, something happened that makes me think now . . ."

That was when Alex made one of her long pauses and then could not remember just what it was that she had thought.

Tapping gently on the table with his pencil, Gaffron waited.

Alex pressed her fingertips against her aching eyes.

" A man at the door," she said after a moment. " There was a man listening at the door while Miss Clyde was talking. Only I don't know if it was a man. I didn't see him. I only heard the footsteps running down the passage and they sounded like a man's. Anyway, the person wasn't wearing high heels. And he went towards the kitchen and disappeared. And there were only two places in that direction where he could have gone. One's the kitchen, the other's that cupboard where the fuses are. Since I've heard about the flex being used, I've been thinking that what he'd overheard made him decide while he was in the cupboard to do the murder. And then he saw the flex there . . ."

Gaffron rewarded her for this theory with one word, " Possibly."

She went on, " When I turned on the light I saw Miss Takahashi on the stairs. I'm not sure how long she'd been there, or whether or not she could have seen the person who was listening at Miss Clyde's door. It was almost dark, so perhaps she couldn't. But I should think she could at least have told if it was a man or a woman."

A silence followed, even longer than usual.

Then in his negligent fashion Gaffron asked, " Any proof that Miss Dale took that first letter ? "

" If she didn't, why was she murdered ? " asked Alex. " I think that letter of Miss Clyde's must have incriminated someone besides herself, and for all I know, Vivian had tried blackmailing that person too."

" Could be the person only thought that Miss Dale was the blackmailer," Gaffron suggested. " Could have been someone else really."

Alex nodded unwillingly.

" Mr. Moorhouse knew Miss Dale," Gaffron remarked next.

" I believe so," said Alex. Till then she had avoided mentioning that fact, out of some obscure caution on Henrietta's account. But now she told him of what Vivian had told her of her acquaintance with Conrad.

" I've no idea if the story's true or not," she concluded. " I don't know Mr. Moorhouse's side of it."

The door opened. Gaffron glanced sideways to see the cause of the interruption. One of the detectives stood there. His face had a bluish look from the cold and he was blowing on his hands to warm them.

" Got any use for a bucketful of coal ? " he asked Gaffron.

Gaffron glanced at the fire, which was adequately stoked, and was shaking his head when the man went on, " Out in the flower-bed under the window of the lounge. With two red candles on top of the heap."

Gaffron cocked an eyebrow at Alex and waited wordlessly to see if she would offer any explanation.

" Well, when the lights went out," she said, " and we thought it was a power-cut, we did think of making up the fire so as to have more light in the room. But it turned out the coal-scuttle was empty. I believe it was Madame Perrier who thought that was queer, because she said there'd been plenty of coal there before dinner. And the candles were missing, too, and I was sure they'd been there before dinner."

" Looks like someone was mighty keen to keep that room

dark for a certain time," said the detective by the door. " And silent, since the radio'd been mucked up, which is pretty rum."

Gaffron frowned as if he found this a reckless squandering of priceless speech.

" Any clock in that room ? " he asked Alex.

" No, I don't believe there is," she answered.

" Anyone in there wearing a watch ? "

" Yes, I was." She showed him her wrist watch, a tiny object ringed with small diamonds.

" Not much good in the dark," he commented.

" But the wireless——" the other man began.

" If the wireless had been on, they could have got the time when the lights went out pretty exactly."

Alex grasped his idea with some excitement.

" Then that's why the electric clock in Miss Clyde's room had been put right," she said. " For some reason it's very important to the murderer that we shouldn't know when the lights went out."

" Could be," said Gaffron. " I suppose you didn't see anyone go near that clock ? "

" I saw several people go near it," she answered. " I stayed by the door myself, but almost everyone else went to the writing-table to see what Miss Clyde had been writing."

" Did you see anyone actually touch the clock ? "

" No."

" That's what everyone else says," he muttered discontentedly. " Which leaves the Jap."

" Miss Takahashi ? "

" Well, she was in the room before all the rest of you, wasn't she ? "

" But what reason could she have had for putting the clock right—unless it was sheer tidy-mindedness."

" Don't know anything about reasons yet," Gaffron said.

After that he let Alex go, telling her that there was no reason why she should not go to bed when she felt like it. So without returning to the sitting-room, she went straight to her room.

Undressing, she sat down at the dressing-table to brush her hair. The strokes of the brush were soothing, though the drumming in her ears went on, almost as loud as the waves pounding on the shingle outside in the darkness. Her eyes prickled with fatigue and her back ached. She was sure that she could not sleep, but at least it would be a relief to lie down on a comfortable bed in a quiet room with her door locked and allow no one to come in to disturb her.

The thought had scarcely formed when someone knocked on her door.

She called out, " Who is it ? "

" Henrietta," was the answer.

" Come in."

Henrietta opened the door.

" I won't stay long," she said, " but I've got to talk to you."

She moved to a chair and dropped into it as if she could hardly have remained on her feet a moment more.

Alex gave her a cigarette and lit one for herself.

Gazing at her with eyes ringed with black shadows, Henrietta said, " If only I hadn't asked you to come here early, you'd never have got dragged into this. Can you forgive me ? "

" But I believe I'm in it as deep as anyone," Alex replied. " It looks as if your aunt's writing to me may have been the cause of it all."

" And that was my fault, too," said Henrietta.

" You couldn't foresee what was going to happen."

" But one should never interfere with people. One should never try to advise and help them," said Henrietta with a shaky note of passion in her voice.

" I'm very inclined to agree with you," said Alex, " though if I go too far along that line, I'll find myself out of a job."

" Who d'you think did it, Alex ? "

Alex's hand jerked a little as she dropped some ash into an ash-tray on the dressing-table.

" Thank God it isn't my business to find out," she said.

" But doesn't this feeling that you're in the same house with someone who's done two horrible murders make you—well, almost want to go out and kill yourself ? "

" It feels quite horrible," said Alex, " but I'm not a suicidal type. And I have a good deal of faith in Inspector Gaffron."

" I didn't like him," said Henrietta. " I thought he was a terrible man. I can imagine him torturing babies."

" I expect he has a number of his own to whom he's an

admirable father," said Alex. " Henrietta, my dear, I've an idea you'd better start controlling your imagination a little."

" Yes, I expect you're right." Henrietta gave a sigh of extreme weariness. " Alex, could these murders have been done by a woman ? "

" I don't know," said Alex.

" I wonder if strangling takes great strength."

Alex looked curiously at the girl's drawn face, then asked, " What woman are you thinking of ? "

" Myself," said Henrietta.

" Well, you are letting your imagination run away with you, aren't you ? " said Alex.

" I mean," said Henrietta, " am I going to be suspected ? After all, my motives were pretty good, weren't they ? I'll inherit this house, which I can sell, I suppose, for what it cost, which was about five thousand pounds. That'll make quite a difference to Conrad and me, you know."

" What about Vivian ? "

" But you know I had a motive for murdering her."

" Are you so sure ? "

Instead of answering, Henrietta let two tears run out of her eyes. She did not seem to notice them, at any rate she did not wipe them away, but only blinked several times.

Alex spoke hurriedly, " Now you're being awfully stupid, Henrietta. What does it matter if Vivian and Conrad used to know each other ? You don't imagine that a nice and attractive man like Conrad hasn't been in love with other women before he met you. It's what he's done since meeting you that counts."

" Yes," said Henrietta sombrely, " that's what counts." She looked down, avoiding Alex's eyes.

" Anyway, no one will think you could be a murderess. And if they try to, we'll find them plenty of other good suspects too," said Alex.

" For instance ? "

" Well, if women are in the running, I believe only Madame Perrier and I have alibis. Both Mrs. Wakely and Miss Takahashi simply say that they were in their rooms, but neither of them can prove that."

" But you don't seriously believe that either of them could have done it. They're both elderly and fairly frail. And Aunt

Jay was a very big, heavy woman, while Vivian was young. I'm sure if either of them had struggled, they could easily have got away from Mrs. Wakely or Miss Takahashi. But I'm quite strong, and I haven't any alibi either. After dinner I helped with the washing up, and then when the Bartons left, I started doing some odd jobs in the kitchen, and when the lights went out I thought it was a power-cut and just lit a candle and carried on till Conrad came in and suggested we should go along to the sitting-room."

" Why does it have to be a woman, then ? " Alex asked. " We've some quite good male suspects, too, haven't we ? "

" Have we ? "

" Yes, of course, there's . . ." But before she had gone any farther, Alex understood the real reason for Henrietta's acute anxiety, and looked at her helplessly. " No," she said after a moment, " it can't have been Conrad."

In a flat and monotonous tone, as if she were reciting something that she had been saying over and over to herself, Henrietta said, " Monsieur Perrier was on the bus. He didn't get here till a few minutes before Tally switched on the lights. There'll be people on the bus who'll be able to corroborate that. Tally was with you except for a minute or two. So there's only Conrad, who says he was in his room. And his room's on the top floor, next to Vivian's." Henrietta stood up abruptly. " Conrad and me, we're the only good suspects," she said. " I think we'd better run away early to-morrow and get married, don't you, then we can't be made to give evidence against one another."

" I'm not sure the suggestion isn't a good one, even if that reason for it is profoundly foolish," said Alex, feeling angry with Henrietta for being so melodramatic about herself and Conrad.

In the sardonic tone that she had used once or twice since coming into the room, Henrietta said, " Is it so foolish ? It happens that Conrad and I know certain things about one another which neither of us would like the police to know."

XII

ANOTHER RESTLESS night, with sleep finally deserting her as soon as the darkness in the room began to turn faintly grey, left Alex with her memory so clouded that for a few minutes she could not think why she should wake with such a feeling of wretchedness and dread. But almost immediately the events of the evening before came back to her, while the day to come, with all that it would contain of further police inquiries, of suspicion and fear, became horrible to contemplate.

She tried hard to escape her thoughts of these things and to plunge back into sleep, but sleep had gone. So she got up and dressed, and again, like yesterday, slipped quietly out of the house and took the cliff path that curved round the little cove. She hoped that no one would follow her this morning, though it was more than probable, she supposed, that a policeman would take an interest in her early departure from the house. But at least a policeman, keeping an eye on her in the way of duty, would not make her enter into conversation with him.

The solitude of the cold, lonely cliffs, deep in silence except for the one sound, so soft and so constant that it only pointed the absence of all other sounds, of the smooth, grey waves crinkling along the edge of the shingle, was a better antidote to feverish thoughts and nightmarish imaginings than the chatter of T. T. Tally. She walked as fast as she could until she was some distance from the house, then she looked back. To-day there was no one else on the path.

Neither was there any boat in the cove. Alex had the frozen scene to herself. It was a scene of grey and silver, under a milky, moonstone-tinted sky. There was something dream-like about the sea's calm. In London Alex had expected to see high waves and breakers. That was how she had thought of the sea in winter, forgetting its other mood of steely stillness, when it lies in a deep quiet, merging with the mists and keeping its threats and portents to itself.

She walked on until she came to the far point of the cove

and could see past the curve of the cliffs to the stretch of coast beyond. There was no cove here, but only cliffs that rose straight out of the sea. The path went no farther in that direction, but turned back on itself, rising steeply, and Alex guessed that if she were to follow it, it would lead her to the ruins of the burnt house. From where she stood she could not see them, because of the slant of the cliff-face, but she knew that they must be almost directly above her.

In starting out that morning, she had had no intention of going to look at the old house, and now when she considered it, the thought repelled her. Yet instead of turning back, she went on.

She found that she had to move with caution, for the frost on the steep path made it glassy, and if she were to lose her footing and slide backwards, she would at the least have a nasty fall. Holding on to tufts of grass, brittle with the frost, and on to boulders beside the path, she worked her way slowly upwards.

After the first ten yards it became easier and she was able to walk briskly again. Ahead of her now she could see the house. She could also see Detective Inspector Gaffron, apparently waiting for her at the end of the path.

She was panting slightly from the climb as she came up to him, her breath making a cloud on the cold air. Characteristically, Gaffron did not reply when she said good-morning, but only gave her a nod, and turning, took a long look, in which he seemed to invite her to join him, at the ruins.

There was nothing very interesting about them. The shell of the house was standing, though a good deal of the roof had fallen in. The windows were gone and all that was left of the window-frames were scraps of flaky, blackened wood. There were no doors, but where the doors had been, the stone-work gaped to show a shadowy chaos within of fallen bricks and timbers. The house had probably been built in the late nineteenth century and could never have had any grace or charm. Apparently it had had battlements and a small turret or two, but even in their ruin these had acquired no trace of the romantic. The only mood that the place expressed to Alex was of a squalid sort of sadness.

" Not very pretty, eh ? " said Gaffron after a while.

" A very nasty mess," said Alex.

" What brought you looking at it then ? " he asked.

" I didn't really come to look at it," she said. " I just couldn't stand it in the other house any longer, so I came out for a walk. But I suppose this is where it all began—Miss Clyde's troubles, I mean."

" Looks like it." He had begun to fill a pipe. " Looks as if someone helped her burn this house down for the insurance, so that she could buy that much better house over there, then murdered her because her conscience wouldn't swallow the corpse that got into the fire."

" Then you believe Mr. Wakely was murdered ? "

" Can't say. Could have been an accident, but even so, it could have been more than she could stand. There's been no evidence so far that he was murdered. No motive, for instance."

" Except the barking dog."

" What's that ? " asked Gaffron, with one of his sidelong glances and a cocked eyebrow.

" Didn't Mrs. Wakely tell you about a barking dog ? " asked Alex.

He shook his head.

" She says her husband told her on the day he died that he was going to the police about a barking dog," said Alex.

" She didn't mention it yesterday to me," said Gaffron.

" And I didn't mention the things Miss Clyde said to me yesterday about a barking dog," said Alex. " There was rather a lot to think of all at once, and I didn't remember it. So far as I can remember it now, Miss Clyde said she was going to count up to five hundred and then write to the police about —a blackmailing bitch, not a barking dog. The barking dog, she said, had nothing to do with it."

" And is there a dog that barks ? " asked Gaffron.

" Only the one in the boat," said Alex, and told him of what she had seen on the previous morning.

When she had finished, he asked, " Ever had anything to do with a murder before ? "

" Never," said Alex.

" People think of all sorts of things to tell one. Any old thing," he said.

" Meaning you aren't very impressed by my barking dog ? "

" Oh, no, I like your dog."

" But you don't take him seriously."

" Well, perhaps you wouldn't mind telling me what you yourself think about it. D'you think it's the password of a secret society, for instance ? Or something to do with—say hydrophobia ? Or a werewolf ? "

Alex frowned. " D'you make a policy of actually trying to stop people telling you things ? " she asked.

He looked surprised. " No, of course not. And you didn't answer my question, did you ? "

" It wasn't the sort of question to answer."

" Well, I meant it to be. What's your own idea about this dog ? "

" I haven't one, except . . ." She did not know how to go on, so she paused. Gaffron, as usual, did not hurry her. At last she said, " Well, suppose Mr. Wakely saw something he wasn't supposed to see, and a dog that was on guard barked, and let somebody know that he'd been seen by Mr. Wakely, and so this person thought that he would have to get rid of Mr. Wakely . . . That's not a very good effort, I'm afraid, but it's the best I can do at the moment."

" I'd say it was a very good effort," said Gaffron, with the nearest approach to a smile that she had yet seen him achieve. " Not too fancy, not too plain. Now suppose you tell me something I'd like to know, Mrs. Summerill. I'd like to know it for sure. Is there any possibility that your secretary was down here some days ago ? During last week-end, say ? "

" No," said Alex in surprise, " I shouldn't think so. Anyway, not that I know of."

" Can't you tell me any more than that ? Could she have been down here ? "

" Well, it's physically possible, I suppose. I didn't see her between Friday afternoon and Monday morning."

" Didn't she tell you anything about what she'd done during the week-end ? "

" Let me think . . . Yes, she said she'd been doing some dressmaking. She was very clever at that sort of thing, in fact at most things, and she was making herself a new dress for the wedding here. And she told me she'd been to a theatre with a friend on Saturday evening."

" D'you know the friend's name ? "

" It was a man called Peter something. Peter Fortman, I

think. There were several men she used to go about with, though I don't believe any of them was particularly important to her."

" Did that description of how she'd spent her week-end seem quite normal to you ? "

" I think so. It does sound normal enough, doesn't it ? "

" I mean, she didn't go out of her way to tell you more than usual or anything like that ? "

Alex shook her head.

He sighed. " That was what I was afraid of. In fact, it would have been the surprise of my life if you'd said anything else. But it complicates things."

" Am I allowed to ask why ? "

" Well, it's this blackmail business. You think, don't you, that Miss Clyde wrote you a letter confessing that she burnt down this house intentionally, and that your Miss Dale stole the letter before it reached you and wrote to Miss Clyde, demanding money for keeping her confidence. And Miss Clyde, knowing that she'd told no one but you what she'd done, leapt to the conclusion that the blackmailing letter came from you and made up her mind to write to us confessing her crime, thereby getting you into plenty of trouble as well. But an accomplice of Miss Clyde's, who didn't want any confessing done, put a stop to that, and while he was at it, killed Miss Dale, because she'd seen the original letter of confession. For all we know, she might have written him a blackmailing letter too. Isn't that what you think happened ? "

" Yes," said Alex.

" Well, it didn't," said Gaffron.

Trying his own technique of silence, Alex waited patiently until it should occur to him to say some more.

Eventually he said, " We've got the blackmailing letter. Miss Clyde had it tucked down the front of her dress, as if it were her most treasured possession. I believe the murderer searched for it hurriedly, but it seems not to have occurred to him to look for it there. The point about the letter is, it was typed on Miss Clyde's own typewriter."

Alex gazed at him incredulously. Then she asked, " Are you sure we're talking about the same letter ? "

" I think so," he said.

" But then Vivian couldn't have written it."

" Unless she came down here specially for the purpose, which I admit isn't likely."

" She can't have had anything to do with it at all, unless, of course . . ."

" Unless she was working with someone here, say Mr. Moorhouse. Wasn't that what you were going to say ? "

" Only I don't believe it," said Alex.

" They knew one another," said Gaffron.

" But they hadn't seen one another for a long time. They weren't even on good terms."

" Who said so ? "

" Well, it was obvious they weren't on good terms. Mr. Moorhouse was furious with Vivian for coming here. He let everyone see it."

" Naturally. If they were working together, it was sheer stupidity on her part to give the connection away."

" But I'm sure there wasn't any connection of that kind. I really don't think they'd seen one another for a long time."

" Then could anyone but Miss Dale have got at your post and stolen Miss Clyde's letter ? "

" Isn't it possible that the letter was never posted ? "

" It's possible, of course. But is it likely? Can you imagine Miss Clyde writing a letter of that sort, addressing it to the well-known Miss Alice Summers at her office and then leaving it lying about or giving it to someone else to post ? Don't you think she'd take it to the post herself and see it safely on its way ? "

" Yes, I suppose so. But then, what did really happen ? Who did take the letter ? "

" Perhaps Miss Dale took it and gave it to somebody here. The alternative is that someone from here went to your office and . . ." He stopped, seeing her change of expression. " So somebody did go," he said.

Alex shook her head vigorously. " It couldn't have had anything to do with it. It's true Henrietta visited me about a fortnight ago, but she wouldn't have had a chance to get at my post. Vivian would have been there all the time that Henrietta was in the office."

Gaffron made a shrugging gesture as if he were giving up both lines of inquiry. But Alex did not feel at all sure that this was so.

They had been walking slowly back towards the house, and now had reached the point where the cliff path, circling the cove, became too narrow for them to continue side by side.

Going ahead, Alex spoke over her shoulder, " Inspector, there's something I'd be glad to know for sure and that is whether or not there was any truth in Vivian's story about her lungs. Had she really spent six years in a sanatorium, or were those six years spent in a different way ? "

" Yes, it's an important point," he said.

" I've been quite unable to make up my mind whether she was an ingenious liar or a quite truthful person," said Alex, " and that's at least one point on which it's easy to check up. This fact that she couldn't have written the blackmailing letter suggests that she may have told the truth more often than I've believed during the last few days."

" And that someone else has told you more lies than you suspected."

" At least that I may have been doing Vivian a great injustice."

Gaffron gave a grunt, as if this were a consideration that he personally would not allow to trouble him much.

It was not only the difficulty of keeping up a conversation on the narrow path that made Alex drop the subject at that point. While she had been speaking of Vivian and her tuberculosis, still in a horrible confusion as to her true feelings about the girl and longing now, because of the horror of her death, to be able to exonerate her, a troublesome sense of something forgotten forced itself into Alex's mind. She had had this sense recurrently ever since, on her journey down to Sharnmouth, she had opened the anonymous letter. A vague echo of something that someone had said had been set up from time to time by other remarks that she had heard. It was something to do with the letter that had never reached her, and it was something important.

Behind her Gaffron had begun to whistle. It was more a hissing sound than a true whistle, almost tuneless. Almost, but not quite, for after a minute or two Alex identified the tune, though more by the rhythm than the melody, as, " I'll see you again."

She tried not to listen but to go on thinking about that

vanished memory. Irritatingly she only found herself thinking about football pools. For a moment she had a quite clear, visual image in her mind of the last football coupon that she had filled in for George, the liftman, at the office. She had filled it in with her eyes shut, but George had told her that it had won him eight shillings. But of all pointless things to think of just then. . . .

She was aware that if ever she tried hard to think about something in particular, her mind was liable to churn up a flood of irrelevancies. Sustained thought had never been her strong point. Probably, therefore, it was very stupid of her now to attempt to lay hold deliberately on a fugitive memory. She would never do it that way.

Besides, it might all be a mistake. Perhaps nothing of any importance had really been said by anyone.

Her thoughts supplied words to Gaffron's hissing imitation of music.

" I'll see you again,
Whenever spring is here again . . ."

" *Again !* "

But that was it. That was the word she had been trying to remember. That was the word that had made that remark of George's important. On the morning when Alex had been so troubled by her photographs of Vivian and when she had been expecting Henrietta to lunch, George had chatted to Alex in the lift, asking her if Henrietta were coming back to the office to work.

" I took Miss Selby up *again* a few minutes ago," he had said.

So Henrietta had gone up twice in the lift that morning. How early the first time had been would be easy to find out by asking George. Perhaps it would turn out to have been before Vivian's arrival at the office. In that case, Henrietta could have looked over Alex's mail for a letter addressed in Miss Clyde's handwriting, or with the Sharnmouth postmark, without anyone being present.

Henrietta had acted very strangely about that visit of hers to London. She had told Conrad that Alex was ill, and Alex that Conrad was ill, thus making certain that she could go to London alone. Then she had insisted on travelling the evening before and staying the night in London, pretending that this was because she was going to pay an early visit to Alex at her house.

It was plain now that it was to the office that her early visit had been paid.

Another elusive memory, made comprehensible by what she had just understood, now yielded itself easily to Alex. On her first evening here, Alex had told Henrietta that she had received a very strange letter that day. Henrietta's reply, in a startled voice, had been the one word, " To-day ? " So she had known nothing of her aunt's writing of the second letter.

At that point a third memory came to Alex, one that she would have been glad to keep suppressed. It was of Daniel Whybrow, in the afternoon of that same day, a fortnight ago, saying : " Did you ever take Henrietta's photograph ? "

XIII

REACHING THE HOUSE, Alex went to the dining-room, finding that breakfast was in progress but that only Tally, Conrad and Henrietta had come down to it.

There was a stiff silence in the room when Alex entered it, a silence which she felt must already have lasted for some time before she appeared. Only Tally gave her something like a smile. Henrietta, looking up from her plate, moved her lips to say what might have been good-morning, but no sound came with it. She was exceedingly pale, with the heavy-eyed look that told of a sleepless night. Conrad was haggard, too, but he also looked angry. Both Conrad and Henrietta were being careful to sit and to move so that they need not look at one another. Tally looked relieved to see someone who might be ready to exchange a few casual remarks with him, and break the spell of antagonism, suspicion, grief, or whatever it was.

" It must be these early morning walks of yours that keep the roses in your cheeks," he said with determined cheerfulness.

" Well, they'd wither pretty soon if I always went walking with Inspector Gaffron," said Alex, as she dropped her coat on to a chair near the door and sat down at the table. "Not an affable man, not the life and soul of anyone's party."

At his mere name, Henrietta gave a curiously violent shudder. It was as if she had just suffered that sensation known as "someone walking over her grave." But her face did not change in its sullen, lifeless pallor.

"He told me a very strange thing," Alex went on, looking first at Henrietta, then at Conrad, then back at Henrietta. "He told me that the blackmailing letter, which Miss Clyde believed I'd written to her, and which I believed Vivian had written, was in fact typed on Miss Clyde's own typewriter here."

Tally was the only one who responded to this. "Blackmail!" he barked in a surprised voice. "Who's talking about black-mail?"

"Everyone," said Conrad.

Neither he nor Henrietta had reacted at all to Alex's information.

"Has the Inspector already told you that?" she asked them.

Henrietta shook her head as if the question merely bored her.

"Look," said Tally, "I'd like to know about this."

Briefly, Alex told him. She ended, "So it seemed clear that Vivian had taken the letter in order to blackmail Miss Clyde. I believe that's what the Inspector thinks, but I believe he thinks, too, that she was working with somebody here. The alternative is that someone from here somehow got at my mail in the office, and of course, if someone knew that the letter had been written and when it had been posted and went to London on purpose to get it, that wouldn't have been impossible."

Tally considered it. "That's the likelier," he said. "If your Vivian took the letter, it'd be a darn stupid thing to send it here to be dealt with. I fancy she'd have been quite capable, by herself, of concocting a nice little letter full of menaces and typing it quietly on the office typewriter. In these particular circumstances that would have been far safer than sending it to an accomplice here. Bit of a queer coincidence too if she had had an accomplice here."

Abruptly Henrietta got up and walked out of the room. Though her face was turned away as she went, Alex felt fairly sure that before Henrietta had reached the door, she was in tears.

Conrad did not move.

All at once Alex became furiously angry with him. " I don't know what's wrong with you two, but I do know you're being perfect fools," she said. " Whatever's happened to you ? "

" Strange as it may seem," said Conrad, " I don't like being treated as if I were a murderer."

" Lord," said Tally, " what wouldn't I give to have a nice girl like Henrietta think I'd got the guts to do a murder or two ? But seriously now, about this blackmail. Did the Inspector tell you, Mrs. Summerill, what the letter said ? "

" No, said Alex.

" Nor, I suppose, what Miss Clyde had confessed to ? "

" I don't think her letter's turned up anywhere yet," said Alex.

" It must be somewhere," said Tally. " Blackmailers have to keep their evidence. And it may even be in this house, or somewhere near here. But I say, that girl Vivian——"

" Yes ? " said Alex.

" Looks as if she was killed by mistake."

Looking down at her plate, Alex's mouth trembled.

" Poor kid," said Tally shortly and got up and walked out.

Waiting until she felt fairly sure that her voice was under control, Alex said, " That thought's been driving me mad since the Inspector told me about the letter being typed here. I was so sure it had come from Vivian. I'd started suspecting her before there was any reason for me to suspect her of anything, simply because there was something strange about her. I suppose I've always been afraid that sooner or later someone would get at my post, and merely having someone new around must have been worrying me more than I realised."

" That wasn't all," said Conrad.

She looked at his strained face, incredibly altered since she had seen him first two days ago, by lines of bitterness and anxiety. Forgetting the anger that she had felt against him a moment before on account of his lack of gentleness to

Henrietta, she said : " Conrad, please tell me what you knew about Vivian. I know you didn't want to before in case it would have been unfair to her. But you can't do her any harm now."

He pushed his chair back, and turning sideways, leant with an elbow on the table and his head on his hand.

" That's quite true, of course," he said, " but I hate to talk about it. It was myself I wanted to spare before, rather than her. Because it must all have been my own fault in some way. And anyway, it hurt. Still, I know I'll have to tell it all to someone sooner or later, and you may be able to help disentangle things for Henrietta. You know, I can't make out why she's treating me as she is at the moment, I honestly can't. Can you ? "

" No," said Alex. " But about Vivian——? "

" Well, we met in Paris," he said, " that first year that one could go abroad after the war. I was engaged to be married at the time. I won't go into that much. Henrietta knows all about it, though she doesn't really know the way it came to an end. I'd been billeted in Beryl's home for a time while she was a nurse in the local hospital. Then, after I'd been transferred, when I got leave, I used to go back to stay with them. She was very sweet and very pretty and very shy and earnest. I believe I was very much in love with her, though in some way it didn't seem to matter much whether or not we did anything about it. I don't suppose that makes sense, does it ? "

Alex gave herself some coffee, but did not answer.

" It was quite a long time before we got around to talking of getting married," Conrad went on, " but eventually we slid into taking it for granted. I was back at the Imperial College then, finishing the degree that had got interrupted by the war. We talked of getting married as soon as I'd got a job. Meanwhile Beryl went on with her nursing. Then I went off to France for a holiday, and in Paris I met Vivian—or Mary as she was calling herself then." He picked up a knife and began jabbing at the tablecloth with it.

" I simply don't know how to describe what happened then," he said. " I suppose you're expecting me to confess that I fell violently in love with her. But I didn't. It's much harder to describe than that. It was as if—as if she took one

109

look at me and decided, ' That's mine ! ' And it was as if she felt that that was all she had to do about it. She simply had to take possession of me and that was that. I didn't grasp it at once. I didn't realise that we were supposed immediately to be madly in love with each other. I was very attracted, of course. She was lovely, as you know, and there was some very strange quality about her, as if she didn't quite belong to this earth. I wouldn't try to say a thing like that except that you knew her, and you'll know what I mean. And in a way, I don't believe she did belong to this earth. I think she was one of those people who live in their own fantasies and when the real world gets mixed into the dreams by mistake, they don't realise that they can't control it as they can the dreams. As I said, I had this queer feeling of having been taken possession of, without my having had anything to do with it. She had the extraordinary force of the single-minded, a sort of power . . ."

" So what did you do about it ? " Alex asked.

" Well, as soon as I began to understand the situation," said Conrad, " which I didn't at first, because I haven't such a wonderful opinion of myself that it was easy for me to take it in, I told her that I was engaged and soon going to be married, and I told her quite a lot about Beryl. That was a mistake, as I found out later. At the time, it didn't seem to worry Vivian in the least, and I began to think I must have got the whole thing wrong. But the next day Vivian had disappeared. Packed up and gone. So that was that, I thought, and settled down to enjoy the rest of my holiday. Only—that wasn't that, by any means. On getting back to England, Vivian had gone straight to Beryl and told her about an imaginary affair that she and I had been having in Paris and begged Beryl to set me free. So waiting at my lodgings when I got back was a letter from Beryl breaking off our engagement, as well as a parcel of all the things I'd ever given her. She was bitterly angry with me, saying that if I was the sort of man who couldn't go off to Paris for a couple of weeks without immediately forgetting all about her, she didn't want anything to do with me. I did every damn thing I could to straighten it out, but it wasn't any good. Vivian had worked it so that Beryl was really finished with me."

" And what happened to her ? " Alex asked.

Conrad laughed. " She got married a few months later to a doctor at the hospital, and at that point she completely forgave me and we all became very good friends and I'm godfather to their son, and somehow the fiction's grown up amongst us all that she jilted me because of the doctor, a very good solution all round, and that, as a matter of fact, is the version that Henrietta knows. I'd hoped I'd never have to try to explain about Vivian to anybody."

" And the next thing you heard about her was when she turned up here ? "

He threw down the knife with which he had been fiddling, so that it clattered amongst some other knives and forks on the table.

" Good God, no, I've never been free of her ! "

He got up and began to prowl about the room while he talked.

" I didn't *see* her till she came here the day before yesterday. But I kept having letters from her, full of mystery, suggesting I wouldn't have to go on waiting for her for very long. She never gave any address, so I couldn't reply that I didn't want anything more to do with her. I'd made up my mind that she wasn't really sane, even if she was clever. Then I came here to this job, and I met Henrietta."

He had stopped his prowling and was standing by the table looking across it at Alex. As he lit a cigarette, Alex saw that his hands were trembling.

" A murder's happened," he said. " Two murders. Well, I'll tell you this—from the time that I met Henrietta I've had murderous thoughts in my mind. If Vivian had tried to get at Henrietta, I'd have been prepared to murder her. And I threatened to do it. I wrote Vivian a letter, telling her that if she interfered, as she did with Beryl, I'd cut her throat. I've been wondering since yesterday when that letter's going to turn up. It's going to be a great help, isn't it ? "

" How did you write to her if you hadn't got her address ? " asked Alex.

" Eventually she did give me an address," said Conrad. " She implied that the period of waiting was now over and asked me to come to see her. So I wrote back, telling her I was going to marry Henrietta and concluding with the threat I've just mentioned. And I felt as if I meant it. Heaven knows if I did or not. Since yesterday I've been trying to persuade myself that I didn't."

" What did you mean yesterday when you said you'd a responsibility towards someone concerning her ? "

" I meant I'd a responsibility towards you. Because you can see what happened, can't you ? As soon as I told her about Henrietta, she immediately set about finding out all she could about her, and realising that Henrietta would be leaving her job soon, wrote to you, apparently by chance, and managed to get the job for herself. It was a chance for her to get to know Henrietta without my knowing that she was on the scene at all. While Henrietta was showing her the job, they spent whole days together, didn't they ? Henrietta took a tremendous liking to her. She talked to me a lot about this Vivian Dale—whom of course I'd known as Mary Carter— and insisted on asking her down for the wedding. Vivian must have been sizing her up, deciding on the best way to go to work on her. I suppose she saw that Henrietta wouldn't be quite such an easy proposition as Beryl. She's got more intelligence, she's maturer, and—I thought—she was more in love with me. Still, Vivian got at her somehow. I've no idea what she did, but the old poison's been at work. And that's partly why I've been telling you all this. Will you help me straighten it out somehow with Henrietta ? Vivian's dead, but she got her work done before she died—unless I can somehow undo it."

" What makes you think that she'd influenced Henrietta in any way ? " said Alex.

" Don't you remember that day when Henrietta and I were to have had lunch with you in London ? " said Conrad. " Henrietta played quite an elaborate trick on me to prevent that. Well, what reason can she have had except that she didn't want me to meet Vivian ? And why shouldn't she have wanted that unless Vivian had somehow arranged things like that ? "

" I think she had a quite different reason for leaving you behind," said Alex, " but I don't want to discuss it until I've talked it over with Henrietta. Did Vivian ever tell you that she'd been in a T.B. sanatorium for six years ? "

" No," he said, obviously surprised.

" According to her story of your meeting in Paris, she was

ill then, but taking a holiday from the sanatorium and not really meaning to go back, because she didn't care much whether she lived or died. But then when you fell in love with her, as she put it, she felt she had something to live for, and she made up her mind to get well. She said she left you without explanation because you'd have insisted on marrying her although she was a possibly incurable invalid. Then when she did get cured, she said, she found you were just about to get married."

He thought it over.

" It may have been true about the T.B.," he said. " It would explain quite a lot, wouldn't it ? The feeling she gave one of not belonging to the normal world, and of having to live in dreams. The rest of it might be what she believed was the truth of the situation, if she had a considerable gift for deluding herself, which she certainly had, in spite of her intelligence. As I've said, I'm sure she was far from normal. But I'm also sure she'd started to get at Henrietta somehow. Henrietta's been looking at me to-day as if there was no doubt in her mind that I'd murdered her aunt and Vivian, and I believe she was looking at me like that yesterday, before the murder happened. Vivian's done something to her, though I've no idea what."

" Why don't you ask her ? "

" I've tried. She'll hardly speak to me."

" As I said, I'm not at all convinced that Henrietta's present attitude towards you has anything to do with Vivian," said Alex. " But I'm afraid I don't understand Henrietta, any better than I did Vivian. I used to think I did, but I don't." She stood up. " I'm going to talk to her and if you're right that Vivian influenced her against you in some way, I'll do what I can to straighten it out. But I'm afraid of something else. I'm afraid there may be something on Henrietta's mind far harder to deal with than Vivian."

" What could there be ? " asked Conrad.

She nearly replied, " A guilty conscience." But seeing his harassed face, she kept the words to herself and went in search of Henrietta.

XIV

SHE FOUND Henrietta in her bedroom. It was on the first floor, a tiny room, almost too small for a bedroom. That was why it was Henrietta's, for it was far too small to let to a paying guest. Henrietta was sitting listlessly on the edge of the bed, looking out of the window. She seemed to know who it was when Alex came in, though she did not look round.

There was one chair in the room, between the wardrobe and the dressing-table. Alex tried sitting on it, but found herself so cramped there that she stood up again.

Still without looking at her, Henrietta said, " I know what you're going to say."

" About the letter ? " said Alex.

" Yes. I took it, of course. I know I ought to have told you, but I thought I would handle it alone."

" What was there to handle ? "

" The whole business of Aunt Jay and her confession. But I blundered horribly."

" Go on and talk about it."

" I must, I suppose. But if you think that I tried to blackmail Aunt Jay——"

" Why should you think I think that ? "

" You may, when I've done."

" Don't you feel that your story's convincing ? " Alex could not help the note of sarcasm in her voice.

At least it made Henrietta turn and look at her. " Perhaps not," she said dully. " You see, I lost the letter."

" Lost it ? When ? Where ? " asked Alex.

" I don't know. That's the point about losing a thing. One's never quite sure just where or when one lost it, is one ? "

" Well, start at the beginning and tell me why you took the letter." Alex sat down at the foot of the bed.

Henrietta looked back at the window.

" I told you in London, didn't I, that I was worried about Aunt Jay ? Seeing her, you must have realised that I'd plenty of reason to be worried. But actually things got worse rather suddenly. She'd been badly upset by the fire, of course, and instead of being pleased with this house, which she'd always wanted while she was in the old one, she seemed to hate it here from the first. But she seemed to be her old self still until a few weeks before Christmas. It was then she started drinking, as she did yesterday, getting quite out of control and not caring who saw her. And between whiles she did a lot of crying and kept telling me that she'd a terrible crime on her conscience. I tried to get her to tell me what was worrying her, but she wouldn't. She said that it wouldn't be safe and that for my own sake I must never know. I was fairly sure by then that she'd had something to do with the fire, but when I asked her questions about it, she just said that she'd got to bear her cross alone and wept a lot more."

" What made you think she'd had something to do with the fire ? "

" Her room, mostly."

" Her room in the old house ? "

" No, here. Haven't you noticed how different it is from the rest of the house ? "

" Yes," said Alex, thinking it over, " it is."

" Well, she was always tremendously attached to all that awful furniture of hers. I think it had come from the house where she'd lived when she was a child. And suddenly, about a fortnight before the fire, she moved it all out of the house into a shed in the garden and started having her room decorated. I thought at the time it was odd. But the result was that when the house was burnt down, the furniture was saved. Everything else in this house was new, paid for out of the insurance money. I chose most of it for her. But just her own room is almost exactly the same as her room was in the old house. That hadn't made me suspicious by itself, but once she started talking about crimes, I began to realise that I'd always been worried by the lucky accident with her furniture, and to wonder if she hadn't been responsible somehow for the fire."

" Was that an awful shock to you, or did it fit in with ideas that you already had about her ? " Alex asked curiously. " I mean, what sort of person did you think your aunt was ? You said that almost as if it didn't surprise you much that she'd committed arson."

" In a way it didn't," said Henrietta. " D'you remember a phrase you used about her ? You called her a formidable old rake with an obvious craving for excitement. Well, that's exactly what she was. When she was young she was an actress for a time, not very successful, but she always spoke of it afterwards as if that had been the peak of her life. It was on the halls, broad comedy stuff and not at all respectable. She didn't live very respectably either. The rest of the family were very ashamed of her. But when both my parents died, it was she who came forward with the offer of a home for me and who gave up touring around and started a boarding-house so that she could look after me."

" That still doesn't quite explain arson," said Alex.

" Well, it does in a way," said Henrietta. " I mean, she'd always loved excitement and a bit of illegality didn't put her off. For instance, she couldn't resist making any black market deals that came her way, and she adored gambling of all sorts. Two summers ago she went to France for a holiday, and the amount of thought and energy she put into getting round the currency restrictions would have staggered you. So would the number of things that she managed to smuggle in when she came back. But at the same time she was generous to every-one, and I'm dead sure, however much she may have blamed herself, that she had nothing whatever to do with the death of poor old Mr. Wakely."

Alex nodded.

Henrietta drew a shaky breath and went on. " Well, it was only after I'd left my job and come back here to live that I realised how bad things were with her. Perhaps she'd been drinking before that—I don't really know. But it was then that she started having attacks of weeping and saying that there was this crime on her conscience. At first I didn't know what to do about it, but then, when she wouldn't confide in me, I got the idea that I might persuade her to confide in you. But all along my idea was that if she did, I'd try to get hold of the letter before it reached you and read it myself. I knew that once it reached you, you'd treat it as completely confi-dential and I'd probably be no nearer to knowing what I ought to do about Aunt Jay, besides having landed you with a problem which I knew you'd find particularly distressing, because of Aunt Jay's connection with me.

" You'd no need to worry about that," said Alex. " I'd have done what I could."

" I know. But I didn't want merely to pass my problems on to you. What I wanted was just to find out what Aunt Jay had on her mind, so that I could help her. Of course the idea was a rotten one, that's plain enough now. But it was the best I could think of at the time. So I got started, persuading her to write to you, telling her that now I'd left you, she needn't be afraid that I'd ever see her letter and that she could rely on you absolutely not to betray her confidence to anyone, whatever it was she had to say. I didn't think she was listening to me, and then late one evening she told me she'd just written to you and suggested that I should walk along with her to post the letter. She'd missed the last post so I knew the letter wouldn't get to you the next day, but would probably be in the first post the day after. Still, I rang you up that evening and said I was coming to London and could I see you. You straight away asked me to lunch and asked if I couldn't bring Conrad. He'd come in whilst I was talking to you, and heard some of it, so I couldn't say no. But next day I made up a telephone call from you about your having woken up with a bad cold and I went off without him. Early the next morning I went to your office, took the letter and went away again. I settled down in a Lyons' to read it and it was more or less what I'd expected, a terrible, pathetic, rambling thing about how Aunt Jay had been tempted and had fallen and had had her house burnt down because it wasn't a paying proposition any more, but that she'd never dreamt anyone would be caught in the fire and that she hadn't had a single good night's sleep since the old man died."

" Wait a moment," said Alex. " The letter did say, did it, that she'd *had* her house burnt down, not simply that she'd burnt it down ? "

" Oh, yes," said Henrietta. " It was clear she meant that someone else had done the actual job for her."

" Did she say who it was ? "

" No."

" Are you sure ? "

Henrietta's foot began to tap on the carpet. " Of course I'm sure. You didn't think I'd have missed a thing like that, do you ? Because whoever it was, was probably a murderer even then. You see, I think that was why Aunt Jay had broken down in the way she had. I think she realised that her scheme to get rid of the white elephant of a house, which to her sort of mind would have seemed morally not much worse than coming through the customs with a few undeclared nylons, had been used by someone else to do a cold-blooded murder. And I think that besides finding her conscience couldn't carry the load, she was terrified for her life."

" If only she'd put the name in the letter," said Alex. " But you haven't told me yet how you lost it."

" I told you I don't know how I lost it." Henrietta's foot tapped harder on the floor.

" Well, was it here or before you left London ? "

" I don't know."

" You must know at least that."

" I don't know anything about it."

" Henrietta, you're lying."

Henrietta took this so calmly that it confirmed Alex in her opinion on this point.

" I tell you," said Henrietta, " I read the letter sitting in that Lyons', and then I think I put it into my bag. I don't remember ever seeing it again."

" What do you mean, you *think* you put it into your bag ? "

" Well, I think I remember doing that. But you know how difficult it is to be sure of anything once you start asking yourself questions about it. I sat in the Lyons' for quite a while, because I had a lot of time to fill in before I could go back to the office again. I had several cups of coffee and read a newspaper. I know I left the newspaper behind on the table, so perhaps the letter was mixed up with it. That could have happened."

" And someone from this house, who had followed you to London and seen you read the letter and leave it behind, picked it up as soon as you went out and brought it back here and typed a blackmailing letter to Miss Clyde on her own typewriter. For God's sake, Henrietta——" Alex jumped up. " Don't be such a fool ! That's a ridiculous story."

" Why is it ridiculous ? " Henrietta asked. Her tone was stubborn but with an undercurrent of hopelessness in it that made her voice quite lifeless.

" Because if you had a letter like that in your possession,

you wouldn't leave it around on teashop tables," said Alex. " You wouldn't even put it in your bag and not look at it again. You'd have kept looking in your bag every little while to see that the letter was still there. At least once or twice during the day you'd have taken it out and re-read it. The moment you got back here, you'd have picked a safe place for the thing."

Henrietta shook her head. " I didn't. And I'm not saying that I did lose the letter in London. I'm only saying I may have."

" But why—why say such an absurd thing ? " Alex pleaded. " What's the object of it ? What are you afraid of ? "

" I'm not afraid," said Henrietta.

" There's no other conceivable reason for such nonsense," said Alex. " I suppose Conrad comes into it somehow. But how ? Why don't you trust me ? Why don't you tell me what the trouble really is ? "

Henrietta's tapping foot became still at the mention of Conrad's name, but her face did not change.

" I don't see how he could come into it," she said. " He never saw the letter."

" Unless he was the person who ' found ' it when you ' lost ' it. Unless he was the person who followed you to London."

" He couldn't have. He did a round of advisory visits that day."

" Oh, then that's why you'd like it to be thought that you lost the letter in London. But no one will believe that story for a moment." Alex had sat down again and her own foot had taken up an impatient tattoo on the floor while she tried to think of some way of wringing sense out of Henrietta, or of making sense of her attitude. " How much of all this did you tell the police last night ? "

" None of it," said Henrietta.

" Well, we'd better go and find Gaffron now and tell him," said Alex, " anyway about how you took the letter. If you'd change your mind about how you lost it, it would be rather a good thing."

" I told you you wouldn't believe me," said Henrietta. " What do you believe, then ? D'you think I've got the letter still ? "

" And used it to blackmail your aunt ? No, I don't.

Though if you go on working so hard to destroy the idea I've had of your character for several years, I may end up believing anything. Oh, Henrietta, I'm in such a muddle about it all. I began by suspecting Vivian, then I stopped suspecting her, then I began again, and now I haven't the faintest idea what to think. Tell me, how much have you ever known about Conrad's connection with Vivian ? When she first came to the office and you were showing her the work, did she never speak about him ? "

An odd smile twisted Henrietta's mouth. " She spoke about him on the first day—and the second—and the third. She wasn't very subtle."

Alex's eyes widened in amazement.

" And I never knew that *you* were subtle ! "

" I don't think I am, I just use my head," said Henrietta. " I didn't believe she really wanted him, she just wanted to keep her hold on him, whatever it was. And I was quite sure he wasn't in love with her. So I thought the best thing was for them to meet before the wedding here where he and I belonged and she didn't, and get it over."

" So that was the real reason you wanted us to come down early—to get that over before the wedding. I see what Vivian meant when she said so bitterly that you could look after yourself."

Something in Alex's tone made Henrietta turn to her with a trace of her normal warmth. She picked up one of Alex's hands and squeezed it.

" I know you're hurt that I didn't confide in you," she said. " But remember that while that sounds quite simple now, it didn't seem simple at the time. I was blundering along, not actually knowing what I was doing. It was all vague and unsure. If I'd tried to confide in you, I shouldn't have known what to say and what not to say."

" And I should have tried to advise you, which you were wise to avoid," said Alex. " Well, now, let's go to Gaffron. But if just once you would listen to advice——"

" No," said Henrietta, " I'm not going to change my story. I lost the letter, and I don't know when or where." But she did not let go of Alex's hand as they left the room.

Gaffron and two other men in plain clothes were in Miss Clyde's room. They appeared to be in the middle of an experiment with the electric clock, stopping it and setting it going again by pressing the switch of the plug on the skirting board near the writing-table. Gaffron stood near to the door while one of the other men pressed the switch with his foot.

" Yes," said Gaffron, watching, " it could have been done that way. He knows that the clock will stop when he turns off the main switch, and start again when the lights go on. Then he knows that if anyone noticed the time when the lights were turned on, the clock will tell them by the amount it's slow, just when the lights were turned off. So before leaving the room, after doing the murder, he turns the clock off and sets it ahead, to a time when he can be pretty sure the murder will have been discovered. And then keeps an eye on his watch and at the right moment he presses the switch with his foot. It's easy to do that without anyone noticing. So the clock is right without anyone having picked it up and reset it. Complicated, perhaps, but possible. Only, why did he bother to do it ? Why did it matter whether people knew what the time was when the light went out ? " He noticed Alex and Henrietta in the doorway. " Yes ? " he said, not looking too pleased at the interruption.

Alex advanced.

" Miss Selby has something she wants to tell you about the letter written to me by her aunt," she said. " She can tell you why I never received it."

" Come in, then." He closed the door behind them and again said, " Yes ? "

Henrietta told her story briefly.

When she finished Gaffron settled into one of his long silences, so that Alex started to wonder whether she and Henrietta were intended to remain in the room or to go.

Eventually he found a few words.

" So you lost this letter. Just left it lying around. Unfortunate." He sounded only half-interested, and to Alex's astonishment but great relief, did not pursue the question. " Have you told this story to anyone else, young woman ? "

" Only to Mrs. Summerill," said Henrietta.

" Then don't tell anyone else. Anyone at all. Understand ? "

" No," said Henrietta. " Why shouldn't I ? "

" Because one young woman's been murdered already because someone thought she'd read that letter. Someone thought his name had been mentioned in the letter as the murderer of Mr. Wakely, and he didn't like that at all, so he killed the person whom he thought had read the letter. Understand now ? "

" Yes," said Henrietta. " Only his name wasn't mentioned in the letter.

" So you say. So I may believe. So he may not believe."

" I see," said Henrietta.

" I hope you do. I've all the work on my hands I can manage. Of course, if you'd like to save me some work . . ."

" What can I do ? " asked Henrietta.

" Find that letter. Find out who got hold of it. Because if we can find out who besides you has seen that letter, that's someone eliminated as the murderer."

" I don't understand that," said Henrietta, returning his sideways glance with a deep frown.

" Think it out," said Gaffron in a tone which showed that the time had come when he had had as much conversation as his nervous system could endure for the moment.

XV

OUTSIDE IN the passage, Henrietta asked, "What did he mean?"

"That's an easy one," said Alex. They went to the sitting-room, which was empty. "If the murderer is the person who helped your aunt to burn down the old house, and if he murdered Vivian because he believed she was the person who'd read your aunt's confession, then the murderer and the person who really got hold of your aunt's confession can't be the same person. So if we can't find the blackmailer, that's one person at least who can't be the murderer."

"Yes," said Henrietta, "I see."

"Don't you think if you tried very hard, you could remember just when you did lose the letter?" Alex suggested.

Sitting down on a window-seat, Henrietta folded her arms on the sill and leant her forehead against the cold glass. She made no reply at all.

"And I used to think you so sensible and level-headed," said Alex.

"Don't you ever lose things?" asked Henrietta.

"But you didn't lose that letter," said Alex.

"I did, I did, I did!"

Alex looked at her helplessly. At that moment she remembered again that this girl was supposed to be getting married next day. Poor Henrietta. Probably there was a wedding dress hanging ready in the wardrobe in that tiny bedroom upstairs. Probably guests had been invited and arrangements made for a honeymoon. Probably too, Henrietta's thoughts strayed to these things so often that she could scarcely think clearly about the murder.

"Of course I know it's in some way to do with Conrad that you're lying," Alex went on.

"I'm not lying," said Henrietta automatically.

"But Conrad himself doesn't seem to like it," said Alex. "At any rate he doesn't like your present attitude to him. He seems to think you suspect him of the murders. That can't be very nice for him."

She thought that this would goad Henrietta to some sort of outburst. But Henrietta again said nothing at all.

Musingly Alex continued, " Well, which is he, I wonder ? The blackmailer or the murderer ? He can't be both. Whichever he is, though, I suppose you'd defend him. That's a very right and proper attitude in a wife. I'm sure I'd do just the same if I were married to a murderer or a blackmailer."

With a long sigh, Henrietta turned and faced Alex.

" I lost the letter," she said. " Really, I lost it. I haven't the faintest idea what happened to it. I——"

Perhaps she would have said more, but the door opened then and Monsieur Perrier came in. He looked curiously at the two women, hesitated and began to say something about fearing that he was intruding. But before he could withdraw, Henrietta had jumped up and thrust past him out of the room.

He stood in the doorway a moment longer, meeting Alex's eyes with a sympathetic but rather puzzled expression. When he smiled, his gold tooth flashed at her.

" I am very sorry for Miss Selby," he said. " She is a very charming young lady. It is very sad that she should have such misfortunes." He closed the door and crossed to the fire. " I cannot conceal I have overheard some of what you have said to each other. It is very sad. I have a great admiration for Miss Selby. I had a great admiration for her aunt. I find Mr. Moorhouse a very excellent young man. I am very sad at their misfortunes."

" Yes, so am I," said Alex inadequately. She still found it difficult to reconcile Monsieur Perrier's slow and solemn speech with his piratical good looks and air of recklessness. He had the appearance all the time, she thought, of acting a part. But his poor English gave him the right to act this part, so that if his behaviour seemed artificial, no one had the right to be suspicious of his sincerity. Wishing that her own French were good enough for her to discover what change might come about in his personality when he had the freedom of his own language, she added, " You and your wife must have known Miss Clyde quite well, if you lived in her house for over a year."

" Ah, yes, very well," he agreed. " She was very kind to

us. She was a very good woman. My wife and I were very fortunate to make her acquaintance. Until she became deranged with her worries, she was always good-humoured and full of laughter. She was a great help to me. This quiet life here is not easy for me, you understand. It is not what I am used to. But Miss Clyde knew this very well and would always try to cheer me when I was in a bad mood. A very good old lady, very wise and amiable."

This eulogy, with each word carefully chosen but spoken tentatively, had the unconvincing sound of an exercise in a grammar book. At the end of it Perrier fixed his eyes on Alex's, as if he were wondering what marks she would give him.

She nodded her head and asked, " How did you happen to find this place ? It's rather off the beaten track, isn't it ? "

" My wife and I became acquainted with Miss Clyde in France," said Perrier. " We met by chance in Nice two years ago, where Miss Clyde was taking a holiday. So when it was decided that my wife and I should remain in England, we remembered this good old lady who had told us of her pension in Sharnmouth. I like Sharnmouth very much. At first it felt very strange to me to lead such a quiet life, but now I have grown accustomed to it, I like it."

" And after all, it hasn't been so quiet, has it ? " said Alex thoughtfully.

Something gleamed in his eyes. " No, that is true."

" A fire, some blackmail and several murders," said Alex.

" Several ? "

" Well, three."

" So you believe that the death of Mr. Wakely was a murder." Perrier made it a statement rather than a question. " And the police, do they believe this too ? "

" I think they do," said Alex.

" What motive do they imagine could make anyone murder such a man ? "

" It seems that he——" She stopped. For some reason her heart had started pounding against her ribs. The look with which Perrier was regarding her had developed a curious intentness, and though she started telling herself that he could not be the murderer because he had been on the bus at the time when the murder had been done, a sense of fear had suddenly surged through her. She remembered Tally's warning that there were things about which it might not be safe to speak in that house. Yet after a moment she heard herself saying the very thing that she guessed was the most dangerous to say. " It seems that he knew something about a barking dog."

Perrier looked a little puzzled and perhaps a little disappointed.

" So that was all, a barking dog ? " he said.

She wondered what he had expected her to say. Her sudden fear of him had not faded yet and she felt sure that she had just done an extremely foolish thing in speaking of the dog. But she could not stop herself going on. " Doesn't that mean anything to you, Monsieur Perrier ? "

He shook his head. " No, it is the first time I have heard about any dog," he said, even more slowly than usual. " But it means something to you, I think. What does it mean ? "

" I don't know," she said. " But Mr. Wakely thought it meant something."

Unexpectedly Perrier gave a broad smile that again showed his gold tooth. " Ah, if that is all . . . You were not acquainted with Mr. Wakely, were you ? "

" No," said Alex.

" But you are acquainted with Mrs. Wakely."

" Yes, of course."

" Well, I never have known a husband and wife so exactly like one another," he said. " Both so grey, so strange, so full of peculiarities, so . . ." He hesitated, then tapped his forehead, still grinning. " It is a type I think to be found very much in England. They fear to eat like other people. They fear their sex. They fear to enjoy themselves. They fear not to be singular. But they are very good people and do no one any harm. If Mr. Wakely had some idea in his mind about a barking dog, it will not have been an important idea to anyone but himself and his wife. It will not have been such an idea as could cause murder." As he said it, he spread out his hands in a gesture that seemed to mean that he was satisfied with the way he had disposed of the matter. His hands were big, brown and looked very strong. When they caught Alex's eye she found that she could not look away from them.

Yet Perrier had been on the bus. He could not have

committed the murders. There was no reason to be afraid of him or his hands.

" I don't know," she said. " But I have a feeling that that dog was important."

" But you, have you heard any dog barking here ? "

This time her sense of caution succeeded in making her hold back any mention of the dog that she had seen in the boat. " Haven't you ? " she asked.

" No. This dog I think is barking up the wrong tree," he said.

" The wrong tree."

" That is an English expression, no ? " he asked gravely.

" Yes . . . Well, perhaps you're right," said Alex. " After all, you were actually here and must know far more about it than I do."

At once she noticed a slight tensing of the long, strong fingers that she could not stop watching. Then he drew his hands back and took hold of the arm of his chair.

" So that is it," he said softly. " You are thinking that I . . . While I have been thinking that you could not . . ." He stopped.

She did not know what he meant. What had he thought she could not think, or do ? But she managed at last to drag her eyes away from his hands and look into his face. To her surprise she found that he was still smiling. It was a sardonic and disturbing smile.

" Ah, well, in such circumstances as these it is natural for all of us to suspect one another," he said, sounding as if he were forgiving her for a breach of good manners. " And it is true that I have killed people in my time. And I did it without difficulty, without scruple. That was perhaps a bad thing and you are aware of this in me."

" Oh, you're speaking of the war," said Alex. " That's different."

" War and peace are not so different as you think," he said. " It is the same people who make both and I am one of those who understand war better than peace . . . But that also was the case with Miss Clyde. Although she was an old lady, she wanted excitement. Perhaps she even wanted danger. We understood one another very well, she and I."

" Are you trying to tell me that Miss Clyde could have killed people ? " asked Alex, startled at this possible meaning in his disconnected remarks. "That she could have been involved in the death of Mr. Wakely?"

"No, no," he said, "but of some crimes, perhaps yes. We all know, do we not, that she helped to burn her own house down? I have known this a long time but now I think it is known to everybody, so I do her no harm in talking about it. You have known of this for some time too, no?"

"No," said Alex, "only for the last couple of days. How could I . . . Oh!" Her heart again gave an uncomfortable thump. "You think I wrote the blackmailing letter to Miss Clyde?"

"Miss Clyde thought so," he said. "When I saw you, I thought that you could not have done so. Yet now I am not sure. . . ." His tone had become harsher, and there was no trace of a smile on his lean, pirate's face.

Flustered and angry, Alex spoke rapidly. "You mean that as soon as you think I might suspect you of some connection with Mr. Wakely's death, you find it convenient to suspect me of something! But don't you know that the blackmailing letter was written on Miss Clyde's own typewriter?"

Plainly it surprised him. He asked sharply, "Is that so? Is that the truth?"

"So the police say."

"Ah," he said, "I did not know that."

She could not tell what he made of the information, but after a moment he nodded his head, as if, once he had had time to get used to the idea, it after all fitted quite well with his own suspicions.

"And so it is someone in this house who is in possession of Miss Clyde's confession," he said. "Yes, now I understand . . . This person is foolish, do you not think so?"

"I do!" said Alex with feeling. She was thinking that if, as Perrier had said, he had overheard some of the conversation between herself and Henrietta, he now knew the very thing that Gaffron had warned them they should keep to themselves. He knew that Henrietta had at least seen Miss Clyde's confession, and that perhaps she still had it hidden somewhere.

But Perrier had been on the bus. There was no need to fear his knowledge of Henrietta's appalling folly. He had been on the bus from Sharnmouth station at the time when the lights had gone out.

But his wife had not. She had been here in this room with Alex. Madame Perrier had been sitting in the chair where her husband now sat. She had been busy with some lacey pink knitting and she had talked. She had gone on and on talking.

As if conjured up by Alex's sudden thoughts of her, Madame Perrier came into the room.

This morning there was a look of anxiety under the heavy make-up on her face. She wore her tightly-fitting black suit, the black patent leather shoes with the tremendous platform soles, some very transparent black nylon stockings, and she had her bundle of pink knitting under her arm. On her jacket was a shiny gilt ornament that Alex had not seen before, and Madame Perrier, noticing that it had caught Alex's eye, smiled at her archly.

" Didn't I tell you so, dear ? " said Madame Perrier, fingering the ornament. " Whenever Pierre goes off by himself, he comes back with some quite unnecessary present for me. I always tell the naughty boy he shouldn't, but I can't cure him. Of course I know it isn't suitable to be wearing anything of the sort to-day, but it cheers me up a little to see it, so I can't resist it. I've dressed all in black apart from that, as I did think I owed that to poor Miss Clyde. Oh, dear we shall have to go away from Sharnmouth now and we were settled here so nicely. Pierre had got used to it and his health had improved so much. Now we shall have to find some other place to stay."

" That is a small thing," said her husband.

" Yes, of course, dear," said Madame Perrier. " I know it is, but there it is and I can't help the way I feel, can I ? And I don't mean any disrespect to poor Miss Clyde. We can't help her in any way by pretending we're enjoying the situation. And though I dread moving, having been so nicely settled, I must say the sooner we go, the better it will suit me. Anyway, Pierre, there's one thing I'm glad about and that is that you chose yesterday to go to London. If you'd been here, you'd have been certain to be suspected before anyone else, what with your being a foreigner and all. But as it is, you can easily prove that you couldn't have had anything to do with it. And I was in here all the evening with Mrs. Summerill, so I couldn't have had anything to do with it either. So I really don't see why the police shouldn't let us leave straight away, do you,

Pierre ? Don't you think we should ask them if we could leave to-day ? I could easily get the packing done this afternoon——"

" No." His wife's rapid chatter seemed to be irritating Perrier. He had stood up and gone towards the door. " We will not ask anything. We will wait and see what passes."

" But Pierre, you were in the bus and I was in here with Mrs. Summerill."

" So you have said more than once." The repetition seemed to annoy him considerably. " The police have not suggested that anyone should leave. When they suggest it, we will do it. Meanwhile there is no need to say the same thing over and over again."

He walked out of the room.

Madame Perrier looked at Alex and shrugged her shoulders.

" Now isn't that stupid ? " she said. " You'd almost think he's got a reason for wanting to stay here. And we could so easily leave and go to Torquay. I've always liked Torquay. We could easily catch the bus from Sharnmouth this afternoon and be there by dinner-time. Still, I know when I'm beaten. Pierre's ever so obstinate and when his mind's made up there's nothing you can do. But it is silly of him, isn't it, when the police know quite well that neither he nor I could possibly have had anything to do with the murder, since Pierre wasn't here at all and I was in here with you ? Still, there you are." She shrugged again and followed her husband out of the room.

But she had insisted on the alibis of herself and her husband once too often. The reiteration had just jolted Alex's mind into remembering that Madame Perrier had not been in this room with her all the evening. In fact, Madame Perrier had been out of the room for several minutes and it had been during those few minutes that the lights had gone out. She had not been gone long enough from the room to have committed two murders, but she had been gone long enough to reach the main switch.

The same was true of Tally. At the actual time when the house had been plunged into darkness, Alex had been in this room quite alone.

She got up nervously and began to walk about in it. Did these facts mean anything ? Was there some puzzle here, the solution of which would shed light on the problem of the murders? Or had it been chance that had taken Madame Perrier out of the room at that particular time? She had said she was leaving the room because she did not like listening to Tally's bad language as he tried to mend the radio, and that, in any case, she never liked to listen to the news.

Alex began to feel she wanted a pencil and paper to start making notes. But just then the door opened again and one of the Barton sisters put her head round it. "There's a gentleman here from London who wants to see you, Mrs. Summerill——" she began.

Alex did not let her finish, for in the hall behind Miss Barton she saw a tall, grey-haired man in a dark overcoat.

"Daniel!" cried Alex.

Probably she had never in her life been so glad to see anyone.

But Daniel Whybrow's face had a gravity that gave his naturally gentle and good-humoured expression a quality which Alex had never seen in it before. He came into the room and closed the door behind him.

"I don't know if I've made a mistake in coming," he said, "but I thought it might be best if I did and told you myself what's happened. Seeing the police here, however, it looks as if you're dealing with the matter already. So I'm sorry if I've butted in."

Alex interrupted him, "What d'you mean, Daniel? What did you come to tell me?"

"About the burglary. But you know about it. The police——"

"No, no, that's nothing to do with a burglary. What burglary?"

"At your house yesterday," said Daniel. "Someone got in and turned the place upside down. Your maid doesn't think that anything has been taken, but somebody searched the place from top to bottom."

XVI

" PERRIER ! "

But at once Alex felt that she should not have said it. She felt that there was danger in the name. At least she should not have said it so loudly, for there were people in this house who listened at doors.

Suddenly it was of the figure that had vanished down the darkened passage the evening before, long before the two murders, that she found herself thinking, the figure that had stood outside Miss Clyde's door, listening while Miss Clyde talked of going to the police. Since the murders Alex had taken for granted that that person had been the murderer. She had believed that it was what that person had overheard while standing with an ear to the door that might have brought about the murders. But that person could not have been Perrier, for Perrier had been in London, searching Alex's house for a letter.

" Perrier, Perrier," she said again, but this time she said it hesitantly, looking up at Daniel in dismay. " It doesn't make sense. You can't be in two places at the same time."

" It's much easier than you'd think," said Daniel. " I've managed it myself more than once. But who is the gentleman ? Do I know him ? "

His tone was light, but his eyes, noting her expression, were watchful and troubled.

" No," said Alex. " But he's the person who searched my house. He must be. That's why he went to London yesterday . . . Daniel, I'm so glad to see you. You can't think what a relief it is just to have you here. In fact, now that you're here, I can't imagine how I lasted as long as this without you. I ought to have rung you up myself as soon as it happened."

" So you ought, of course," said Daniel, patting her hand, which had taken a tight hold of his sleeve. " In general, I entirely agree. Only what did happen ? "

" You really haven't heard ? " she said. " You haven't seen the papers this morning ? "

" I've seen the papers," said Daniel, " but that doesn't seem to help much."

" Perhaps it hasn't got into them yet." She turned away from him, going back to her chair. It seemed almost incredible to her that anyone could exist who did not know that murder had been done here the night before. It also seemed extremely difficult to put the fact into words. But at last she managed to tell Daniel of the two deaths of how they had been discovered, of how the lights had gone out and even of the clock in Miss Clyde's room that had been right when it ought to have been wrong. She knew that she told the story incoherently. Details that she had not considered till then seemed in the telling to become so important that she could not stop talking about them, while she left out other really important things.

When she stopped Daniel said nothing for such a surprisingly long time that his silence almost made her think that he did not believe her. Then she began to think that she must have told the story so badly that he could not make head or tail of it.

" What are you thinking about ? " she asked, trying to read his expression. It seemed to her that a look almost of satisfaction had appeared on his face, yet this surely could not be so.

As if he himself felt that there was something in his expression that ought not to have been there, he looked away from her.

" I daren't tell you what I was thinking about at just that moment," he said. " It was one of those appalling and inappropriate thoughts that come to the most well-meaning of us at the worst possible moments. I sometimes think I'm particularly liable to them. But now to return to this burglary at your house. I can quite understand that it seems rather insignificant compared with what's happened here, but all the same I think you should know just what did occur. Your maid discovered it when she arrived this morning and had the excellent idea of telephoning to me about it instead of to the police. I went straight round there and when I saw that plainly it wasn't an ordinary burglary, I decided to come down here and tell you about it privately, since I didn't feel sure that you'd want the police in on it at all. Did I do right ? "

" Yes," said Alex. " Oh, yes, most certainly, particularly since it brought you down here just when I need you so badly."

" Wait a moment," he said. " Let me tell you what I found at your house. A window at the back had been broken and then opened—the window of your dining-room. Someone stood in the flowerbed to do it and climbed in through the window, bringing some earth on his shoes. That makes me think it happened in the afternoon."

" How d'you arrive at that ? " she asked.

" Because there was a heavy frost in the morning and again at night," said Daniel, " but in the afternoon, for a time, the sun shone and it became quite mild, so that at least the surface of the ground would have softened and some earth stuck to the man's shoes. If he had stood on the flowerbed during the night when the frost had come back, he wouldn't even have left a footprint."

" You're quite a detective, aren't you, Daniel ? " she said. " It was really very clever of you to think that out. Of course, it must have been in the afternoon, because the Perrier man left here by a morning train and got back by the evening. He must have gone to London just for the purpose of searching my house. He wanted to get back that confession of Miss Clyde's. Someone searched my room and Vivian's on the first evening here. I thought at the time it was Miss Clyde, but it looks now as if it may have been Perrier."

" At any rate, apart from the broken window, he did no damage," said Daniel, " and your maid said she couldn't see any sign of anything having been taken. But your desk and your files and your cupboards and drawers had all been ransacked and the mess resulting isn't a pretty sight. I'm afraid you'll have a bad time getting your files in order again. But it was because of those files that I didn't call in the police. I know your feeling about the letters you get, and I thought you might not want the police hunting through them."

She nodded. " Yes, you were quite right."

" But I think you'll have to tell the police about it now," he said.

" Yes, I suppose so. It all helps to give Perrier an alibi, doesn't it ? And yet . . ."

She paused for so long that this time it was Daniel who asked, " What are you thinking ? "

" Why should Perrier be so interested in that letter unless he's the murderer ? But he can't be the murderer, because he was in the bus on the way here from Sharnmouth when the murder happened."

" Are you so sure of that ? "

" I can't see any way round the facts," she answered.

" Let's go over them again," said Daniel. " But let's go a bit more slowly this time and I'll ask questions as you go along. Then perhaps I'll be able to take in a bit more clearly than I have so far all the funny business with the lights and the coal-scuttle and the clock and everything. I can't pretend I've got any clear picture of events in my mind at the moment."

Alex smiled. Studying his lined, mobile face, she felt her-self surprisingly cheered by the sight of it. " D'you know, Daniel, I've an odd idea in my head that you're enjoying this," she said. " That couldn't possibly be true, could it ? "

" What do you think yourself ? " he asked. " Wasn't it you who said I was far too civilised to attend hangings or witch-burnings ? "

" Yes, but . . ."

" Well, you're quite right, I am," he said. " I'm not sorry that I missed the sight of that beautiful girl, or that fantastic old woman, done to death. No, I don't regret having missed that at all. But at the same time . . . Well, you remember I said just now that I'd had an appalling and inappropriate thought which I didn't dare tell you about ? "

" Yes," said Alex.

" Well, it was a thought of great foolishness and great vanity." He stroked a hand backwards over his grey hair in a gesture which Alex knew betrayed a certain embarrassment. " As you probably know, the earliest detective stories ever written are in the *Apocrypha*. Susannah and the Elders and the story of Bel and the Dragon. And the detective's name was Daniel . . . Well, I suppose my little effort with the earth from the flowerbed yesterday whetted my appetite for detecting. So when I heard of the murders just now I im-mediately developed slight delusions of grandeur. But now, let's see what I can do when I really try. Go back to this business of the lights going out . . ."

All over again Alex told him of everything that had happened the evening before. This time Daniel prompted her with

135

frequent questions so that the telling took far longer. Then gradually she strayed back over the events of the two days before, to the point when she had opened the anonymous letter in the car. It was the deepest relief to her to talk and her one fear whilst she was doing so was that someone would come into the room and interrupt her.

But the house was strangely quiet. It seemed that each person was keeping to himself. The only interruption was when Daniel murmured that he was infernally hungry and that he hoped food of some sort would be available soon. Replying that murder no doubt upset the normal routine of a household and that one should not complain, Alex went on talking. She caught herself telling some parts of the story several times, but when she did this, Daniel did not check her, in fact, he seemed to listen to these repetitions with particular care, as if something of special interest might be deduced from the slight variations in each telling.

In the midst of one of these repetitions Alex stopped herself.

" No, I know I've told you all that before. I think I must really have told you everything," she said. " So now let's see what light you can shed on it. What about the lights for instance, and what about the clock ? "

" Ah yes, the clock that wouldn't stop, even for a murder. Well, except that somebody wanted to make us think about time, I don't see yet . . ." He paused. He glanced round the room, looking for a clock. " There are all sorts of ways of thinking about time, aren't there ? You can think forwards and backwards, sensibly and deludedly, obviously and strangely. You can let it obsess your imagination or you can ignore it. I'm pretty good myself at ignoring it."

" I'm afraid I haven't the faintest idea what you're trying to say," said Alex.

" Nor have I, at the moment," he answered. " I'm just splashing around with words to see what happens. And I'm certainly not trying to say anything profound."

Alex did not quite believe him. She thought that some idea had already formed in his mind, but that he did not want to discuss it. She told him impatiently to go on.

" Let's go carefully into Monsieur Perrier's alibi," said Daniel, " and see what it really means—if, in fact, it means anything. As I understand it, no one knows for certain at just what time the lights went out and it looks as if care had been taken that no one should be too sure about it. The wireless had been put out of order and the candles and the coal had been removed, all to make sure, apparently, that there shouldn't be any light to speak of in here when the electricity failed. Yet there's a general impression that it was soon after nine o'clock when that happened, because Mr. Tally had come in here just a few minutes before to turn on the nine o'clock news. Well, now, what strikes you specially about all that ? "

" Of course, that if Perrier was involved in the murders, he had an accomplice here," said Alex. " Even if he was here at the time of the murder, he can't have been here when the wireless lead was cut and the coal and the candles were tipped out of the windows."

" Quite true," said Daniel, " though I meant something else. Yet perhaps the two things are linked up. What I did mean was that the really striking thing about all this jiggery-pokery with the lights and the radio is its uncertainty. Suppose it had occurred to you, as you sat here, to light a match and look at your watch. Suppose someone in some other room had happened to be looking at a watch just when the lights went out. Any alibi then that depended on a few minutes here or there would have been blown sky high. Actually it seems that no one did look at a watch and so a slight confusion about the time element has come into the case. But what a rash thing it would have been on the murderer's part to rely on that. There's Tally's habit of listening to the news to be considered also. Didn't Madame Perrier tell you he always did it ? Didn't everyone in the house know of it ? So the murderer must have known that there was no possibility of misleading people about the time by more than a very small amount. And Tally, at least, was liable to have his mind on the exact time, trying to get the radio to work so that he shouldn't miss the whole of his beloved news. All of which makes me wonder."

" You mean," said Alex, " you wonder if the coal and the candles weren't got rid of, and the wireless lead cut for some reason that really had nothing to do with concealing the time. For instance . . ." She began to grow excited. " For instance, it might all have been done simply because Perrier couldn't have done it. An alibi upside down, so to speak.

Someone who couldn't have done the murders could have done that, then Perrier, who couldn't have done that, did the murders ! "

" Whom d'you mean," said Daniel, " when you say someone who couldn't have done the murders ? "

" Madame Perrier, of course."

Daniel nodded. " It's possible. But it still doesn't tell us how Perrier could have got here in time to do two murders when he was supposed to be on the bus. Let's go over it stage by stage. Tally comes in to turn on the news, presumably at just nine o'clock, or a minute or two before. He finds the wireless won't work and tinkers about with it for a few minutes. Then Madame Perrier goes out of the room. Say she went out at five minutes past nine. She turns out the lights . . . Perrier gets off the bus at nine fifteen. He walks up the lane to the house, taking at least another five minutes. That makes it nine twenty. He claims he went straight to the sitting-room and told you all that there wasn't any general power-cut. Tally goes to the switch-box, tinkers about a little more . . . How long do you suppose that went on? You were with him, weren't you ? "

Alex nodded and suddenly, remembering what had happened when she went with Tally to the switch-box, she felt herself, greatly to her annoyance, blushing. She hoped Daniel was too absorbed in his reasoning to notice it.

" Not more than five minutes at the most," she said.

" That means that the lights came on again about nine twenty-five, or nine thirty," said Daniel. " In fact, they were out for rather less than half an hour. And Perrier was in the house, according to that reckoning, for ten minutes at the very outside. I think that's scarcely an adequate length of time for strangling two women. But I can see two other possibilities . . ."

" That in fact it was much later than nine twenty when he came into the sitting-room," said Alex.

" Yes, having been in the house for some time beforehand. That would mean that in reality you all sat in the darkness for much longer than you believe. I think that isn't impossible. Unaccustomed darkness does confuse one's sense of time. It would also explain why the clock in Miss Clyde's room was put right. If it had been, say, three-quarters of an hour slow, it would have given the whole show away. But there are some things about that idea that I don't like."

" And they are ? "

" Again the uncertainty. Suppose someone had looked at the clock before Perrier or his wife could get at it to put it right. The alibi would have then been bust straight away. Also, how could he have known that he would find Vivian Dale in her bedroom ? Miss Clyde he could have been fairly sure of finding, but wasn't it more likely that Vivian would be in the sitting-room with the rest of you than upstairs alone ? It would mean that her murder must have been more or less unpremeditated."

" Is that impossible ? "

" No—in fact, it may have been that in any case. No one can have known that she'd spend the evening up there alone."

A thought stirred uneasily in Alex's mind. She thrust it away from her. " You said you could see two possible ways how Perrier could have done the murders," she said. " What's the second."

" That his accomplice wasn't his wife, but Tally," said Daniel. " It's on Tally's desire to hear the news that you all base your belief that the lights went out soon after nine. Well, suppose that when Tally came in to turn on the wireless, it wasn't nine o'clock, but nine-fifteen. Then he goes out of the room for a minute or two to turn off the lights. Perrier could have come into the house only a few moments later and had the full half hour of darkness for the crimes. But again I don't like the idea."

" Because of the uncertainty of the whole thing ? "

" Yes. For such an intricate plan, it's too full of holes. And that's what makes me think that we're thinking about time in the wrong way. We're thinking about it as we were meant to think about it, and getting into a hopeless confusion. I repeat, there are all sorts of ways of thinking about time."

Alex gave a sigh. " At any rate it couldn't have been Tally who put the clock right because he stayed beside me, only just inside the door, and never went near the clock or the switch. If he and Perrier were working together, putting the clock right must have been one of Perrier's jobs. But, as you say, uncertain and risky. All the same, it looks as if Perrier *could* have done the murders. And he did search my house for Miss

Clyde's confession. And in my opinion, he's a very suspicious character——"

She stopped. She suddenly noticed that the sitting-room door, which she had been sure was closed, had opened about an inch.

As she looked at it, the door opened farther. Quite noiselessly and with a look of great mystery on her face, Miss Takahashi came into the room. Standing still just inside the room, she closed the door as noiselessly as she had opened it, then she looked at Daniel, with a shy but penetrating gaze, Alex feeling that Miss Takahashi was getting ready to go into one of her bewildering fits of silent giggles, hastily introduced them to one another.

Both bowed and Miss Takahashi advanced cautiously across the room.

" Very funny house to come and visit now," she observed, only just above a whisper. " Very funny situation. Very difficult for me to work when there is so much else to think about, so I come down to see Mrs. Summerill and tell her what I think. I think murder is very funny business. I think this is very funny house. I think perhaps I should tell Mrs. Summerill something I know, because I think perhaps I am not safe till I tell it, but when other people besides myself know it, then it is no good for the murderer to kill me. Very dangerous to be only person who has knowledge of something, so I tell Mrs. Summerill what I know, because I think I am not safe here in this very funny house, also I cannot work while I am thinking of not being safe, so I think I will tell Mrs. Summerill——"

" Yes, Miss Takahashi, what is it you know that you want to tell me ? " Alex asked, cutting across the flow of repetitions.

" I tell you who listened at the door yesterday while you talked to Miss Clyde," said Miss Takahashi. " I am standing on the staircase and I see him clearly. I am standing on the staircase and I see him go to the door and put his ear to it. I am standing on the staircase——"

" Yes, who was it ? " said Alex.

" Tally," said Miss Takahashi.

XVII

ALEX AND DANIEL looked at one another.

Miss Takahashi went on quickly. " Now you tell everyone you know what I know, then I am not in any danger. There is no danger in knowing what everyone knows."

Daniel said interestedly, " So you think Mr. Tally is the murderer, do you, Miss Takahashi ? Have you any special reason for thinking that ? "

At once Miss Takahashi looked scared and evasive.

" No, no, I do not think anything, I only think it is very dangerous to know anything that no one else knows. But now you know what I know and you tell everybody——"

" I wonder if there's anything else you know that no one else knows," Daniel said, speaking quietly and thoughtfully, as if to himself, rather than to Miss Takahashi.

The remark seemed somehow to embarrass her deeply. Looking at the floor, she murmured indistinctly, " No, no, I do not know anything. Very funny man, Mr. Tally, talks so much about himself, you never learn anything about him. Very funny. No, I do not know anything." Without waiting to risk being questioned any further, she darted soundlessly from the room.

" An odd, but rather penetrating little woman," said Daniel, looking after her. " That's a rather suggestive description of your friend Tally, who kept you talking in the hall. Would you say it was correct ? "

" Yes, I think perhaps it is," said Alex, trying to ignore the remark about talking in the hall. " But d'you really think she thinks he's the murderer and liable to kill her for having seen him listening at the door ? "

" What is there against the idea ? " asked Daniel.

Alex thought it over. " The clock," she said presently, " and the time element in general, and the business with the lights."

" What's wrong with them ? "

" He never touched the clock," said Alex. " I know he

didn't. And all the time the lights were out, he was in the sitting-room all but a minute or two. I admit he could have been the person who turned the lights out during that minute or two, but he couldn't have committed two murders. So if he did do the murders, he'd have had to do them before the lights went out, and in that case, why all the tricks with the lights and the clock? They don't give him an alibi for the time before nine o'clock, which in his case would be the important time."

" Still, I wonder if Miss Takahashi doesn't actually know something that she hasn't told anyone," said Daniel.

" About Tally?"

" Not necessarily."

" I rather suspect Tally of listening at doors a good deal." said Alex. " He won't admit it, but I've an idea that when he says he works for an insurance company, what he means is that he's a detective, tracking down insurance frauds. I think something must have leaked out sometime last autumn about Miss Clyde's arson, and he was sent here to look into it. And I think Miss Clyde must have realised what he was after, because it was about then, Henrietta told me, that her aunt's condition got much worse and that she seemed to become terrified of something or someone."

" Well, I'll look forward to meeting him," said Daniel. " At lunch, which I'm looking forward to more still. D'you think by any chance a discreet inquiry about it would hurry someone up? A very considerate inquiry, naturally, the domestic circumstances being what they are. But still, a question, just to keep the thought alive."

" I'll see what I can do," said Alex, and went out in search of Henrietta.

She did not find her, but she found a Miss Barton laying the table in the dining-room. Presently a sparse, cold lunch appeared at which all Miss Clyde's paying guests assembled, except for Conrad. Neither he nor Henrietta came to the meal. Alex went upstairs to look for them in their rooms, but did not find them.

" I expect they've gone out for a quiet walk together, poor things," said Madame Perrier. " You know, I'm so sorry for them both. I could cry when I think of it. Just fancy having all this happen the day before one's wedding. Not that I'd take any notice of it, if I were them. I'd just go ahead and get married and be blowed to everything."

"Perhaps that's what they're doing now," said Tally.

He said it casually, with no appearance of dropping a hint, but the words gave Alex a jolt. She remembered Henrietta's suggestion that that was what she and Conrad ought to do and the reason that she had given for suggesting it.

Daniel was studying each person at the table with undisguised interest. But he seemed to be paying more attention to Mrs. Wakely than to anyone else. In a few minutes he had her talking about compost, which seemed neither to irritate nor to bore him, while Mrs. Wakely, responding to him with animation, plainly found him the most intelligent listener that she had had for a long time.

Tally was less talkative than usual and looked moody and rather ill-humoured. Perhaps this was because Miss Takahashi, quite suddenly and without any explanation, announced that she had seen him listening at Miss Clyde's door the evening before. He seemed not to know what to make of the accusation and shrugged his shoulders at it. Glancing from Daniel to Alex, he seemed to be trying to guess at the relationship between them, coming to conclusions that brought a sardonic glint to his bulging brown eyes.

"Well, well," he seemed to be saying to himself, "well, well, who'd have thought it?" After lunch, however, when he succeeded in speaking to Alex by herself, it was in a quiet, serious tone.

"Remember me saying I'd some photographs of my kid?" he said. "Well, I've got them here, if you'd care to see them. Don't bother with them if you aren't interested, but I thought that perhaps . . ." He paused wistfully, thrusting a hand towards the pocket inside his coat.

Alex reassured him that she would be delighted to see the photographs. Bringing a folder out of his pocket, he took out a handful of prints and handed them to her one at a time. Alex glanced round to see what had happened to Daniel. He was still talking to Mrs. Wakely.

"Daniel, do look," Alex called out to him. "Mr. Tally's showing me some photographs of his little girl."

As Daniel came towards them, she looked at the first photograph.

It was a very charming picture of a little girl of seven or eight. A likeness to her father was just discernible. It lay in the big dark eyes and the short blob of a nose. But the child's eyes were without the bulging, pug-dog look of her father's and her nose was a dainty trifle instead of being coarsely shapeless. She had a mop of fair, windblown curls and a wide, laughing mouth that showed the gaps in her teeth. She looked an engaging, confident child who had enjoyed posing for the photographs and perhaps had a certain art in doing so. She was dressed in a short, checked gingham dress and sandals. The background was of some seaside esplanade, perhaps Bournemouth, where she was at school.

" You'd never have thought I could have done it, would you ? " said Tally in a rapt tone, gazing over Alex's shoulder at the snap-shot, as if he had never seen it before.

" What's her name ? " asked Alex.

" Sally," he said. " Sally Tally. Sounds sort of silly, don't it, but it was her own idea. Really she's called Marylin, but she never took to it, and one day started telling people her name was Sally. She's like that, full of cute little ideas of her own and as independent as they come." He put the photograph back into the folder and gave Alex the next. All the photographs were much the same, except that they showed Sally at different stages of growth. At all stages, she was certainly a child that any parent might be proud of. There was one picture of her as a baby of a year or so, in the arms of a plump, blonde young woman. Tally did not let Alex and Daniel look at this photograph for as long as the rest. When they had seen them all, he gathered the pictures together and put them back into his pocket.

" Been boring you, I expect," he said, though without looking in the least as if he thought this possible. " But she's a fine kid, isn't she ? I can tell you, I think the world of her. And yet I never knew that it would work out like that when I took up with May, I never thought even of wanting a kid. Then there she was one day and she's been everything to me ever since. Not that it's easy for me to know if I'm doing the right thing for her. You don't need to tell me that I spoil her, I know I do. But you're only a kid once and you may as well enjoy yourself if you can, that's the way I think about it. Being a kid isn't much fun, according to my experience. Hard words and hard knocks, that's what it mostly meant to me. Still, I don't blame my poor old Ma. She never got anything out of life but hard work and worry and she meant well by us in her way. I wish my kid had a mother. That's where I've gone wrong. I guess I ought to have married again so Sally could have a real home and not have to spend her holidays gallivanting round hotels with me. But somehow the right sort of woman never would look twice at me. Why should she, I ask you? I haven't got looks or money or even anything out of the ordinary in the way of brains. And I'm not cultured and I've got vulgar tastes and when I get really drunk I'm terrible. Besides, whenever I meet the kind of woman I could really go for, she's always hooked up with somebody else. Somebody tall and handsome."

Grinning, he gave a little slap to the pocket where he had stowed the photographs, as if, after all, he was quite content with things as they were, and went out.

When he had gone, Daniel remarked, " I think your Miss Takahashi described him rather well."

" You know, I believe he has a silent sort of yearning for Henrietta," said Alex. " And Conrad is tall and handsome."

" So am I," said Daniel. " And when men start showing women photographs of their children and talking of wanting to find a mother for them——"

" Really, Daniel ! Anyway, I'm not ' hooked up ' with you."

" He may easily have been deceived by appearances. But talking of Conrad and Henrietta, d'you think it's conceivable that they've gone off to get married ? "

" I don't think so. But . . . Well, I just don't know where I am with Henrietta at the moment. Or anyone else if it comes to that."

" I'd like to meet them as soon as possible," said Daniel. " Meanwhile, as they aren't around, d'you think we might take a walk along the cliffs ? There's nothing like sea air for clearing the mind."

" I suppose you mean you want to look at the ruin of the old house," said Alex.

" No, I don't see any special value in that," said Daniel, " but there are one or two other things I shouldn't mind taking a look at."

" Well, wait while I get my coat," said Alex.

She went upstairs to fetch it. As she reached the landing, she saw Mrs. Wakely coming out of the bathroom. The bathroom door, standing open behind her, revealed an array of aggressively sensible underwear, hanging up to dry on a string above the bath. Alex remembered Miss Takahashi's indignant description of Mrs. Wakely's habit of leaving her more intimate belongings in the bathroom. Mrs. Wakely gave Alex quite the most human smile that Alex had yet seen on her face.

" What a charming man your friend is, Mrs. Summerill," she said. " A man of real intelligence, as anyone can see. It's a long time since I've had such an interesting conversation as we had at lunch. I've been thinking it over and it's occurred to me that he might care to have some literature on the subject. I'd gladly give him some pamphlets that I happen to have, and lend him one or two of the more significant books. Would he care for that, do you think ? As you know, I never thrust my beliefs down people's throats—I don't believe in doing that, it never leads to anything—but he seemed to me to take a genuine interest in the subject, so that if you think he'd like it, I'd go and put together a little collection of worth-while things for him to take away with him. He won't be staying, I suppose ? He'll be returning to London to-day ? "

Alex had no idea what had been behind Daniel's noticeable friendliness to Mrs. Wakely at lunch, but thought that he might as well take the responsibility for its consequences himself. So Alex assured Mrs. Wakely that she was sure Mr. Whybrow would be delighted to have some good books to read about compost, but also that she had not the faintest idea how long he was staying.

" I see," said Mrs. Wakely, and seemed unexpectedly troubled by this latter piece of information.

As she went on to her room, Alex went to her own and fetched her coat. But she and Daniel did not go out for a walk. When she came downstairs again, she found him in conversation with Conrad. They were in the sitting-room, where a Miss Barton had belatedly delivered a tray of coffee. Both men turned to Alex eagerly when she came into the room.

" Isn't Henrietta here ? " Conrad asked.

Daniel added, " It seems we were wrong in thinking she was with Mr. Moorhouse."

Alex poured out coffee for the three of them. " Where have you been ? " she asked Conrad.

" Out by myself," he answered. " The way that Henrietta's been treating me this morning hasn't made me particularly want to search her out."

" You're both so stupid," said Alex. " Now of all times to be acting like this ! You're as bad as she is."

" How ought one to act towards a woman who suspects one of being a murderer ? " asked Conrad.

" I've no experience of it myself," said Daniel, " but I suspect in the same way as you'll handle most of the other minor differences of your marriage."

" And how do you know she suspects you of being a murderer ? " asked Alex. " Has she said so in so many words ? "

" No," said Conrad. " But she's quite good at looking her suspicions."

" Looks can mean all sorts of things," said Daniel. " They're even more ambiguous than words, which are bad enough. They might mean, for instance, that she thinks you suspect her of something."

" But that's absurd," said Conrad.

" You know it isn't," said Alex. " You were pretty suspicious about that trip of hers to London when she didn't want you along."

" But that could have had nothing to do with all this," said Conrad. " It was a fortnight ago."

" It could have had quite a lot to do with all this," said Alex. " D'you know why it was she wanted to go to London alone ? "

" No," said Conrad, " but it can't have been anything important. You said so yourself when we first talked about it. And when I said I thought it was connected with Vivian, you said you were sure it wasn't." He said this too emphatically, with an overbright, uneasy look in his eyes.

" Well, I was quite right," said Alex, " it had nothing whatever to do with Vivian. But it did have something to do with——"

She got no further, for, to her surprise, Daniel raised his normally quiet voice to cut across her sentence with the words, " By the way, do you know about the eavesdropper whom Mrs. Summerill surprised outside Miss Clyde's door yesterday evening ? Miss Takahashi has identified this person as Mr. Tally."

The change of subject brought more confusion into Conrad's gaze.

" Tally ? " he said, but his thoughts were plainly following some path of their own. " Well, I wouldn't put it past him. Tally . . . I'd say he was capable of anything."

" Including murder ? " asked Daniel.

" Why not ? " Conrad turned to Alex again. " You were saying something about Henrietta's trip to London . . ."

But Alex by now had understood the reason for Daniel's brusque interruption. It had been a reminder of Gaffron's warning that for Henrietta's safety no one else should be told that Henrietta had read Miss Clyde's letter of confession. That Daniel thought it necessary to keep this knowledge from Conrad as well as from the other people in the house was a shock to her, for she had not been able yet to bring herself to believe in the possibility of Conrad's guilt. But after all, she had no reason for trusting him more than anyone else, except that he happened to be engaged to Henrietta, which, since Henrietta herself was full of distrust for him, was not really an adequate reason.

" Yes, I was saying it had nothing to do with Vivian," said Alex.

He recognised the evasion and frowned, but did not pursue the matter. Instead, he gulped his coffee and left the room.

As soon as he had gone, Alex exclaimed, " But you don't really suspect him, Daniel ! "

" A precaution." Daniel put his coffee cup down and lit a cigarette. He added sombrely, " I hope unnecessary."

" Telling him about the eavesdropping, that was just a precaution, too ? " she asked.

" That's all."

" But of what importance could that be to Conrad. Why should it matter to him if Tally was seen ? "

" Suppose Tally wasn't seen ? "

" But Miss Takahashi said she saw him."

" Yes, she said so, and it may be true that she believes it. But it was dark in the passage, wasn't it ? "

" You couldn't confuse Tally and Conrad. Conrad's the taller of the two by inches."

" I agree."

" Then what are you getting at ? "

Thrusting an arm through hers, he replied, " At what you've just said. I think myself you couldn't confuse them. But Miss Takahashi was standing on the staircase, wasn't she ? She was looking down. That can give one a very misleading idea of height. Now, let's go for that walk." He drew her towards the door. But before they reached it, he changed his mind. " Wait—I've just thought of something. That main switch—where exactly is it ? "

" In a cupboard by the kitchen."

" Show it me, will you ? "

Alex took him along the passage. The kitchen door was closed and the light in the passage was dim. She switched on a light, then pushed open the cupboard door.

She did not hear her own scream. Yet she knew by a feeling in her throat that she had cried out wildly.

On the floor of the cupboard in a heap, with blood clotting on her forehead, lay Henrietta.

XVIII

SHE WAS NOT dead.

She was not, at that moment, even unconscious. She appeared just to have struggled back to consciousness and to be making a desperate effort to hold on to it and not lose herself again in the threatening darkness. Her eyes were open, gazing uncertainly towards the light, but the two faces before her seemed to mean nothing to her.

Daniel knelt down beside her and took her hand.

She managed to focus her eyes on his face and ask hoarsely, " Who are you ? "

" Never mind about that yet," he said. " How do you feel ? "

" Awful," she said.

" Where does it hurt ? "

" My head." She lifted a hand and felt the top of her head, but winced at the touch of her own fingers.

" Nowhere else ? " asked Daniel.

" I don't think so."

" Then I think we'll get you out of here," he said. " You don't look very comfortable there among the brooms and mops."

" Are you the doctor ? "

" Unluckily, no," he said. " We'll get him along, but meanwhile we'll get you on to a sofa. It can't be any fun, sitting in a dark cupboard." He slid an arm behind her. " Now can you move at all or will you leave it all to me ? "

" Oh, I think I can manage." Carefully exploring the use of her own limbs, she got to her feet with only a little assistance. As she did so, Alex came forward to take her arm.

" This is a silly business, getting conked on the head, isn't it ? " Henrietta said to her with an attempt at cheerfulness, though her face was grey-white. " Where's Conrad ? "

" We'll get him," said Daniel, his arm still about her as they started along the passage. " That's right, you're doing fine."

" If you aren't the doctor, I suppose you're the police," said Henrietta.

" Not even that," he said. " I'm no one for you to worry about."

" He's Daniel Whybrow, a friend of mine," said Alex. " You must have heard me speak of him."

" Oh, of course," said Henrietta, " you were always ringing up the office. We've often talked on the telephone. I always had a suspicion that you and Alex were secretly married."

" Being conked must be making you a little light-headed," said Daniel.

" I dare say," Henrietta agreed. " Anyway, I'm very glad to see that you seem to be as nice as you sounded on the telephone. I'm so glad it was you who found me in the cupboard and not . . ." She stopped and raising a hand quickly laid it over her eyes as if to shut out some unbearable sight.

" Do you know who conked you ? " he asked, but his tone suggested that the question was of relatively small importance.

" No," she said. " That was what was so horrible about lying in there and thinking that if I called out, the wrong person might hear me. When you opened the cupboard door just now I was petrified with fear."

" Well, don't try talking too much all at once," said Daniel.

" There'll be plenty of time for that later on when you're feeling a bit better."

They had entered the sitting-room. Henrietta sat down thankfully on a sofa, smiling up at Alex as she arranged some cushions under the girl's head.

" Who's your doctor ? " Alex asked her. " I'll ring him up straight away."

" I really don't think there's any need," said Henrietta. " I'm feeling better every moment."

" All the same, we'll get him along," said Alex. " Who is he ? "

Henrietta gave her the name of a local doctor. Going to the telephone, Alex left a message for him, asking him to call as soon as possible. When she returned to the sitting-room, she found Daniel delicately exploring the wound on Henrietta's head.

" That's nothing much, at any rate," he said. " All round, from the look of things, you've had a rather lucky escape. Now the next question is, whom shall we look for first to tell about your adventure, the police or your Conrad ? "

" Conrad," said Henrietta quickly.

" Are you sure ? "

She frowned at him before she answered. " Yes, of course. There's no need for the police to know about this at all."

" There is, you know," said Daniel.

" I'd far sooner not tell them," said Henrietta.

" I'm afraid there's no choice. But as they don't seem to be on the spot and as Mr. Moorhouse is probably upstairs in his room, we could quite justifiably tell him about it before the police arrive—if you're sure that's what you want."

" Yes, of course I want that," said Henrietta.

" All right, I'll go and find him," said Daniel, "and telephone the police while I'm about it." He went out.

Stirring restlessly on the sofa, Henrietta asked, " Why did he talk like that, as if I might not want to see Conrad ? "

" I suppose because he's been told by me, and by Conrad himself, that you've been acting as if you suspected Conrad of being involved in the murder," said Alex. " But I shouldn't try to talk now. The police will want to ask you a lot of questions presently, and you may as well rest while you can."

The advice had no effect on Henrietta. Her face, which

Alex had always thought of in the past as so calm and cheerful, became stormy with anger.

" You told Mr. Whybrow that I suspected Conrad of the murder ? You tried to make him suspicious of Conrad ? I'll never forgive that, never. It's—it's unforgivable. And from you, of all people ! "

" And from Conrad," Alex reminded her.

" Oh, that's different," said Henrietta. " It's just like him to get some silly idea in his head about me. But you ! "

" And I suppose it's just like you to get some silly idea in your head about Conrad and I mustn't criticise that either," said Alex. " However, I do criticise it. I think that the two of you have been doing every single thing that in my column I've advised those about to marry not to do. And you must have typed out hundreds and hundreds of letters about the stupidity of beginning with an attitude of distrust and so on and so on, and it plainly hasn't had any effect on you at all. It's dreadfully disheartening. D'you know, I've practically made up my mind to give up that column. I've always been quite sincere about it and I can't work when I don't feel sincere, but now . . ."

Henrietta's temper subsided. She managed a subdued smile.

" Don't worry, you'll calm down," she said. " One gets over most things, as you always used to tell people. But Alex, you're quite, quite wrong if you think I suspect Conrad of the murder. I don't. As a matter of fact, I can prove he didn't do it, if I have to." But there was no happiness in her voice as she said this, and the trace of a smile had gone again from her face, leaving it utterly woebegone.

This made Alex more troubled than she had been yet by anything that the girl had said. For she felt that this attitude of Henrietta's was caused, not by mere distrust or suspicion, but by knowledge. Henrietta must have discovered, or believed that she had discovered, something about Conrad not much less dreadful to her than the discovery of him as a murderer would have been.

" What d'you mean, if you have to ? " Alex asked. " If you have real proof of that sort about anyone here, you ought to produce it."

" Ought I ? " Henrietta smiled again, but this time it was not a pleasant smile. " That sounds very simple. Only it just happens that the situation isn't simple. It . . ." The hardness went suddenly out of her voice and tears came into her eyes. " Oh, Alex, how long does it take one to get to know a person whom one loves well enough to know for sure what things they'll do and what things they simply couldn't ever do because they're the sort of person they are ? "

" All one's life, perhaps," said Alex. " After all, one never even knows for sure what one's capable of oneself."

" It never occurred to me until a short time ago that I didn't know Conrad," said Henrietta. " I just loved him and I didn't think about anything else. Then I did get to know something about him . . . Yet I don't seem to stop loving him."

" This thing that you know . . . ? "

" No, I don't want to talk about it. If I have to, for his own sake, I will, but not otherwise. It can't affect anyone else."

Alex sighed. " Well, if you would talk about it, you might just possibly find out that this thing you think you know is some sort of illusion, but if you won't talk then you've just got to settle down to the idea of giving up your marriage. In your place, I know which risk I'd take."

" Do you ? " The unpleasant little smile reappeared on Henrietta's face. " As I said, that sounds simple. Only it isn't simple." She moved restlessly. " Why doesn't Conrad come ? Mr. Whybrow's an awfully long time finding him."

" They're coming now," said Alex, who heard footsteps on the stairs. " Actually it hasn't been a long time."

Yet it had been a longer time than she had expected. She had been assuming that at the first words of the attack on Henrietta, Conrad would come racing down the stairs and would have to be restrained, in his passion of anxiety, from gathering the possibly seriously injured Henrietta into his arms to comfort and protect her and to reassure himself. But the steps on the stairs were not at all hasty, and when the door opened, Conrad allowed Daniel to enter the room ahead of him, then remained standing in the doorway, apparently without any desire to approach Henrietta.

Alex noticed the flash of bitter disappointment that crossed Henrietta's face. She also noticed that Conrad's face was extremely pale. He spoke in a voice which was obviously intended to be unemotional, but which came out hoarsely and jerkily.

" I'm very sorry that this has happened to you, Henrietta."

" I'm all right," she answered shortly. " You needn't worry about me."

" I haven't heard yet just how it happened," he said.

" Someone hit me on the head and pushed me into the broom cupboard. I was just opening the cupboard when it happened. And that's all I know. I didn't see who did it and I don't know whether the person meant to come back later and finish me, or whether I was merely wanted out of the way for a little."

" Perhaps," said Daniel, who had placed himself on the hearthrug with his back to the fire, " Mr. Moorhouse can tell us a little more about that."

Henrietta turned on him at once. " What d'you mean by that, Mr. Whybrow ? "

Alex also had looked at Daniel in surprise. There was a sternness in his voice that she was sure she had never heard before. He was looking challengingly at Conrad. But Alex knew Daniel well enough to realise that although he was looking straight at Conrad, his attention was all on Henrietta.

" Are you suggesting," said Henrietta furiously, " that it was Conrad who attacked me ? "

Daniel did not reply. Conrad also said nothing, which seemed to Alex very strange. He was trying to meet Daniel's gaze steadily, but there was a great anxiety in his eyes.

" Well, that's nonsense ! " said Henrietta, sitting up on the sofa, forgetting all about her injured head. " I know he didn't."

" You're perhaps prejudiced in his favour, Miss Selby," said Daniel, still in the cold tones of judgment. " You may be less inclined than other people, particularly the police, to look at the facts."

" What facts ? " Henrietta demanded.

" I think they can keep until Inspector Gaffron gets here, and I think you should remain lying down until the doctor has seen you."

Still Conrad said nothing at all.

" It's all nonsense," said Henrietta. " The person who hit me on the head is the person who thinks that Aunt Jay named him as her accomplice in the letter she wrote to Alex, confessing about the burning down of the old house. But that couldn't be Conrad."

" Why not ? " asked Daniel.

" Because Conrad has read the letter."

Conrad's head jerked in surprise. Giving up his effort to meet Daniel's glare, he looked in plain astonishment at Henrietta.

" When on earth could I have read that letter ? " he asked.

" When you took it out of my bag that evening after I got back from London," she said.

He still looked as amazed as ever. But Daniel was smiling now, with a rather appealing air of being extremely pleased with himself. Something had just happened in the way that he had hoped. But neither Henrietta nor Conrad paid any attention to him. Conrad had advanced a few steps towards the sofa.

" I've never even had my hands on your bag," he said.

" You have," said Henrietta, " I saw you. Don't try to make out you've forgotten."

" I swear to you, I've never seen that letter," he said. " And I never even knew till just now that you'd ever seen it. When did you ? "

" When I went to London and took it out of Alex's office," said Henrietta.

" Then what did you do with it ? "

" I brought it home. It was in my bag. And you took it out of my bag."

" I tell you, I've never touched your bag, unless I've picked it up sometime to hand it to you . . ." He stopped. An uncertain look of recollection came into his eyes.

" You've decided to remember it now, have you ? " asked Henrietta in a savage voice. As he did not answer, she went on, " I'd put it down for a moment on the table in the hall. I'd just come in and Aunt Jay had heard me and called out so wildly that I thought I'd better go to her at once. But the letter was in my bag and I had some idea I'd better not take it into the room with me. So I dropped it and my coat on the table and went in to her. I was there only two or three minutes, but when I came out you were in the hall, holding the bag. It was open and while I looked at you, you closed it. You gave it to me. For just that moment I thought nothing about it. I thought the bag must have fallen down and you'd simply picked it up. But when I got upstairs, the letter was missing."

"And that's what you've had against me all this time," said Conrad. "You thought that I'd taken that letter out of your bag."

"At first I didn't know what to think," said Henrietta. "Whichever way I looked at it, it didn't make any sense."

"And does it make sense now, that I should have done such a thing?"

"No," said Henrietta violently. "It doesn't. I can't—I simply can't see you doing a thing like that. And at first I couldn't see why you should have done it. Only I *did* see you. And you said nothing about it, and the letter didn't reappear and then when Alex got here I heard how it had been used to blackmail Aunt Jay."

"But Henrietta, darling," he said and went and sat on the sofa beside her, taking up both her hands very gently in his, "I was only picking up the bag. It was on the floor, open, and I picked it up and closed it and handed it to you. That's all I did. I swear that's absolutely all."

Henrietta had started trembling. It was clear that she was longing to believe him, but struggling at the same time not to do so.

Before she could say anything, Daniel spoke. "The question is, Mr. Moorhouse, when you went into the hall and saw the bag on the floor, did you see anyone else there, or on the staircase?"

Conrad considered it. "Yes, I think I did. In fact, I spoke to her. But at the time I didn't think anything of it. I never imagined she'd have touched Henrietta's bag. I thought it had just fallen off the table."

"She?" said Henrietta excitedly. "Whom on earth do you mean?"

"Mrs. Wakely," said Conrad.

Henrietta turned quickly to Daniel, as if he could assure her that this was an impossibility. But Daniel nodded.

"That's what I was rather expecting to hear," he said.

"Oh, come now," Alex broke in, "this Daniel-come-to-judgment line is all very well, but you shouldn't try going too far. Until Conrad told you, you can't have had the faintest idea that Mrs. Wakely had taken the letter. So please don't put on airs."

Henrietta was still looking at Daniel. She said, thoughtfully, " I believe you did know Conrad was going to say Mrs. Wakely. But how did you know ? "

" I thought it was, practically speaking, obvious," said Daniel, trying not very successfully to sound modest. " I thought it probable, Miss Selby, that you believed, or half-believed, that Mr. Moorhouse had the letter and was the person who had tried to blackmail your aunt. Your story of simply losing the letter was as unconvincing as any story I'd ever heard and I thought you could only be telling it in an attempt to conceal the fact that you knew the letter had been stolen from you. Further, I thought that the only person you'd be likely to protect in that manner was your fiancé. I realised too that you were making him pay for this protection by forcing him to endure a great bitterness in your attitude towards him. But I did not feel at all convinced myself that Mr. Moorhouse had the letter, so I was anxious to get the actual story of the theft. For this reason I slightly over-emphasised my belief in his being guilty of the murders. I thought that might provoke you to supply his alibi. Being very anxious himself to find out what you thought you had against him, he agreed to co-operate with me."

" So that's why you were such a long time fetching him," said Henrietta.

" Yes—but I think you'll find the delay was worth while," said Daniel.

" But you still haven't told us how you guessed it was Mrs. Wakely," said Alex, refusing to be sidetracked.

" Chiefly because I had reasons of my own, which I won't go into at the moment, for eliminating everyone else," said Daniel, " though I wasn't quite certain of Miss Takahashi. But choosing between her and Mrs. Wakely, I plumped for Mrs. Wakely. After all, she'd practically told you, Alex, that she was staying here to try to discover the truth about her husband's death. That meant that she must be doing a lot of listening and poking and prying. Perhaps she actually knew from eavesdropping that that letter had been written and she may have guessed that Miss Selby had gone to London to get it back. But even if that wasn't so, she was just the person to look into other people's handbags and drawers and cupboards."

" But is she the kind of person to use blackmail ? " Alex asked, still doubting.

" Remember that blackmailing can be a peculiarly torturing form of revenge as well as a means of augmenting one's income," said Daniel. " She's a woman of violent feelings, egotistical and self-righteous. I think she would like herself in the rôle of the avenger."

" If you're right," said Conrad, " how are we going to get the letter from her ? "

" She hasn't got the letter now," said Daniel.

Henrietta asked quickly : " Who has it then, because that person's in danger."

" I have," said Daniel and brought the letter out of his pocket.

XIX

THEY WATCHED him as he unfolded two sheets of thin note-paper, closely covered in handwriting. Alex thought of how much the loss of that letter had meant to her. But as she looked at Daniel, so modestly triumphant in his new rôle of private investigator and enjoying to the full the drama of the moment, she found herself wanting to laugh. When he handed her the letter, however, and she began to read it, with Conrad and Henrietta looking over her shoulders, the laughter died.

The letter was a crazy and pathetic self-accusation. Yet the crime of arson and the defrauding of an insurance company were mentioned only casually. Henrietta had been right about her aunt's ideas of morality. The burning of the house seemed to have impressed Miss Clyde as a reckless and extravagant thing to have done, but there was no sign in the letter that she had found it an unbearable load on her conscience. It was the death of Mr. Wakely that had been more than her mind could endure. For months she had tortured herself with thoughts of the nature of his death, of his fears and his sufferings as the flames surrounded him. But she made no unambiguous statement that she believed his death to have been murder, and though she hinted at this half a dozen times, she named no accomplice. Indeed, the letter was really a curiously harmless one, which in some circumstances might have been taken for the ramblings of the mentally diseased rather than as a confession of crimes that had ever taken place. If her hints had not been confirmed by her own murder and that of Vivian Dale, those two sheets of writing would probably have brought her into the care of a doctor, rather than to the notice of the police.

Alex read the letter to the end before she asked Daniel, " How did you find this ? "

" Well, in a sense by a method I've always tried to use in my photographic work," he said, " but that's a bit complicated, so let's just say, I found it in the bathroom."

" Good heavens, amongst Mrs. Wakely's best woollen underwear," said Conrad. " Is that really where she hid it ? The cunning old witch,"

" I really don't think photography sounds appropriate in the circumstances," said Alex.

" I only meant," said Daniel, " that having picked on Mrs. Wakely as the culprit, I tried to make a rapid study of the postures and the gestures that were natural to her—in this case, of course, the mental postures and gestures. If you don't do that with a photographic subject, you can never make a person look in the least like himself. You'll make him take up some posture in which he feels unreal and uncomfortable, and you'll make him look exactly like the last hundred people you've photographed. He may be very pleased with the result, because he may prefer looking like other people to looking like himself——"

" Yes, yes," said Alex, " but let's stick to the point. You saw Mrs. Wakely's underwear hanging in the bathroom and so you thought that the bathroom was just the sort of place where she might hide other rather private possessions. And you made a lucky guess. But just exactly where in that bathroom did you find it ? "

He smiled at her. " I'm sorry you don't like my higher flights of thought. As a matter of fact, it was quite easy. There was a towel hanging on the line among the wet clothes and the towel happened to be dry. I thought that queer, so I examined the towel. The hem at one end of it felt stiff and I found the letter had been pushed inside it."

"I suppose she thought her room might be searched," said Henrietta. "The letter's probably been there for days, for any of us to find. But what do we do now? Shall we call her?"

"I think at this stage we should wait for the police," said Daniel. "We've collected a good many things to tell them and I think they might prefer to hear them and then to handle Mrs. Wakely without our help. They might feel a little left out of it if we take things too far."

Conrad remarked, "I can hear a car now. It's probably Gaffron."

But it was the doctor. He was a startled and indignant elderly man who seemed to regard everyone in the room as being probably concerned in the attack on Henrietta, and who insisted on remaining until the police appeared, but who then transferred his anger to Gaffron, for not having provided protection for Henrietta. All the inhabitants of the house, the doctor implied, ought to have been placed under guard the day before, and preferably been lodged in gaol. However, he confirmed what Henrietta herself kept saying that her injuries were not serious. A small dressing for the cut on her head and orders that she should rest were the only treatment he gave her. Gaffron listened to him stolidly, waited until he left, then settled down to get an account of the attack on Henrietta.

He also wanted an explanation of the presence of Daniel Whybrow. Daniel told him of the breaking and entering at Alex's house, and also of his efforts at deduction, or, as Alex preferred to call it, his guesswork, which had led him to the discovery of Miss Clyde's letter in the bathroom. Gaffron took the letter without comment and read it through. When he had done so, he turned to one of his men and ordered him to bring to the room, one by one, all the other people in the house, leaving Mrs. Wakely to the last.

Madame Perrier was brought in first, then her husband, then Tally, then Miss Takahashi. To each in turn Gaffron handed the letter to read, asking, when that had been done, if the person had ever seen the letter before. Each denied having done so. When Mrs. Wakely came in, his method was different. He did not give her the letter, but only allowed her a glimpse of it before folding it and putting it away in a pocket. She was unprepared for the sight of the letter in his possession and did not conceal the shock it gave her.

Gaffron nodded heavily, as if the blenching of her face had been a remark.

" Now, let's have the story." That was all he said.

She put out a shaky hand, feeling for a chair. Conrad pulled one towards her. As she sat down, she took a handkerchief from her pocket and began to pull at it with both hands.

" These people," she said, looking round the room, yet managing not to meet the eyes of anyone in it. " Is it necessary . . . ? "

" They're all mixed up in it, one way or another," said Gaffron. " It'll save time if they hear what you've got to say."

She breathed deeply two or three times and her face flushed painfully.

Then she burst out. " Well, I had a right to do it. I had a right to find out the truth about my husband's death. That's all I wanted. I only put demands for money into my letter to conceal who it came from. If I'd simply threatened her with the police, she'd have guessed at once who it was. Then I shouldn't have been safe. She'd have set her thugs on to me, the ones who did the killing for her. And those were the ones I wanted to know about. When I'd got their names, I'd have gone to the police. That's all I meant to do. I'm not a blackmailer, I didn't want her money."

Gaffron treated this with one of his intimidating silences.

After a moment, with the hysteria in her voice increasing, she went on, " I suppose you want to know how I got the letter. Well, I knew it had been written. I'd overheard her telling Henrietta so. Then next day Henrietta went to London, so I guessed what she'd gone for. So I waited my chance and I looked in her bag when she left it in the hall, and I found it. But I was disappointed with it. It didn't tell me all I needed to know. I had to think out a way of getting more information from her. So when I'd thought very carefully, I wrote a letter myself and got a friend of mine in London to post it for me. I arranged for an accommodation address, and it never occurred to me that Miss Clyde would leap to the conclusion it was Mrs. Summerill who was threatening her and would write to her again. I never wanted Mrs. Summerill or her secretary to be suspected and I never wanted Miss Clyde to pay me any money. I only wanted to find out who'd murdered Roland and when I'd done that I was going to see that that person went to the gallows and was hanged by the neck until he was dead ! " It ended in violent weeping.

Nodding again, Gaffron waited until her sobs had subsided, then muttered, " Well, that's that, at any rate." But he looked and sounded very glum, as if the folly of human beings and their unavoidable company and conversation bored and depressed him beyond endurance.

Blowing her nose hard, Mrs. Wakely asked, " Is that all you want from me ? "

He nodded.

She got up and stumbled out of the room.

When she had gone, he said, apparently to himself : " If one single person in this house had used his head, we shouldn't have had any murders."

" I don't agree," said Daniel. " If there's murder in one, one'll get around to it somehow."

Gaffron looked unimpressed. " At least they've all seen the letter, so there shouldn't be any more unnecessary attacks. How are you feeling now, Miss Selby ? "

Henrietta replied that she felt all right except for a bit of a headache, but that if she was not needed for the moment, she would like to lie down. The curious fact was that but for a slight pallor, she was looking as if knocks on the head agreed with her very well. There was a brightness in her face that had not been there for some time, a look of hope and cheerfulness that made her look her proper age again. She was sitting close to Conrad, her wariness of him quite gone.

Gaffron replied that he had no need for either her or Conrad and the two of them went out together. The sight seemed, if anything, to increase Gaffron's glumness. As the door closed on them, he actually scowled at it. Then he gave Daniel one of his thoughtful, sidelong looks.

" Now this affair yesterday at Mrs. Summerill's house," he said, " let's hear it again."

Daniel repeated his account of the telephone message from

Alex's maid, and the signs he had found that the house had been searched, not burgled.

"All for this letter that we've got here and that doesn't tell us anything we didn't know already," said Gaffron, when Daniel stopped. "And you think Perrier's the one who went after it."

"He's the only one from here who could have done so," said Alex. "No one else was absent for long enough."

"In that case, it makes him look like the man we're after for the arson and the probable murder of Wakely," said Gaffron, "only that time he had an alibi, too. The gentleman with too many alibis . . ."

"If he isn't the murderer, why was he after the letter ? " asked Alex.

"That's something I think we'll ask him shortly," said Gaffron. "It could be, of course, that he'd had the idea that getting at your files might be a profitable thing to do. The fact is, though, there are a good many things we know about Monsieur Perrier, since for reasons of our own, we investigated him pretty carefully some time ago, and we never came across anything that suggested he took any interest in blackmail."

"Are we allowed to ask what these reasons were that made you investigate him ? " asked Daniel.

"It was just on account of an idea we'd got that something not quite legal was going on along this bit of coast," said Gaffron. "We investigated a lot of people whose presence, one way or another, was a bit difficult to explain, but we never got anything. The trouble is, the people you really need on those occasions are usually people who've been living in the place all their lives, doing some normal job in a normal way and only going on the crook in their spare time. All the full-time suspicious characters generally turn out to be artists, or novelists, or archaeologists, or nervous-breakdown cases and all as law-abiding as they know how to be."

"I suppose you're talking about smuggling," said Daniel.

Gaffron nodded. "Only we never could find where the stuff was coming ashore, though there've been good quantities of it. It's all small-time stuff, nylons, watches, so on, and we haven't really much evidence about it, except that too much of that sort of thing has been turning up in the neighbourhood, and that a load was washed up on the coast a little way from here, stuff that had been ditched when things went wrong somehow. Anyway, we didn't manage to tie Perrier up in it."

" But what did you find out about him ? " Alex asked.

"Nothing to his discredit," said Gaffron. " In fact, very much the other way round. He was a fisherman's son in a village near Marseilles, and went to work himself in the Marseilles docks. Then he worked his way up slowly till he owned a fleet of small pleasure boats—the shilling-sick type of thing, operating along the coast there. By the time the war came, he was reasonably well-off and with that part being Vichy France, he needn't have done a thing. But one day he cleared off by himself in one of his own boats and turned up sometime later at Gibraltar. He joined the Free French Marine and was torpedoed twice and badly wounded in the chest and the head. There's a silver plate in his skull and he's not fit for work of any kind. By the way, talking of illness, Mrs. Summerill, you asked me to tell you if Vivian Dale was really a consumptive. Well, she was. She'd been bad with it, and it looked as if the illness had got going again recently. I don't believe she'd have lasted much longer, anyway. Perrier has had trouble with his lungs too, but the head's the real danger. He met his wife in England during the war when she was with an Ensa troupe. She's got a bit of money in house property in England, and they just manage to get along on it. There's your story."

Alex frowned as she thought it over.

" It's a thing we all hate to recognise," she remarked, " but men can be heroes and criminals at the same time. It seems to me that a man like that, who must have a lot of the spirit of adventure in him, but who finds himself forced into complete inactivity, might easily start thinking out schemes about things like smuggling, which most people don't take very seriously as a crime unless it involves something like dope."

" Or murder," said Gaffron. " But for these murders here, including Wakely's, if that was a murder, Perrier has a cast-iron alibi."

" I wonder . . ." said Alex. " Mr. Whybrow and I have been discussing it and it does seem just possible . . . I admit I can't quite straighten it out, but if someone this end was working with him, his wife, perhaps, or Mr. Tally . . ." She stopped and looked at Daniel for help.

Rather unwillingly, Daniel repeated the argument that nearly destroyed the Frenchman's alibi. But before Gaffron could start picking holes in it, Daniel himself pointed out its inadequacies. " As I said to Mrs. Summerill before, the time element is far too tricky. If the idea was to make the people in the house think that the lights went out sooner than they actually did, so that the time of Perrier's arrival would be estimated wrongly, there were far too many risks of the thing going wrong. A chance look at a watch by someone at the wrong moment, and the whole scheme would have been blown sky-high. And I think Perrier would have had to have both his wife and Tally as accomplices, since both of these seemed to have had their minds on the time when the news started, one because he liked to listen to it, the other because she liked to avoid it. But if that were so, why did they both go out of the room just before the lights went out ? I can't see any reason for that. And there is another difficulty. Perrier went to London apparently believing that Mrs. Summerill had Miss Clyde's letter. He searched her house and failed to find the letter. Then, if he was the murderer, he must have made up his mind straight away that it was Vivian Dale who had the letter and that she must be murdered. But how did he know, having been away all day and coming into the house presumably only after the lights had been turned out, that she would be in her room ? Miss Clyde's habits may have been such that he could count on finding her in her room after dinner, but he had no such knowledge of Vivian Dale. No, I'm inclined to think we're running off down a false trail when we bother too much with upsetting Perrier's alibi."

Gaffron nodded in complete agreement.

But Alex would not give it up. Taking her forehead between her hands, she tried hard to make her thoughts come clearer.

" But this time element must mean something," she said, " and I can't see that it means anything to anybody but Perrier. It doesn't give anybody else an alibi, yet the clock was put right for some reason."

" That's something we can't be sure of," Daniel muttered.

" Eh ? " said Gaffron.

" I mean it may have been done almost automatically by the murderer," said Daniel, " when he found himself near the clock, and without thinking clearly that he was doing it. A sort of muddled feeling that he'd got to obscure all his traces. In any case, I suspect that we're thinking quite wrongly here about time. If it does mean anything, it means something different from what it appears to mean."

" But Perrier did go to London and search my house for the letter," said Alex, " and he did go near the clock. So he could have been the one who put it right and . . ." A tide of excitement suddenly welled up in her, so that she did not notice the change of expression that came to Daniel's face at that moment. " And he could have known where to find Vivian ! "

" How's that ? " asked Gaffron.

" Vivian's room faced towards the road," said Alex. " If the lights were still on when Perrier came up the lane, he could have seen that her lights were on and that therefore she was probably in her room. If he'd gone there the moment the lights went out, he was certain to find her . . . Daniel, why are you looking at me like that ? " For Daniel was staring at her as if she had just said something that had startled him beyond words.

He took a moment to pull himself together. Still looking slightly dazed, he muttered : " The alibi . . . you've just shown me how the alibi was worked. Why didn't I see it straight off ? It's so damn simple . . ."

Gaffron was not listening to him.

" At any rate, I think it's time we asked Monsieur Perrier a question or two about his trip to London," he said, and going to the door, called one of his men to find Perrier and bring him to the sitting-room.

XX

PERRIER CAME IN briskly, seeming sure of himself but wary. For the first time Alex looked carefully for the signs of illness in his face and thought that she recognised them now, not in any shadows or lines that she had not noticed before, but in the impersonal expression that comes so often to the faces of people who have had to some extent to withdraw from life. It is a look that can mask good and evil, sympathy and hatred, and make the nature of the person who insists on wearing this mask of normal health as much of a mystery to anyone who knows him as his concealed pains and fears.

Perrier at first remained standing near the door, a tall and apparently powerful figure. " I can assist in some way ? " he said to Gaffron, as if in pleased surprise at this being possible.

" Perhaps," said Gaffron in his usual, reluctant way, so that it might have been supposed that he disliked being assisted, preferring to fish up the solutions of all his problems out of the silent depths of his own consciousness. "Perhaps. It's about this business at Mrs. Summerill's house." Having said that much, he waited.

Perrier's eyebrows went up. He seemed for a moment to be uncertain whether or not to admit that he understood what Gaffron was talking about. Then with a wry smile he turned to Alex, shrugging his shoulders.

" I am caught—yes, it was I," he said.

" We know that," said Gaffron and again waited, leaving Perrier to sort out by himself all the unasked questions.

Perrier chose to ignore them and went on addressing Alex. " I ask your pardon, Madame. For any damage I have done, I will compensate. But I humbly ask your pardon for the foolish suspicion that took me searching your house. Having once seen you, I should have known better." Then he too left it at that, standing there easily, apparently ready to consider the matter closed.

This forced Gaffron into saying impatiently, " All right,

all right—question is though, why was it your business to suspect anyone ? "

" It was not my business," said Perrier, so simply that it might have been an exercise in grammar, a demonstration that he could use the negative.

" Well, then, whose was it ? " asked Gaffron.

" It was the business of Miss Clyde," said Perrier.

" She sent you."

" Certainly.'

Gaffron's look suddenly reminded Alex of Henrietta's idea that he might be capable of torturing babies.

" So she gave you orders, did she ? " he said.

" Certainly not," said Perrier. " She requested my assistance."

" Oh. Just like that. Please help me to burgle this lady's house."

" No, not at all like that," said Perrier, as earnestly as usual. " It is a long story."

The admission seemed to make Gaffron feel that he was getting somewhere. " Sit down then and tell it," he said.

Perrier took a chair. " Perhaps I shall not tell it comprehensibly," he suggested.

" More than likely," said Graffon.

" But I am glad to tell it to Mrs. Summerill," said Perrier, " because I wish to ask her pardon humbly for listening to Miss Clyde's suspicions."

" We've had that part," said Gaffron.

" It is the important part," said Perrier.

Alex felt inclined to agree with him, but saw that Gaffron did not. Nor, it seemed, did Daniel, for to judge by his expression, he was not troubling to listen to Perrier at all. Daniel was looking at the Frenchman, but it was with a wide-eyed and unblinking stare of the kind that someone deeply and confusedly engaged in mental arithmetic, and longing for paper and pencil that were not available, might fix on a spot on the wall.

" The story begins long ago in France," said Perrier. " Two years ago when my wife and I became acquainted with Miss Clyde. It is then that I come to like Miss Clyde very much. We become very good friends. We trust one another. That is the beginning."

" Well, and Instalment Two ? " said Gaffron.

" That is when my wife and I come to live in Sharnmouth, in the old house across the cove," said Perrier. " We are very comfortable there, not because it is such a nice house as this one, but because Miss Clyde is a very good and gay old lady, very good to us. Then one evening the house goes up in fire and Mrs. Wakely is killed. This is very bad."

" Quite bad," Gaffron agreed.

" I tell you from the first I have suspected things," said Perrier, " but I have known nothing for sure. Besides, I am a foreigner and I do not want to make trouble for anybody or myself either. So I leave it to the police and they are satisfied, so I am satisfied too."

" Nice of you," said Gaffron.

" But it is only natural," Perrier replied with what might or might not have been an irony to match the Inspector's.

Gaffron chewed the knuckles of his thumb and did a little more waiting.

" You understand," Perrier went on, " it has been easy for me for a long time to see that all is not well with Miss Clyde. Soon after we come to this house from the hotel where my wife and I have gone to stay when the house is burnt down, we see that it is not at all the same any more. Miss Clyde is not well and has become very unhappy. She broods. I speak to her, I say, ' You are troubling yourself about this old man. This is not good. It will not help.' She weeps but she will not answer me. Several times I try to make her confide in me, but she will not, so I give up. But I tell her I am her friend and if she wishes it ever, I will help her. Then we talk no more about it till this week."

Gaffron took his thumb out of his mouth. " This week ? When ? "

" It was Tuesday," said Perrier. " Miss Clyde asks me to come to her room. I notice she is a little—well, she has been drinking a little, and she is excited. She catches me by the arm and she looks into my face. ' Pierre,' she says, ' you have said once, if I ask it, you will help me.' I say certainly and she says, ' Have you ever burgled a house.' ' No,' I say. ' Do you think you could if you tried ? ' she asks me. ' Yes,' I say, ' I think it is probable.' ' Very well,' she says, ' now I will tell you just what I want you to do . . .' So she tells me that on the next day a lady is coming here from London who has a letter of hers that she must have back, because this lady, she tells me, is trying to blackmail her for what she has written in this letter. She says to me then, ' Pierre, I think you have always known, I am guilty of burning my house down. I do not do it myself, but someone has done it for me while we are all at the cinema, someone I pay to do it, so I am guilty. But I swear to you I never knew anyone would die in the fire. I am a bad woman but not a murderess.' Then she weeps and drinks a little more gin and goes on. She says she felt the need to confess to someone, so she has written to this lady, Mrs. Summerill, thinking she will be kind to her and help her, but instead she has written back threatening her and demanding money. I become very indignant when I hear this. I think it is terrible and I say I will help in any way I can."

" So off you went to London and broke into Mrs. Summerill's house ? " said Gaffron.

" Alas, yes," said Perrier. " It is true that when I see Mrs Summerill on Wednesday evening I am surprised that such a charming lady should be a blackmailer. But in my life I have known more surprising things even than that. Nothing is impossible in the way of evil, that is my belief."

" Comforting notion," said Gaffron.

Perrier shrugged his shoulders. " That does not concern me. What concerns me is to burgle this lady's house. This is a new and very interesting experience for me. Miss Clyde tells me she knows from her niece, who has worked for Mrs. Summerill, that a woman comes to the house in the morning to clean, but in the afternoon it will be empty. This I find is true, for first I ring the bell many times, but no one answers. So then I walk to the back of the house, break a window and enter. It is very quick, very easy. But I search and I do not find the letter. Soon I begin to feel there is something wrong, for this house that I am in, it feels like a good house, a nice house, not a house where a blackmailing lady hides her secrets. It comes to me as I search that Miss Clyde has made a mistake and it is not Mrs. Summerill who has threatened her but somebody else. I think then of the secretary, the beautiful secretary . . ."

" So did someone else," said Gaffron.

Perrier spread out his hands. " I am glad to hear you say

someone else, Inspector, for I think that if you knew how to do it, you would suspect me of her murder."

The words seemed to bring Daniel's attention back to earth. The glazed look faded from his eyes. For a moment they looked steadily into Perrier's face, then Daniel remarked, " However, we don't know how to do it. Mrs. Summerill and I have spent half the day trying to break your alibi down, and we seem to get pretty near doing it sometimes but at the last moment it always beats us."

Perrier smiled. " I am very fortunate."

" As a matter of fact, I think you are," said Daniel. " Clocks are tricky things to rely on for one's safety. The chances of a clock going fast or slow——"

" But Miss Clyde's clock was right, was it not ? " said Perrier.

Alex interrupted, " Inspector, d'you mind if I put a question to Monsieur Perrier ? "

Gaffron grunted his permission.

" Monsieur Perrier," said Alex, " you can see this house from the main road, can't you ? "

Perrier nodded.

" You can see it from the bus ? " she asked.

" Yes, certainly," he said.

" Did you look towards the house yesterday while you were still on the bus ? "

" Yes, I did," he said, " and I noticed then that it was already in darkness. That is what you were going to ask me, was it not ? "

" Yes," she said, " *but do you think anyone else on the bus noticed it ?* "

For the first time since he had come into the room, Perrier looked unsure himself. He hesitated, then, as if groping for the difficult English words, he began, " Madame, I think . . ."

He got no farther, for Daniel suddenly jumped to his feet, shouting, " The clock was right ! "

Even Gaffron managed to look really astonished.

" The clock was right," Daniel exclaimed again, " and you've been letting the woman go around by herself ! God, what fools we are ! Come on quick ! Anything could happen ! "

He plunged for the door.

Gaffron looked for a moment as if he thought Daniel had

gone raving mad, but did not take more than an instant to make up his mind to follow.

Daniel was taking the stairs three at a time. But half-way up them, it seemed to occur to him that he did not know his way about the house. He stood still.

" Which way ? " he demanded.

" Where the hell d'you want to go ? " asked Gaffron, catching up with him.

" Her room—Miss Takahashi's ! "

" What the devil ? " But Gaffron did not stop to argue it out, for Daniel, assuming that in any case Miss Takahashi's room must be higher up, was once more racing up the stairs. Gaffron, staying at his heels, directed him up the next flight of stairs to the top floor of the house.

Alex had also started following. But she could not run upstairs as fast as the two men and they had reached the top by the time that she had begun on the second staircase. She was aware, as she hurried, that they had both suddenly come to a standstill above her. Then she heard one of the men moving again.

At the same moment she heard Daniel say, " Don't come any farther, Alex."

But she did not take it in and ran up the remainder of the stairs. Daniel, who was standing at the top, caught her arm and would not let her go on. But she had come far enough to see the sight from which he had hoped to save her.

The door of Miss Takahashi's was open and Miss Takahashi was sitting at the table in the middle of the room. She was sitting with her arms flung out across the table and her head fallen forward on her arms. The thick plait of her grey hair had come uncoiled and was hanging over one shoulder. From between her shoulders something protruded. It was the long bone handle of a knife. Behind her and facing Gaffron, with a wild expression like that of a trapped animal, was Conrad Moorhouse.

XXI

" No, no," said Alex, in a whisper, " no, it can't be."

She started to follow Gaffron into the room. Daniel made as if to stop her, but went with her instead, keeping his hold on her arm. In a sick daze, she saw Gaffron go towards Conrad, who made no effort to retreat from him. She heard the formula of arrest and the official warning. Then she heard Conrad say in a low voice, " I didn't do it."

" Of course he didn't ! " she cried out. " He couldn't have ! He——"

She felt Daniel's fingers tighten on her arm, warning her to keep silent.

" God knows why anyone should have done it ! " Conrad went on, sounding angrier. " What harm had she done anyone ? What power had she over anyone ? What could she have known or told ? "

" If you wish to make a statement—— " Gaffron began, but at that moment there was a cry from the doorway and Henrietta rushed into the room.

Conrad, seeing her, said, " Take her out ! Take her out ! "

But Henrietta ran to him and threw her arms round him, pressing her face against his shoulder.

Conrad drew a shuddering breath, then repeated for her, " I didn't do it, Henrietta darling, I didn't do it."

There were other people on the landing now, Tally, the two Perriers, Mrs. Wakely and two policemen.

" I came in here only a moment before you did," Conrad said, looking past Henrietta at Gaffron. " I saw as much as you did, that's all."

" What brought you in here, then ? " Gaffron asked, then immediately reminded Conrad that he was not obliged to answer any questions.

But Conrad seemed to feel no hesitation in answering.

" I was in my room and I heard a noise in here and it worried me. I came to look and I found this."

" What kind of noise ? " asked Gaffron.

" Someone moving about," said Conrad. " One never heard Miss Takahashi moving about. She always crept about in slippers. But this person moved with quite firm footsteps. Then I heard her door shut and someone go downstairs. For a few minutes I didn't think much about it, then I suddenly realised that although I'd heard footsteps I hadn't heard voices. So I wondered if anyone had been up to anything in here and I came along to see. I wasn't even sure that Miss Takahashi herself was here at all."

" But why should anyone kill Miss Takahashi ? " Alex asked in what she imagined was a normal voice, but nobody seemed to hear it. She was wondering what dangerous knowledge the shy little woman could have possessed that had led to her murder. She had told what she herself appeared to believe was her most dangerous secret, the fact that it had been Tally whom she had seen eavesdropping at Miss Clyde's door. But once told, any danger that that might have held for her was gone. Plainly it was the wrong secret that she had told. In something else that she had known there had existed a greater menace.

" What did she know ? " Alex demanded and this time her voice came out so loudly that everyone looked at her in surprise.

" She knew that the clock was right," said Daniel. " Or she may have known. That was enough for our murderer. Her murderer's a ruthless fellow. He was taking no risks."

" But we all know that the clock was put right," Madame Perrier broke in excitedly. " That doesn't mean anything, except that someone did it to get you all muddled about time, so that you should start suspecting Pierre. I know that's why it was done. But it's not true. Pierre was on the bus and no one can prove anything else ! "

" No," said Daniel quietly, " no one can prove anything else, and there's no reason why they should try to. But what Miss Takahashi knew, or may have known, was that the clock was right when she first went into Miss Clyde's room. She went in ahead of the rest of you, didn't she ? She found the key lying in the hall and she recognised what key it was and she went to Miss Clyde's room and let herself in. And if at that moment it happened that she looked at the electric clock on the writing-table, she must have seen that it told the right time."

" But it can't have," said Conrad. " The current had been turned off for something like half an hour."

" But if the murders had been done before the lights were turned out," said Daniel, " and the clock put forward then to a certain time, all that the murderer then had to do, in order to provide himself with a rather curious sort of alibi, was to take care to turn the main switch on again at just that moment."

" Don't move, anybody ! "

The words came from Thomas Theodore Tally, citizen of the world, graduate of the University of Hard Knocks. He was facing the room from the doorway with a revolver in his hand.

" Don't think I mind using this on any of you," he said, " so take my advice and keep still. You're smart all right, brother, but you can amuse yourselves working out the rest of it while I'm on my way."

He took a step backwards, the door slammed and the key turned on the outside of it.

XXII

A CAR DROVE away from the house. They saw it from the window, accelerating along the bumpy lane and swinging out at high speed into the main road. A moment later the lock of the door of Miss Takahashi's room gave with a crack as Gaffron hurled his weight against it. He ran down the stairs, calling out orders to his men as they followed him. While Gaffron snatched up the telephone, the other policemen drove off after Tally.

In Miss Takahashi's room Alex was saying, " But I was sure Tally was the one person who couldn't have tampered with the clock. He was standing beside me all the time we were in the room, we were only just inside the door . . ."

" That's just what you were meant to be sure of," said Daniel. He was looking round the room. " I don't think we have to stay in here," he added. " Suppose we go downstairs."

Silently they trooped out on to the landing, Daniel coming last and drawing the door to behind him. But the broken latch would not hold and the door swung open again. As Alex started down the stairs she had a last glimpse of the room, and it was a long time before she could forget it, a rather bare room, very tidy, with hardly any personal belongings to be seen but a few books, and no pictures on the walls except a scroll in Japanese characters and a small portrait of Shelley.

Gaffron coming upstairs again as the rest went down, said to Daniel, " D'you mind coming back with me for a moment ? "

So Daniel returned to Miss Takahashi's room while the others went silently to the sitting-room.

Henrietta quickly switched on all the lights and started building up the fire into a big blaze. It made Alex realise with surprise how dark it had become. Going from one tall window to the next, she drew the curtains, shutting out the greenish bleakness of the evening sky. Conrad fetched glasses and poured out drinks for everyone. But in spite of the roaring fire and the lights and the drinks, the room seemed shadowy and cold and no one had anything to say to anyone else.

The Perriers sat down side by side and so did Conrad and Henrietta. Her hand slid into his, but they did not speak to one another. Mrs. Wakely withdrew to a corner of the room and sat there white-faced and bewildered-looking, her lips moving occasionally, as if she were uneasily muttering self-justifications to herself. Alex sat down on a window seat, sipping the brandy that Conrad had given her and wishing that Daniel would come down.

He did not reappear until after some more police had arrived at the house. A few minutes after their tramping up and down the stairs had broken the silence, he came quietly into the sitting-room. Seeing the brandy, he helped himself. He looked as if he did not want to do any more talking. But the faces of everyone in the room had turned towards him with questions in their eyes.

Giving a sigh, he sat down beside Alex.

" It'd be better if you had it from the Inspector," he said, " but I'll tell you what I can. I don't really know anything about it though. I mean I don't know anything about the smuggling or the barking dog. It's true we've just found one of those whistle things in Tally's room. Those things they use at sheep-dog trials, you know. People can't hear them at all, but dogs can hear them at a tremendous distance. And that's what your husband must have found out about, Mrs. Wakely. The reason that the dog barked . . . I'm sorry . . ." He brushed a hand across his forehead. " I'm not putting it clearly, I know."

Hoarse-voiced from the far corner of the room, Mrs. Wakely asked, " Did that man Tally kill my husband ? "

" Yes," said Daniel.

" But he wasn't in the neighbourhood at all at that time," said Henrietta. " He only came here last autumn, about the same time as Conrad."

" He wasn't staying in the neighbourhood then," said Daniel. " But he used to come around, selling insurance. He sold some to your aunt, which is how he made her acquaintance. Gaffron had got hold of those facts about him. Tally used also, I think—but this part is guesswork—to come along the cliff path here on certain dates, at night or in the early morning, and meet a boat that came ashore with bundles of smuggled goods. The boat was a rowing-boat which probably put out from Sharnmouth to meet a French trawler, then rowed in here to be met by Tally, who took over the contraband, then rowed back to Sharnmouth, perhaps with a few lobsters to explain the trip, or something of that sort. And they'd worked out a rather neat method of signalling whether or not the coast was clear for the boat to land here. There was a dog in the boat, trained to bark when he heard a certain whistle. Tally had the whistle, a much less conspicuous thing to use than a flashing light or a flag. He could hold it hidden in his hand and put his hand to his mouth, and even someone standing quite close to him wouldn't hear or see anything unusual. But the dog in the boat would start barking and then the boat wouldn't come in to the shore. I dare say it worked very well for a time. But then Mr. and Mrs. Wakely came here and they happened to be interested, Mr. Wakely in particular, in herbs and birds and insects, and so they were always about on the cliffs at odd times of the day and night. At a certain point it must have struck Mr. Wakely that he met a certain man on the cliffs rather often and that whenever he met this man, there was also a boat near the beach, with a dog in it. That's not a very common thing to see, after all. And further, when he met this man, the dog in the boat always started barking. Mr. Wakely must have started putting two and two together. But unfortunately he must somehow have let Tally know that he had done this. Perhaps he actually caught the smugglers red-handed and let them know that he had. But whatever the incident was, that made him decide that he had evidence which he ought to take to the police, it also made up Tally's mind to murder him."

" Then Tally wasn't any kind of detective ? " said Alex. " He wasn't here to investigate the fire for the insurance company ? I was quite wrong about that ? "

" Quite wrong," said Daniel, " though it was your telling me how Tally had allowed you to believe that about him that was the first thing that started me off thinking rather curiously about him. For if he was a detective, he was certainly a crooked one, going in for blackmail on the side, because no detective on earth could have stayed long in this house, anyway during the last few months, without getting all the facts about the fire out of Miss Clyde. He'd only to notice the way that Miss Clyde had saved all her own treasures from the fire to have a lever to get her to make the confession that she was longing to make."

" Then the burning of the house was simply a part of the murder of my husband ? " said Mrs. Wakely.

" No, I think it was more complicated than that," said Daniel. " Tally went in for complicated schemes, that was his trouble. The dog and the clock and so on—all very ingenious, but very dangerous as soon as someone else who was a little ingenious started to think about them."

Mrs. Wakely nodded. " Roland had a very ingenious mind," she said. " Very alert, yet at the same time very profound. He was never deceived by appearances, and he could cut through a tangle of prejudices with a surgeon's knife. For instance, when he and I first began to think about the problem of the systematic poisoning of the soil——"

Hurriedly Conrad interrupted, " I suppose it was useful to Tally to have Miss Clyde in his power."

Mrs. Wakely, who appeared to have recovered enough to want to ride her hobby-horse as usual, turned on him with an irritated frown and was about to plunge into one of her lectures, when Daniel, his voice slightly raised, replied to Conrad. " Yes. I think that was an important part of the scheme. I think that in the first place, long before Tally had started to worry over Mr. Wakely, the burning of the house must have seemed to him a good thing to do for its own sake. Because, of course, it isn't likely that an idea like that could be sown in Miss Clyde's mind and a plan for carrying it out developed, all in a few days. The date for the fire may have been chosen because Tally had decided to kill Mr. Wakely, but the decision to do it must have been arrived at some time before."

" But what was the purpose of it ? " asked Henrietta.

" Just money," said Daniel.

" The insurance money ? " said Conrad.

" That to begin with," said Daniel. " Afterwards, black-mail. I imagine Miss Clyde believed she was getting the job done for a down-payment out of the insurance money, but when Tally turned up again and said he was going to move in here, she must have realised that she'd acquired a burden for life. Somehow I don't think Tally was paying her anything for his room and his keep, and he was probably squeezing her dry of the little money that she had over for herself. What he'd have done when it no longer suited him to stay here, we can't tell, but he might have tried forcing her into selling the house and giving him most of the proceeds. While he stayed here, he was in a very good position for meeting the boat, but that sort of enterprise always winds up sooner or later, and when that happened, it isn't likely that Tally would have remained satisfied with Sharnmouth for long."

"So that's what he was doing yesterday morning on the cliff-path," said Alex, "when he said he'd come out to stop me wandering around the ruins of the old house. He was signalling to the boat."

Daniel nodded. "Tally really had a very nice little set-up here," he said. "But a blackmailer's situation isn't always as enviable as one might think. There's one danger always hanging over him and that is that he may drive his victim to desperation. When that happens, power really changes hands. The blackmailer risks not only losing his profits, but finding the law closing in on him. In fact, to be successful, he has to be a very nice judge of character. That's where Tally failed. He didn't realise how intolerable Miss Clyde had already found the burden of even an unknowing complicity in Mr. Wakely's death, or that when the man whom she knew to be a murderer moved into her house and ate her food and talked with her and her guests, she would become so distracted that she would actually go to the police to ease her conscience. Rather a crude man, in fact, and therefore not as successful in his profession as he might have been."

"So it was when he was eavesdropping outside Miss Clyde's door," said Alex, "and heard her say that when she had counted to five hundred she would write to the police, that he made up his mind to kill her."

"I suppose so," said Daniel, "but as in the case of Mr. Wakely's death, he must have had his scheme ready beforehand. There was so much elaboration. But that was deliberate, to introduce a sense of confusion and contradictoriness. He wanted people to think about time and about light and darkness, and to feel sure that the clock having been put right, apparently after you had all gone into Miss Clyde's room, was to conceal the length of time that the light had been out, just as the radio-lead having been cut was supposed to mean that it was important that no one should know the precise time when the lights went out. He created a web of misleading circumstances in which Monsieur Perrier very nearly became entangled. In fact, the question of time, in itself, was quite unimportant. Both murders had been committed before the lights went out."

"Which Tally himself pointed out was a possibility," said Conrad.

"Did he?" said Daniel. "He was acute then, in some ways. He knew that would occur to someone sooner or later, so he got in with it first. The real object of all the elaborations, however, was to make everyone think about the clock, not about time. Who had gone near the clock? Who could have put it right? Not Tally, because he had been standing next to Mrs. Summerill, near the doorway, and had never approached the clock or the switch. That was his alibi, you see. He hadn't any alibi for the real time of the murders, but apparently he had an unassailable one for that other action that he had made look so important. But a certain accident happened and it was that that led to the third, or rather the fourth murder, a murder which may have been as unnecessary as Miss Dale's, since it's quite likely that Miss Takahashi never looked at the clock at all when she went into Miss Clyde's room. It was the accident of Miss Takahashi finding the key in the hall after Tally had deliberately dropped it. Plainly he'd expected it to be found when there were plenty of witnesses to its finding, so that a number of people would have gone to Miss Clyde's room at the same time."

Perrier spoke. "But if I had not come in when I did and said that there was no power-cut, what would he have done then about switching on the lights?"

"He'd have found some other reason for doing it at the precise moment he had chosen," said Daniel. "As it was, he took Mrs. Summerill along with him as a witness to the fact that he did nothing but switch on the lights, and I believe he kept her talking for some minutes. What I don't think she noticed was a glance at his watch, which must have been what terminated the conversation at a given moment."

Mrs. Wakely stood up. "I suppose they'll catch him,"

she said. " I'm going upstairs now to start packing. Henrietta, I shall be leaving in the morning. I've stayed on all these months for one purpose only, and that, thanks to Mr. Whybrow, has been accomplished. Mr. Whybrow, if you'll give me your address, I'll be very happy to post you some of our more interesting literature."

She bowed to him sedately and went out.

" Dignified exit of Second Blackmailer," muttered Conrad. " I suppose she won't get into any trouble. Big crimes make small ones rather lose their lustre."

" I hope they do," said Henrietta, " because several of us have done things that we ought not to have done."

" That is true," said Perrier.

Madame Perrier chimed in, " Mr. Whybrow, it looks to me as if Pierre and I should thank you, too. I don't know if that Tally was aiming to tangle Pierre up in all his nonsense with lights and times and so on, but that's what could easily have happened."

Perrier got up and shook Daniel by the hand.

" Yes, indeed," he said. Then he and his wife also went out.

" And I certainly should thank you," said Conrad.

Daniel began to look embarrassed by all these acclamations. " Speaking just for myself, I could do with a little more of that brandy," he said.

Henrietta got up quickly to refill his glass.

" I wonder where he's making for," she said. " London, I suppose."

" Or Bournemouth," said Alex.

" Or perhaps in the very opposite direction to Bournemouth," said Daniel.

Alex gave him a quick look. " Yes, I suppose you're right. I believe he really cared for that child. And he wanted her to have everything. What will she have now ? What will become of her ? "

" But they'll catch him," said Daniel, " if he doesn't drive into a tree or over the cliffs. From the way he started off from here, that looked rather probable." He sipped some brandy. " This detecting business takes it out of one," he said. " I think I'll go back to photography"

" I won't," said Alex. " I've a camera going begging.

Henrietta, would you like a camera as an extra little wedding present ? "

" Nonsense," said Daniel. " I gave you that camera and you aren't giving it away to anybody. Besides, isn't there a wedding group for you to take to-morrow ? "

" As a matter of fact," said Henrietta, " I was going to ask you both . . . we wired round to all the other guests, of course, telling them not to come, but we didn't tell the vicar not to come and we shall need two witnesses . . ." She stopped, looking at him questioningly.

" My dear, I should be very honoured," said Daniel. And now, can I help myself to that brandy again ? "

Henrietta brought him the bottle. As he helped himself, she and Conrad went out together.

It felt strange that all of a sudden there was nothing more to be said, no more questions to be asked, no more doubts to be answered. In the silence the fire crackled cheerfully and the warmth of it began to fill the room.

Daniel noticed Alex looking at him.

" Don't worry, there are certain times when nothing on earth would make me drunk," he said. " To-night I could finish this bottle, as I probably shall, and it'll have no effect on me at all, which is a pity."

" Actually," said Alex thoughtfully, " I've never seen you drunk. I've seen you drink a great deal on occasion. but I've never seen you drunk. And apparently there are quite a lot of other things about you that I've never seen before."

" Well, there's a first time for everything," said Daniel. " And considering how long we've known each other, there are rather a number of avenues we haven't explored. For instance . . ."

" I think we've done enough exploring for one day," said Alex.

" Do you ? I'm not at all sure," said Daniel. " And after another couple of glasses of this brandy, although I shall still be stark sober, I may be even less sure about it. Which is a pleasant thought. I've been feeling horribly sure of myself for the last hour or so and I can't say I really enjoyed the experience."

" I, on the other hand, should be glad to feel sure about any single thing," said Alex. " But I don't. There's nothing I'm sure about, nothing at all."

" That's the best news I've heard for a long time," said Daniel. " It'll make it so much more interesting to explore those avenues. And after all, it's time we did that."

" Only not to-night," said Alex. " To-night you just stick to that brandy, if that's what suits you."

" It might suit you too," said Daniel.

Alex considered it. " Yes, I think it probably would," she said, and held out her glass to him.

THE END

>>> If you've enjoyed this book and would like to discover more great vintage crime and thriller titles, as well as the most exciting crime and thriller authors writing today, visit: >>>

The Murder Room
Where Criminal Minds Meet

themurderroom.com

www.ingramcontent.com/pod-product-compliance
Ingram Content Group UK Ltd.
Pitfield, Milton Keynes, MK11 3LW, UK
UKHW022311280225
455674UK00004B/255

9 781471 906947